Out Cold

From the Library of
Daisy Jones

Out Cold

DAAMON SPELLER

Urban
soul

URBAN BOOKS

http://www.kensingtonbooks.com

This is a work of fiction. Any references or similarities to actual events, real people, living or dead, or to real locales are intended to give the novel a sense of reality. Any similarity in other names, characters, places, and incidents is entirely coincidental.

URBAN SOUL is published by

Urban Books
1199 Straight Path
West Babylon, NY 11704

ISBN-13: 978-1-59983-053-7
ISBN-10: 1-59983-053-1

First Printing: February 2009

10 9 8 7 6 5 4 3 2 1

Printed in the United States of America

This one's dedicated to my birthplace, NYC, and the borough of Queens. To the eighties and early nineties, when old school was the new school. To keepin' on till the break of dawn and house music all night long. If you were there and remember, sit back and reminisce. If you weren't . . . well, you better ask somebody.

ACKNOWLEDGMENTS

Writing a novel isn't easy. It's hard work. But I love what I do. It gives me an incredible sense of accomplishment to know that I've done something that only a very small percentage of people in this universe are capable of doing. So, let me take a moment to reach out to those who in some form or another have had a hand in this latest incredible accomplishment.

My superagent, Audra Barrett, for doing what you do and doing it well. Jami Shepard, for your critical eye and creative input throughout the creation of this novel. (We make a great team. ☺) April Proctor, for embracing this narrative from the get-go and constantly staying on my back to hurry up and get it done. Kevin Taylor . . . just got four words for you, bruh: Those were the days ☺!!! To all the bookstores and book clubs who have promoted me and, most importantly, to the readers who purchased *A Box of White Chocolate,* read it, and GOT IT, thanks for your past and future support. I never tire of hearing what you have to say and think.

Lastly, Lorraine Speller—no person on earth has had a greater influence on me. Enough said.

Daamon

email: tds_writes@verizon.net
web: www.daamonspeller.com

JAMAICA, QUEENS,
1986 . . .

THE GOOD LIFE

1

RANDALL CRAWFORD

Let me make something clear right off the bat: I'm no ladies' man. Just your average, conservative kinda guy. A one-woman kinda guy. My problem isn't meeting honeys. I just always seem to end up in the "friend zone." I meet girl. Girl tells me how personable she finds me. Girl uses words like "open" and "free" to describe how I make her feel. Girl and I subsequently spend many evenings snuggled up together while she talks me deaf, dumb, and blind about her ex-boyfriend, current no-good boyfriend, or the guy she's presently trying to get with. The latter is never me. In fact, it's gotten so bad these days that when a honey tells me I'm a "nice guy," I don't even hang around to hear what she has to say next.

I'm the polar opposite of Dirk, my best friend since elementary school. He and I grew up a few houses away from each other on 199th Street in St. Albans, Queens. A lot of folks don't understand our friendship—and neither do I at times. I don't know, I guess we just sorta balance one another out. I reel him in when he goes too far, and he casts me out when I don't go far enough.

Unlike me, Dirk's been a chick magnet as long as I can remember. He lost his virginity at 15. He's six one, light-skinned, with a curly fade. And here in the eighties, his type's the shit. But who knows? Hopefully us chocolate bruhs will start getting some love come the nineties.

Neither Dirk nor I attended college after graduating from August Martin High in 1982. My aunt Ethel, head of human resources at United Trust Life Insurance in Midtown Manhattan, got both of us entry-level jobs at the company right out of high school. Dirk's is in the claims unit and mine is in the accounting department. We decided to delay college—or skip it altogether—and give these gigs a shot. The starting salary for two 18-year-olds, living at home, with few if any expenses, was too tempting to pass up. That, plus we were eager to get out on our own anyway.

We each made great progress in our positions at United Trust and saw our entry-level salaries increase nicely in just two years. By our twentieth birthdays—while other people our age were broke college students eating Ramen noodles and fretting about the student loans they were going to have to repay—Dirk and I were each already clocking close to $20,000. So, in the spring of 1984, we copped an apartment off Francis Lewis Boulevard and Hillside Avenue, and moved in together.

2

DIRKSTEN FRANCIS

I've got three vices. Honeys would be number one. Sex would be the second. My third? That would be New York City's nightlife. Since turning 21 a year ago, I've become a regular on the club scene. Randall thinks I'm out of control in regard to all three of my vices. Dude's the complete opposite of me. Not only in personality but in appearance, too: five eight, 155, chocolate brown, horn-rimmed eyeglasses, and an Afro.

Randall's got a good heart, though. *Too* good a heart if you ask me. He's notorious for letting honeys cuddle and tell him all about their "issues"—without giving him any. I guess chicks feel comfortable enough to do that kind of stuff with him because he's so "sensitive." Such a "nice guy."

Honeys know better than to try that with me!

Randall's always telling me I'll never meet anything but skeezers and bimbos in the nightclubs I frequent. You'd think by now he'd realize that's fine by me 'cause I like 'em scandalous and brainless—so as long as they've got big butts and/or jugs, too. C'mon. It's not like me and a honey are gonna be discussing the fundamentals of trigonometry before we get undressed. Booty kills only need enough smarts to remember their phone number, scribble it on a drink napkin, and pass it along to me.

I will give R credit for this, however. He deals with a much classier grade of female than I do. I admire that about him. Really. It gives me something to . . . *aspire* to. And one of these days, I'm only going to deal with classy women, too— but it ain't gonna be *today*. I'm only 22 years old, yow mean? And in the "boxing ring of love," I've got zero plans on becoming what I think Randall already has: an early-round TKO waiting to happen. So that said and until further notice, I've got one and only one principle when it comes to the opposite sex: treat 'em like a boxing match.

Stick and move. Bob and weave.

3

RANDALL

I just celebrated my twenty-second birthday with a slammin' party. It was more like a bachelor party. Dirk threw me a guys-only affair at our apartment, complete with strippers he hired, who I recognized as dancers at Bentley's, a Manhattan nightclub Dirk likes to frequent. How he got these girls to perform at *my* birthday party I had no idea. In any event, they really turned things out in Apartment 3B.

Unfortunately, we had to cut the festivities short around 11:00 PM. My neighbors called the NYPD on us because of all the noise we were making. I guess it was just as well since one of our best friends from back in high school, Raymond Walker, aka "French Fry" (so named for his favorite food) had too much to drink and was beginning to trash the place. Dirk said he'd clean up and let everyone out, so I thanked my guests for a great party and retired to my room. My head was throbbing from all the noise and alcohol. I was so out of it, I dived into bed without even taking off my clothes. I was asleep as soon as my head hit the pillow.

I was awakened a few hours later by the sound of our television. Figured everyone had gone home so I changed into my pajamas and went into the living room. Didn't find Dirk but did find one of the strippers he had hired, who went by the name of "Kat."

"Uh, where's Dirk?" I asked her, wondering why she was still in my apartment.

"Since the police preempted y'all's little party, he and a few of your boys decided to continue it over at the Silver Shadow."

"Where's the rest of your crew?"

"They've gone home. Their work is done."

Their work?

Kat had gotten comfy with her feet up on my couch as she watched ESPN's *SportsCenter* like she paid rent here, too. Looking half-black and half-Filipino, she stood about five-two, had jet-black hair that reached her shoulders, and possessed a shape like a Coca-Cola bottle.

"Hey, Kat—"

"Shavonda."

"Excuse me?"

"My name's Shavonda. Kat's my performing name."

"Sorry. Shavonda. Why, um . . . are you still here?"

"I decided to stick around and wait for you to wake up so we could get better acquainted. Dirk said you'd be cool with that."

Oh, he did, did he?

"Look, Kat—"

"Shavonda."

"Shavonda. I've got a headache, so I doubt I'd be good company right now. Can I get a rain check?"

"Why don't you get back in bed and let me bring you something for that headache in a second. You a Mets or Yankees fan, Randall?"

"Yankees."

"Yankees? How you gon' be a Yankees fan living in Queens? That's bugged, dude. You're supposed to be a Mets fan."

Ask me if I care, I thought.

Kat had changed out of her striptease getup—a leopard-patterned catsuit with a matching mask and lifelike whiskers—into a tight, cutoff T-shirt that accentuated her ample breasts and flat stomach. She was also wearing a pair of jeans so fitted they looked as if someone had spray-painted them on her.

"Don't take too long. My headache's a monster," I told her.

I headed back to my room, where I lay on my bed and closed my eyes. Moments later, Kat entered my bedroom with a glass of water in her hand and two Tylenol tablets.

"Take this. It'll do the trick," she said.

I swallowed the Tylenol, laid the glass on my nightstand, and lay back down. Glanced over at her as she sat on the edge of my bed staring at me.

"Is there something I can do for you?" I asked.

"Is there anything else I can do for *you?*" she replied.

"Um . . . you wanna dance for me again? You were great tonight."

She laughed.

"Dancing isn't my *only* talent, Randall. Your head hurt too much for me to show you another one?"

The pain in my head suddenly took a backseat to the sensation in my pajama bottoms.

"What headache?" I chuckled.

Kat wasted no time. Pounced on me like a . . . cat. Straddled me and began performing a striptease out of her clothes, starting with her T-shirt. In the midst of doing so, she started singing that Taana Gardner jam "Heartbeat."

I sure hoped *singing* wasn't the other talent she was referring to.

Kat was turning me on—horrific crooning aside. I could feel my heart pounding against the inside of my chest. She cupped her right breast in her left hand, raised it to her mouth, and began licking her nipple slowly and seductively. Repeated the same act with her left breast, never taking her eyes off me in the process. Thought I was going to hyperventilate.

Next, she stood over me on the bed and resumed her slow, seductive striptease, slithering out of those painted-on jeans she was wearing. She also resumed her god-awful singing.

". . . Heartbeat, you make me feel so weak . . ."

In no time, Kat had stripped down to nothing but her dental floss panties.

This is definitely a better cure for a headache than Tylenol.

Kat got back down on the bed and straddled me again. Began tickling my navel with her tongue. Had a brotha feeling like Neil Armstrong—ready to blast off. I had to take my mind someplace else in order to keep from having an accident on myself. After teasing me a while longer with the tongue-in-navel business, she pulled down my pajama pants, springing my Johnson like an escapee from Rikers.

Sensing that now was probably a good time for me to do something other than just lie here, something to show Kat that I had a few "talents" of my own, I lurched forward and tried to kiss her.

BAM!

Our heads collided. She buckled like a stunned prize-fighter.

"Shit, muthafucker!" she scolded me, rubbing her head.

"Sorry." My headache was back for an entirely new reason.

Like the song "Set It Off," I guess Kat figured she'd better get this party started quickly before I *seriously* injured her. She reached into the pocket of her jeans that were lying on the bed, took out a condom, and ordered me to lie back. I obeyed. She skillfully dressed my Johnson—now harder than Chinese arithmetic—then inexplicably froze like a mannequin, stared at it for a few seconds, then stared back at me.

Oh, Lawd. Is she gonna ask me is this all I'm working with? (I don't exactly live up to that black male myth, okay?)

"You want it from the back, don't you?" she asked.

"Huh?"

Silence.

Ooooh.

"Y-yes, I d-do. I want it from the back."

DUH!!!

Kat turned around, propped herself up on her hands and knees, and struck a pose.

Sweet Mary, mother of Jesus!

Now *I* felt like singing a song.

I moved in behind her like I was Joe Montana. Palmed her beautiful compact ass in both my hands . . .

"Hut one . . . hut two . . . hut three . . ."

She didn't find that humorous in the least.

"*What* the fuck are you doing?" she asked incredulously.

I had no earthly clue.

Suddenly in a panic not to blow my best chance ever at actually getting some, I grabbed hold of my Johnson and headed for the Promised Land.

Evidently, my aim wasn't very good.

"Hell, naw, muthafucka. Not *there* you ain't!"

Oops.

"Sorry, Kat."

"For the last fuckin' time. My name's *Sha-von-da,* dammit!"

Shavonda Dammit's vocabulary left a lot to be desired. (Right along with her sense of humor.) I had become totally unglued. Even worse, I was still fumbling around behind her trying to . . . you know.

Allow me to digress here to say that it's a good thing a guy's first time isn't weighted with the same significance of being "special" as a woman's. This was turning out to be anything *but* special. I definitely wasn't representin' in Apartment 3B tonight. (Striking out with the bases loaded would be more apropos.)

Kat must've lost her last ounce of patience with me because she began to critique my sexual competence in an expletive-laced tirade that I won't bother repeating. (Insert your imagination here.) In utter exasperation with me, she reached between her thighs, grabbed hold of my Johnson, and brought me to that place I had yet to visit in twenty-two years.

I lasted all of 59½ seconds. In my delirium, I think I may have even told Kat I loved her before I passed out.

4

DIRK

There was something else besides money that motivated me to jump at that job offer from Randall's aunt Ethel right after high school. An escape from the home life I'd come to know.

My mother drinks like a fish. She's only 45, and was a total fox when my pops met her back in 1961. But her drinking over the years has stripped her of that beauty she once possessed. Nowadays, she looks like she's at least 55.

My parents have been married twenty-three years. How, I can't begin to fathom. They fight like cats and dogs. Cowboys and Indians. Jews and Arabs. Back and forth. Forth and back. Him about her drinking. Her about his lack of interest in her. I've never been able to figure out whether his lack of interest is the result of her drinking or her drinking is the result of his lack of interest.

My father's a prolific womanizer. I think the only thing that has kept him around is me and my little sister, Rhonda. The man has his faults but loves his kids. My sister's almost 16. And if I know my pops like I think I do, he's just counting down the days til her eighteenth birthday. When that day comes, he's outta there.

My pops has got a chick-on-the-side these days who he doesn't even *try* to conceal anymore. She's 25. Twenty-three years his junior. What does my moms think about this? Remarkably, she doesn't seem to give a shit so as long as he pays the mortgage, keeps the lights on, and breaks her off a little chump change for her frequent treks to One Stop Liquors on Linden Boulevard. That's where her guy-on-the-side lives. His name's Johnnie. Johnnie Walker.

I was chillin' at the Silver Shadow with French Fry and a few other dudes who came to R's party when Shavonda beeped me on my pager with the mission-accomplished code: 777. That meant the coast was clear and I could come home now.

I got back to our apartment around 2:30 AM to find Randall sitting up in his bathrobe, watching TV with a silly grin on his face.

"How you feeling, birthday boy?"

"Man, you ain't gonna believe what happened after y'all left. That stripper, Kat, the one you told could hang around? I waxed it, Dee. Knocked it outta the park!"

"Say *whaaaat?*"

"Yo, check this out. I found her business card. I'm calling her and see if she wants to—"

"Whoa. Slow your roll there, Ca-*niggula*. Please don't do that."

"Why?"

"Shavonda ain't that kind of chick."

"How did you know her name was—"

"She's a freak-for-hire, Randall."

Silence engulfed the room.

"So, what are you saying, Dirk? What happened tonight didn't have anything to do with me?"

Now, I felt bad.

"No. I hit that, too, on my twentieth birthday."

All of R's gusto evaporated like a pot of boiling water.

"As many times as we've seen that girl dancing at Bentley's you never told me you knew her—let alone had *sex* with her."

"You're my boy, R, but I don't tell you *everything.* Shavonda owed me a little favor, okay?"

"So this whole thing tonight was a setup?"

"Mmm . . . yes. But, hey. If that blissful look I saw on your face when I came through the door is any indication, I'd say it was well worth it, yow mean?"

Randall shook his head at me, called me "out cold," then turned and headed back to his room.

"Randall."

"What, Dirk?"

"That's the umpteenth time you've called me that. What the hell does 'out cold' mean?"

"Just a term I use to describe those I believe to be unconscious. Without shame. Oblivious to consequence. Those who just don't give a shit in some respect or another."

"Ah, I get it. It's like a state of mind."

"Exactly."

"Out cold. *Hmph.* I like that, Randall."

"I'm going to bed, Dirk. Thanks again for the party. And the 'birthday gift' especially."

5

RANDALL

I'm probably going to hell.

I haven't been to church since 1984. That's two years ago when I was still living at home with my parents. And if not for that reason, then for what I'm about to say. If I *ever* see the inside of a church again it'll be *too* soon.

My father, Miles Crawford, is the Bible-thumpin' pastor of First Savior, a small Baptist church on Farmers Boulevard. Everyone loves them some Pastor Crawford at First Savior. Especially those tight-skirted, flamboyant-hat-wearing heifers in the congregation. If you ask me, my father—or PC, as I often refer to him—took the Word of God a bit *too* far in our house.

Now, I suppose the fact that our family damn near *lived* in First Savior might have a little something to do with my indifference toward church nowadays. Here's what I wanna know. What happened to the days when church was a *Sunday* affair? Following Sunday services, we'd be back at First Savior on Mondays for Bible Study. Tuesdays, Youth Ministry. We'd get a breather on Wednesdays, then have to reconvene on Thursdays

for Family Service. Fridays, Revival. Before you could catch
your breath, Sunday had rolled back around. For me, going to
church was like being on a circular freeway with no exits. One
big, endless loopty-loop.

I'd listen to my father give these passionate sermons each
and every Sunday. He'd scream, holler, say his amens, Praise
the Lords, and his favorite: "You need Jesus." He'd practice
those performances in front of the mirror at home sometimes
a week in advance. Yes, I did say *performances.*

It goes without saying that when you're a child of a well-
respected pastor in the community, the last thing that's toler-
able is any un-Christian-like behavior. That said, however,
you've probably noticed, too, that in nearly every God-
fearing, religious family, there's usually that one child in the
brood who never bothered to read the memo on this. In the
Crawford family that would be my youngest sister, Lori.

Lori's been a rebel without a pause since she came out of
the womb. Started smoking reefer at 12 and had her first child
at 15. At 24, she's already had three kids by three different
men. She's currently working part time and living back home
with my parents.

She, like the rest of my siblings, resented PC's religious fa-
naticism. But unlike her brother and sisters, who kept their
mouths shut and endeavored to be good soldiers, she hasn't.
For reasons only known to Lori, she's been on an ongoing mission to be as big a pain in our father's ass as she can be. PC's so
fed up with her he doesn't know what to do or where to turn.
It's no secret he'd prefer Lori and her kids to be out of his
house. Can't say I blame him. True, they're my nieces and
nephews, but my sister's kids are also three of the most *ignant-*
ass kids I've ever seen in my goddamn life! I think the only
reason PC hasn't put Lori out yet is because he's worried how
that might make him look in the eyes of his congregation.

Image is everything to my father.

* * *

I met this honey at the Lexington and 53rd Street subway station a few weeks ago. Short, petite, brown-skinned, and very fine. I'd see her nearly every evening after work at roughly the same time and spot on the subway platform. She'd always board the next-to-last car of the F train. I smiled and spoke each and every time I saw her. No extended conversation, just the obligatory "How are you?" kind of thing. Well, after several days of this, I summoned the inner fortitude to do a little more than smile and say hello to her. I asked what her name was. Myesha, she said. Told me she worked in public relations for McCann Publishing over on 47th and Third.

From that day forward, I timed my departures from work every evening so that Myesha and I would meet up on the subway platform. If I arrived and didn't see her, I'd let a few trains come and go just in case I was a little early, she was a little late, or vice versa. Got her digits in no time and immediately commenced catching feelings for her.

Myesha and I started spending time together outside of the New York City underground. I'd go visit her at her apartment in the Queensbridge housing projects, or she'd come over and visit me at my apartment. During one of Myesha's visits, she stayed so late she ended up spending the night. Slept in my bed with me. Nothing happened, though. I didn't even try to get any. Felt like our relationship was still in a "best-not-to-bust-a-move-yet" window. Well, that and something Myesha said to me right before closing her eyes and drifting off to sleep: *"'Randall, make sure your skin don't touch mine.'"*

This is all to say that I got a call from Myesha this morning. She asked if I'd like to go shopping with her in Midtown this afternoon. My initial reaction? Hell, no! I don't like shopping in Midtown—or with women. As for the latter, they're too damn slow and too damn indecisive. Furthermore, it's mid-December and 24 degrees outside. I told her I'd think about it and call her back after I had finished my breakfast.

Over pancakes and sausage, I came to the conclusion that I liked being in Myesha's company more than I disliked shopping with a woman in Midtown Manhattan, in the freezing cold.

She and I were hand in hand, sashaying up, down, and around 34th Street in the bitter cold hitting all of her favorite stores from Conway's to Macy's, and everything in between. I was even carrying some of her bags. We had already been out for what seemed like an eternity to me. I was running out of gas and getting hungry. But there was one more store Myesha said we *had* to hit before we could get out of the cold and get back to her place. An intimate-apparel joint called Bare Necessities.

"This is the last store today," she assured me as we stepped inside the small, cramped boutique. "You're not embarrassed to be in here with me, are you?"

"Naw."

Truth? I would have gone in *any* store with her if it meant getting out of the friggin' cold.

Myesha was as giddy as she could be, asking my opinion on all kinds of ling-er-ree: bras, teddies, dental floss panties.

"You like that, Randall? Oh, wait. What do you think about *this?*" she asked, holding up one item after another for my opinion.

"If I could *see* you in some of this stuff, I could give you a much better opinion," I joked. (I was dead serious, actually.)

"You *would* like that, wouldn't you?" she purred.

Myesha was barely five feet tall and weighed no more than a buck-ten. All of it tits and ass at that. Would I? *Do ducks quack?* I wanted to answer her. The thought alone of seeing Myesha in some dental floss had my Johnson doing gymnastics inside of my BVDs.

Following what seemed like an eternity inside the boutique

(like I said, too damn slow, and too damn indecisive), she finally settled on several items and we hopped the subway back to Queens.

Back at Myesha's warm, toasty apartment, I quickly got out of my ski jacket, hat, gloves, and scarf, and made myself comfortable. Meanwhile, she grabbed her many shopping bags and disappeared into her bedroom. Reappeared ten minutes later in nothing but a fishnet chemise with matching G-string.

Hallelujah, let the heavens rejoice!

"You like?" she asked, giving me a view of her from every conceivable angle.

"H-h-hell, yeah," I st-st-stuttered.

"Good. Don't move. I'll be right back."

I *couldn't* move.

Myesha returned to the living room modeling a different piece of ling-er-ee for me. And repeated the presentation several more times until she had modeled every single item she had bought this afternoon. Then she ordered Chinese. We ate (with her fully clothed again), then snuggled on her sofa, and began watching *High Plains Drifter* on HBO starring Clint Eastwood.

There was little question in my mind how we were going to cap off this evening. I could barely mask the excitement circulating through my veins (or my Johnson, which was harder than my ninth-grade algebra class.) Best part? This time it wasn't going to be any setup. No "gift" from Dirk.

Now it was time to bust-a-move.

Oozing with confidence, I pressed my cheek against Myesha's. "So, tell me. Who's the lucky guy that's gonna be helping you *out of* all those sexy little items you just modeled?"

"Eric, I hope."

She said that with the straightest face.

"Eric?"

"Uh-huh. This guy I met out in L.A."

"L.A.?"

If this was her idea of a joke, she needed to say "gotcha" quick, fast, and in a hurry.

"Mmm-hmm. Guess I didn't tell you, huh? I met him at the FMPA conference."

"What's that?"

"A conference I attend annually for my job. Eric and I have been talking on the phone for several weeks now . . ."

Um . . . yoo-hoo, Boo. Remember me? We've been talking for several weeks!

". . . and he's coming to New York to see me over the Christmas holiday. I'm so excited."

My Johnson went limp as a wet noodle.

It suddenly dawned on me that none of what took place this afternoon was for my benefit at all, but that of some cat, three thousand miles away, who had probably been chillin' in 65-degree weather all day. I wasn't getting anything more than a hard-on and some Chinese takeout tonight.

This was some *bullshit.*

"Thanks for braving the cold and shopping with me today. I really wanted to get a man's opinion on the lingerie. I think Eric's gonna be pleased . . ."

Shut the eff up, Myesha. Puh-leeze!

". . . I couldn't have tried those things on in front of *any* guy. Most would have read more into it. But not you, Randall. That's why you're my pal. You're such a nice guy."

I don't know how I got here, but here I was again. Back in the friend zone. Same shit, different girl. I didn't have to go home, but I had to get the hell out of Myesha's apartment.

"Wow, look at the time. That beef and broccoli was slam-min', girl. Gotta go. Bye." I leaped off the sofa, picked up my broken face off the floor, and stuffed it in my back pocket. Put on my ski jacket, scarf, gloves, and hat, and made a beeline for the door. Myesha followed me.

"You okay, Randall?"

"Mmm-hmm."

"You seem a bit annoyed all of a sudden."

Ya think?

"I'm fine, Myesha."

"Okay. Well, do you have to leave so soon? I thought you'd be sticking around a little longer."

For what?

"I really need to get going. We've been out all day and I need to take care of some things at home that I've totally forgotten about," I lied.

"I guess you're right. Well, look, if I don't see you before, have a Merry Christmas, all right?"

I slithered out of the projects back to the subway station, walking as fast as I could in the frigid December air that felt ten times colder now.

SIX MONTHS LATER . . .

6

DIRK

I settled into my cubicle at United Trust and prepared to partake of my customary morning breakfast: toasted corn muffin with butter, small coffee, and the *New York Daily News*. I noticed the voice mail light flashing on my phone, so I dialed in to check the message before getting my grub on.

> *"Hey, big bro. Mommy and Daddy were at it again last night. I don't exactly know what sparked this one, but she threw a glass at him. Daddy stormed out of the house and she followed out right behind him, tipsy—like what else is new—and got behind the wheel. Please call me when you get a chance."*

I lost my appetite.

I decided to drive over to the house after work and investigate this latest rhubarb Rhonda had told me about. Had my own set of keys so I didn't bother to ring the bell. Inside, I found my father lounging in his favorite recliner watching

The Cosby Show with a plate in his lap of fried chicken, collard greens, and potato salad.

"What chu doing here, Dirksten?"

"Nice to see you, too, old man. Where's the lady of the house?"

"Downstairs," he said, laying down his fork on his plate and picking his teeth with his pinky nail.

"Rhonda told me what happened. You wanna talk about it?"

"What the hell is *it,* Dirksten?"

"Your confrontation with Ma."

"There's at least a half dozen of those a week. You need to be more specific."

"The one last night."

"My baby girl can sure run her mouth."

"Ma threw a glass at you?"

"Your mama's *always* throwing shit. Cups, plates, tantrums."

"Any reason she might have had to do that?"

Before he could answer, my mother came upstairs from the basement.

"Hey, baby, I didn't know you were here. You hungry? Want me to fix you a plate?"

"Sure. I'll be back," I said to my father.

I followed my mother into the kitchen, grabbed a Heineken out of the fridge, and took a seat at the dinner table while she fixed me a plate. She seemed totally sober for a change.

"I heard things got a bit testy in here last night. Ma, you know you shouldn't be driving when you're—"

"Do you know that bitch had the nerve to call this house?"

"Who?"

She looked at me with her hands on her hips.

"Uh-uh."

"Uh-huh!"

"What she want?"

"I dunno. Called here asking to speak to Henry. Bitch

didn't even acknowledge me, Dirksten. You know the other woman can't disrespect the wife that way unless she thinks she can get away with it. She obviously does, so I don't have to tell you who gave her that idea. You know I don't give a shit what your father does when he's running the streets with that young tramp, but I'll be damned if I'm gon' let her disrespect me in my own house!"

"That's messed up." *Out cold* is what I wanted to say, but she wouldn't have understood and I didn't feel like explaining.

"I'm waiting for that bitch to open a can of *bold-itis* and bring her young ass on over here. I'll beat her like a drum, Dirksten," she said, dancing on her toes and doing a Muhammad Ali shadowboxing routine.

She had me in tears I was laughing so hard. Her technique wasn't half-bad, actually. I was glad to see she was trying to keep a sense of humor about the situation.

She stopped throwing left jabs and right hooks long enough to hand me my food. The aroma made my mouth water. I said a silent grace and started grubbin'.

"I hope when you get married and start cheating on your wife, you at least have the decency not to *flaunt* it in her face."

"No, you didn't just go there, Ma."

"Chile, please. I birthed you, Dirksten. Changed your shitty diapers and washed your little monkey before you knew what it was or what it did. A mother knows shit. Like I *knows* you're running around right now trying to stick that little monkey in every and any hole that'll let you. That's the reason you were in a hurry to get out of this house. You knew you weren't gonna be able to carry on like that under my roof. That behavior ain't gon' stop once you get married. The apple don't fall far from the tree."

"Meaning?"

"Meaning you're your father's son. I know this much. You

best not come telling me you got some heifer pregnant. I ain't helping raise no more kids. Especially no *illegitimate* ones. Ain't happening. Ain't gon' be none of that drama up in here, like what's going on over at the Crawfords' with . . . What's that chile's name again?"

"Lori."

"What is wrong with that heifer? Can't she keep her damn legs closed?"

I didn't know if that was a rhetorical question or what.

"These collard greens are the bomb."

"Poor Miles," she continued, ignoring my compliment of her culinary skills. "That man's just trying to be a shepherd for the Lord and make it to heaven. Shame that daughter of his is going to be his undoing one day. You just better watch yourself with these little hussies out here, Dirksten. They see a good-looking young man with a decent job, a car, a little money in his pocket, and they start—"

"You worry too much," I said, interrupting what I knew was about to be a long monologue. "If I ever get married— and that's a mighty big *if*—I'm never gonna be unfaithful to my wife. I ain't gon' cheat on her, either."

"You're so silly."

"Look, I promise you no illegitimate grandkids if you promise me something."

"What?"

"No more driving while you're intoxicated."

"The only thing I've *got* to do is stay the color I am and die! I ain't got to promise nobody shit! Now hurry up, finish eating, and get out of my kitchen so I can clean up in here. Give Randall my love when you get home." She kissed me on top of my head and left the kitchen.

I couldn't help but laugh to myself as I rinsed my dirty dishes in the sink. That chat reminded me of what a cool, funny, and personable mother I had had before she got involved with Johnnie Walker.

When I returned to the dining room, Pops was still lounging in his recliner, looking like a vegetable, with a remote control in his hand.

"I'm fixin' to leave. Bookmark our discussion 'cause we will continue it at some point," I told him.

"I can hardly wait," he said sarcastically, never taking his eyes off the television.

7

DIRK

I took a peek at myself in the rearview mirror to make sure I didn't have any boogers in my nose. Opened the glove box and took out the bottle of Pierre Cardin cologne I kept stashed in there. Applied a few dabs to my pressure points. Killed the ignition, stepped out my 1979 Cutlass Supreme, locked the doors, and activated the car alarm. (This ain't Manhattan, Kansas.) Stepped back and gave a final look-see in the car window.

Somebody's gon' get hurt tonight!

I preferred doing this solo. Made any extracurricular activity I wanted to engage in during the wee hours of the morning a lot easier to navigate. However, Randall had been tagging along with me a lot of late. And whenever he did, he insisted on driving his new pride and joy: a 1981 Datsun 200SX he bought a few months back. In other words, making himself a huge cog in my routine. Guess he's just got nothing better to do right now than hang with "Mr. Saturday Night." (What R calls me.)

I flashed my ID to the doorman, stepped inside of Bentley's, and slid the cashier the damage for the evening. Now, unlike most of these amateur macks in this place, I didn't immediately go on the prowl, foaming at the mouth for a supermodel. I did as I always do: made my way over to the bar, copped my customary Amaretto and OJ, and carved out a good vantage point from which I could do what I believe is the first thing a *real* mack does in the first ten to fifteen minutes inside of a club. *Observe.*

As I nursed my drink (I'm no lush like my mama. One drink is about all I can handle), I spotted a honey on the dance floor that caught my eye. Wondered how many drinks it would take to anesthetize her better judgment—and inhibitions if she had any. Two, was my guess. She was on the petite side. Not one of those full-figured honeys. Takes *four or five* drinks to loosen up those big heifers. Sorta like the difference between fueling up R's Japanese compact and a minivan. I didn't have the patience—or the loot—to mess with no big heifer tonight. But I digress . . .

Honey dip was a bit ugly in the face—but cute in the waist. In other words, the type of honey a bruh can always find having a good time in the club slinging booty everywhere. The type of honey who ain't afraid to work up a sweat 'cause she just got her "hair did." Supermodels only want to stand around looking cute. Posing. Acting like they're going to be discovered by the Wilhelmina agency if they just stand completely motionless long enough. *Shyyyt.* Bunk them prissy, high-maintenance heifers.

Now, if the honey I'm scheming on just so happens to have much-better-than-average looks, well, I'm just one lucky fellow, aren't I? Conversely, if she's way beyond just a *little* ugly in the face—but still cute in the waist—I'll throw a paper bag over her head before leaving the club with her. And if in the extreme case she just looks like a straight cookie monster, I'll throw a paper bag over her head and mine, too. (That's what guys in the club call a "two bagger.") Perfect cheek-bones don't mean a goddamn thing in the dark, yow mean?

Anyway, observation time was over. I knocked out the rest of my drink and stuck a fresh piece of Juicy Fruit in my mouth. It was time to roll up this honey, hit the dance floor, and get my "BBF" on. (That's big booty freakin'.) How do I know she'd even be with that? Simple. I saw her BBFin' the hell out of another dude while I was in "observe mode" earlier. After a little contact on the dance floor and two drinks, she just might let me hit those skins. Because there's one common denominator—aside from the love of dance and house music—as to why we're all in this club tonight: it's to find someone . . . some are hoping it will last forever; the rest, for just a few hours. I'm a card-carrying member of the latter group.

In the past three months alone, I've put to bed five different honeys I've met in one club or another in this city. My scores included a skinny honey, a full-figured honey, one with a god-awful weave, a college grad, and a high school dropout. Won't bother to go into detail about all of them, but I will at least tell you about one of them. Charmaine. My booty kill with the god-awful weave.

Charmaine was an unwed mother, with three young kids at home. But that didn't stop her from coming to Bentley's every Friday night dressed in something more revealing than she wore the previous week. She told me clubbin' was her release from a stressful job and the responsibilities of single parenthood. "I'm a good mother *six* days a week," she whispered in my ear, then proceeded to BBF the hell outta me to Fonda Rae's "Over Like A Fat Rat." So what if Charmaine snatched the tail off a carriage horse in Central Park and glued it to the top of her head? The backyard was busy and a "two-bagger" she wasn't. In quick order, Charmaine became my Friday-night regular.

We'd get the party started by hitting the dance floor and taking things as far as we could without being arrested for public indecency. Raze's "Break 4 Love" was our favorite jam to get freaky to. Around midnight, the DJ, Sugar Daddy, would stop the music so Bentley's resident strippers could take the stage. Shavonda and her crew on level one of the club, male strippers on level two. That's when Charmaine and I would bust the joint.

She'd follow behind me in her Dodge Aries K, while I drove around Lower Manhattan in search of a suitable booty palace. The Holiday Inn? Marriott? *Shyyyyt!* (She wasn't my *girl.*) Any accommodations that were a step above fleabag status would do the trick for what we had in mind. And once we found a suitable spot, we'd waste little time unleashing all that sexual tension we'd built up for each other on the dance floor earlier. Warning: always have a box of hats handy, and for security reasons—yours, not hers—never handle your business on a booty kill's turf.

What I loved most about Charmaine and the others was that they understood exactly what we were doing and never tried to make it out to be more than it was. When the deed was done, they didn't ask things like, "When am I going to see you again?" or "Are you going to call me?" Catching feelings ain't an option in this game. Like Tina sang: "What's love got to do with it?"

Much to my chagrin, Randall played chauffeur tonight, but this time, we hit a different club. The Red Parrot on West 57th. Things didn't exactly work out the way I had hoped with that petite honey dip from last week, so I was on a mission to "bounce back" tonight.

I was chillin' at the bar, sippin' my habitual Amaretto and OJ, when someone tapped me on my shoulder.

"Would you mind ordering a Cosmopolitan for me?" a

female voice asked. "The bartender's acting like he doesn't see me standing here."

I spun around on the bar stool to get a glimpse at who was making this request. My mouth dropped open. A redbone with long honey-blondish hair, and a pair of stunning green eyes. A supermodel if I'd ever seen one. I gathered myself, got the bartender's attention, and copped that Cosmo she wanted.

"How much is that?" she asked.

"It's on me. Just tell me one thing, sweetie."

"What's that?"

"Your name and who gave you those pretty green eyes?"

"That's *two* things," she replied with a hint of sass.

"True dat. How 'bout your name for now?"

"It's Madison."

"Pleased to meet you, Madison. I'm Dirk." I shook Madison's hand, taking notice of her manicured nails, which were of a respectable length. I stay clear of honeys with those long-ass claws. Don't tell me they don't have trouble wiping their ass. But I digress . . .

"You are *extremely* fine, Madison. Not only that, you look good."

She laughed. Took a sip of her Cosmo. My eyes followed the glass straight to her lips, smothered in burgundy lipstick.

"Thank you, Dirk."

I was so taken with this girl's fineness that I totally forgot Randall was sitting next to me. He reminded me by clearing his throat loudly.

"Excuse my manners, Madison. Uh, this is my boy, Randall. Randall, Madison."

"Pleased to meet you, Randall."

"Pleasure's all mine," R responded to her in some sort of weak Billy Dee Williams impersonation. (I wanted to pop him upside his head.)

Just then the DJ started spinning Eric B. & Rakim's "I Know

You Got Soul." Folks went bananas whenever that jam was played. I wasn't in any hurry to hit the dance floor, though. I was pleasantly preoccupied—until Randall took Madison's drink from her, handed it to me, grabbed her by the hand, and raced off to the dance floor with her, nearly all in one motion. Whatever he was drinking must've been spiked with some confidence.

Randall *can't* dance.

Damn. I was just fixin' to lay the Francis mack on Madison, too. I wasn't going to sweat it, though. No need. A voluptuous Puerto Rican honey slid into the empty bar stool Randall vacated.

"*Que pasa,* Mami?"

8

RANDALL

I'm far from the forward type, but the Long Island Iced Tea had me feeling confident. Besides, Dirk always said *never* ask a honey, "Would you like to dance?" It was a wimpy question that only set a guy up for rejection. "If you see something you like and she's dancing alone, with another girl, or just standing around posing like a supermodel, roll up on her and *make* her dance with you," he always said.

I've got a little more rhythm than the average white boy in Topeka, Kansas, so I just did a little one-two step, and tried to converse with Madison above the amplified scratches of Eric B. & Rakim's lyrical flow.

"It's been a long time, I shouldn't have left you
Without a strong rhyme to step to . . ."

"YOU COME HERE OFTEN, MADISON?"
"NAW, THIS IS MY FIRST TIME."
"DO YOU LIVE IN MANHATTAN?"

"QUEENS."

"WHAT PART?"

"HUH?"

"WHAT PART OF QUEENS DO YOU LIVE IN?"

"LAURELTON."

Yes! Madison was not only fine but an "around the way" girl, too.

"WHERE DO YOU LIVE, RANDALL?"

"QUEENS VILLAGE."

Madison and I remained on the dance floor for a few more songs: Alicia Myers' "I Want To Thank You" and the Fatback Band's "I Found Lovin'"—Bentley's national anthem and my personal favorite. Afterward, we moseyed back on over to the bar. Found Dirk so busy mackin' some honey he didn't even notice we had returned. I wasn't about to disturb his groove since I had a nice one of my own going for a change. I even got Madison another Cosmopolitan and I *never* buy a honey a drink.

I learned Madison was a bit older than me, 28, and rented a basement apartment in a single-family house off Merrick Road. She asked about Dirk. Couldn't tell if it was interest on her part or if she was just making conversation.

When Dirk finally came up for air, he noticed us, excused himself from the girl he was mackin', and made his way over.

"Madison, right? Can I wrestle this good man away from you for a quick second?" he asked.

"A *quick* second," she told him.

Dirk pulled me aside.

"I like the way you whisked that honey dip away with the quickness, R."

"Brotha's gotta do what he's gotta do, Dee."

"I ain't mad atcha. Whassup with that? She ain't no joke!"

"I'll give you the scoop on the way home."

"That's what I need to talk to you about. You're gonna have to roll out of here without me tonight."

"Again?"

"See that girl I was talking to at the bar?"

"The Puerto Rican one?"

"She's Dominican. Try not to get the two confused. 'Ricans and Dominicans hate that. Anyway, I'm taking her to breakfast."

"Breakfast?"

"She's gonna be calling me *Papi Chulo* in an hour or less," Dirk said, looking at his watch. "She's from the Boogie Down."

"South Bronx, huh? So is that where you're taking her for 'breakfast'?"

"What I tell you about that?"

"Right. I forget. Never on their turf."

"Never, ever, ever!"

"How you getting back home?"

"Hmm, let me see. I suppose I'll take yet another expensive cab ride home." He sounded annoyed with that option. "I've gotta find a more economical way to do this."

"Here's an idea. *Stop* doing it. It ain't like you can't get booty for free, Dirk."

"Booty ain't free, Randall. It's never *free*. You'll learn, Grasshopper. Besides, I *can't* stop chasin' it. I think I've become addicted to this game."

"Well, in that case, I'm sure you'll figure out something. Have a good time, be careful, and make her say my name, too," I laughed.

We joined back up with Madison who was waiting patiently for us at the bar.

"Hope I didn't keep him from you too long," Dirk told her. "It was nice meeting you, Madison. I'm sorry we didn't get to chat more."

"Same here," she replied.

Dirk promptly exited the club with his Puerto Rican . . . I mean, Dominican honey.

* * *

It was 2:00 AM when I walked out the front door of the Red Parrot with Madison. I was so hyped I think I could have *jogged* all the way back home to Queens. I walked her to her car, secured her digits, jumped in my 200SX, and pumped WBLS. The image of Madison's long hair, light skin, and green eyes was all that permeated my thoughts as I made my way from the West Side to the East Side of Manhattan to get on the 59th Street Bridge. I thought about Dirk for a moment, too. Namely, how easily tits and ass can send him off into the night to do Lord knows what, with Lord knows who.

9

MADISON JONES

I'm a go-getter. If I want something, I go get it. Got that gene from my parents. They're both very successful go-getters. Dad's a surgeon and my mother's a psychiatrist. They've been married thirty-three years and have raised three great kids during that time.

I'm originally from Newburgh, a suburban town in Upstate New York. Newburgh was cool to grow up in, but by the time I finished my sophomore year at Syracuse University I knew I wasn't going back there. After graduating in 1981, I felt ready to take on the world . . . well, the borough of Manhattan anyway. I just couldn't wait to get a job and move to New York City, where I could immerse myself in its cultural happenings. Back then that was mostly partying in the city's myriad of bars and nightclubs. These days, it's Broadway shows, museums, and trendy restaurants in SoHo.

Social pursuits aside, I also knew that living in New York could mean big things for me careerwise. I have a solid plan when it comes to my career. I'd like to become the editor-in-chief of a major fashion magazine like *Vogue* some day. On my very first interview after college, I landed an editorial assistant position at the headquarters for *Trendy* magazine. One of New York's up-and-coming fashion publications. My starting salary was okay, but simply no match for the rents in Manhattan. Especially for a 22-year-old, who wasn't keen on having a roommate. So, I had to go with Plan B: find a reasonably priced apartment *near* Manhattan instead. The Bronx and Brooklyn were a bit too seedy for a prissy Upstate girl like myself, so I ended up settling on a small basement apartment in a single-family home in Queens. Never imagined I'd still be living there six years later, but the rent's cheap, and my landlord's an awesome kind of fellow. Furthermore, living in Queens has afforded me the opportunity to save lots of money. I've already saved enough for a down payment on a home. But I'm still waiting to pull the trigger on that move. I've always had this fantasy of me and my *husband* buying our first home together.

I was engaged once—to a white guy. Graham Browning. Star linebacker on the Syracuse University football team. We met when I was a freshman and he was a junior. Graham was the first boy to get my cookies. I loved that boy more than I loved myself. We planned on getting married after I graduated, but those plans came to an abrupt halt one afternoon when I returned to my dorm room from study hall and walked in on him sexin' my Irish roommate, Irene McGinty, doggy style.

Back in college, I loved guys like Graham—star athlete with a body to die for. But I don't necessarily need a "looker" anymore. I just want a guy who's decent-looking, trustworthy, and loves me to death. Mostly trustworthy. Fidelity is still one of my biggest issues where men are concerned. Following the debacle with Graham, I promised myself never to get involved again with a man I even *suspect* might be the type to take comfort in the bosom of another woman over me. I don't *ever* want to go through that pain and hurt again. Especially when I'm the type of woman who could *never* be unfaithful to her man.

It's been three years and counting now since I've been involved with anyone to any degree of significance, but I'm hoping I'll meet Mr. Wonderful soon. Because when it comes to love and happiness, I've got a solid plan for that, too. I want to be married by the time I'm 30, and have two, maybe three kids by the time I'm 35. Anything less is unacceptable.

Last night was the first and last time I'm going to the Red Parrot. The joint was swarming with half-naked girls looking like hookers who'd just come in from doing a shift on 12th Avenue. The guys weren't much better. A bunch of ain't-saying-nothing brothas, with way too much gold around their necks. Have I outgrown the club scene or what? The only reason I was there in the first place was on account of my girlfriend Fatima, whose choices in men leave a lot to be desired if you ask me. She'd been depressed of late over her current relationship with a married NBA player. Fatima says he plays for the hometown Knicks—she's a basketball fanatic—but won't tell me his name. All she will say is that he's like the thirteenth man on a twelve-man team. A "pine" brotha, she calls him. (As in never leaves the bench.) She may as well have gone ahead and told me his name since I don't even follow the NBA.

Anyway, she said she needed to get out and shake her ass for a few hours and blow off some steam. Well, Pine Brotha calls her shortly before she's leaving to meet me. She tells him of our plans. He tells her they need to talk. Fatima never makes it to the Red Parrot. I didn't have to guess why.

So, there I was, stood up in that modern-day Sodom and Gomorrah set to music. The night would have been a total bust if not for the fact that I met Randall. Not half-bad-looking, he was dressed really nice in a black short-sleeved shirt worn over gray pleated slacks, with cuffed hems. His butt looked nice and firm in those slacks, too. No gold chains hung from his neck, either. I loved the way his pearly white teeth contrasted with his chocolate-brown skin.

I wasn't quite sure what to make of the Afro, though.

Randall had absolutely no rhythm whatsoever. But he did seem like the type of guy a sista would enjoy snuggling on a sofa with while watching an old Clint Eastwood Western.

I met Randall's roommate also. Dirk: Six one, with wavy hair, and skin as fair as mine. Pretty boy if I ever saw one. I found myself attracted to him initially, but something about him oozed "womanizer." I'm pretty sure my instincts are right because he left Randall at the Red Parrot to go and have sex with some Latino girl he had just met.

Nevertheless, I'm glad I opted not to be "Tammy"—my alter ego when I'm simply not in the mood to meet any guys and/or listen to their weak-ass raps. I gave Randall my number. Something I rarely give a guy I meet in a nightclub. But I think the brotha has potential. Besides, the big 3-0 is fast approaching, and, like I said, I'm ready to settle down, get my house with the white picket fence on Long Island, and have my 2.5 babies.

10

RANDALL

I thought of waiting for a couple of days before calling Madison. Didn't want to seem anxious. But who was I fooling? All sorts of clichés were running through my head. *"When you're slow you blow"* being the main one. I called her the very next night and asked if we could get together. She said we could. I was hyped.

I decided to take Madison to the movies at the Sunrise Multiplex at Green Acres Mall. We planned on catching the nine o'clock showing of Spike Lee's sophomore flick, *School Daze*. I showered, changed, and got to her crib in Laurelton at 7:45 PM. Yes, I was early; the theater was only fifteen minutes from her crib, but I wanted to make this date last as long as possible. (Second dates are far from automatic for me.)

I dressed summer chic in an orange short-sleeved shirt worn outside my pleated navy blue print shorts I got from the Gap. I was also rocking the brand-new Air Force 1 Nikes I copped on Delancey Street. Madison wore a formfitting denim miniskirt, a sleeveless top, and a pair of sandals that showed off her pretty feet and painted toes that matched her nails. She was wearing a jacket the night we met at the Parrot, so I couldn't tell what was going on out back. She left little question about that tonight. I was *very* pleased.

I played it safe when we got to the movie. Didn't attempt any physical contact whatsoever. (Though it was killing me not to put my arm around Madison during the flick.) She wasn't an expensive date, either. Didn't ask for popcorn, a Klondike bar, or a large soda before the movie. Good. (I'm tight when it comes to spending money on anyone other than myself.)

It was close to midnight when I pulled up in front of Madison's crib. We both thought *School Daze* was whack. Not nearly as good as Spike's first joint, *She's Gotta Have It*. She asked if I'd like to come in for a minute. Would I? *Do ducks quack?* I wanted to answer.

Inside, she offered me a glass of water after apologizing for not having anything else to offer. Next, she grabbed my hand and said, "Let me give you a tour of my place." It was the first time our skin had touched all night. Gave me goose bumps. My "tour" took about a New York minute. Madison's place was half the size of the phone booth Dirk and I lived in. Cozy nonetheless. Smelt of coconut incense, with plants, pictures, and funky knickknacks all over.

Madison's lips were moving a mile a minute, but I wasn't hearing a thing she was saying. I was too transfixed on her green eyes and her luscious lips. Lips I wanted to kiss in the worst way. I glanced at my watch: 12:15 AM. Less would have to be more tonight. I needed to end our date on a high note in order to boost my chances of getting a second one.

"I better get going," I told her. "We've both gotta go to work in the morning." She walked me back outside.

"Thanks for the movie, Randall. I had a really nice time. Let's do it again. Call me," she said, giving me a hug.

This was a good date.

* * *

Me, Dirk, and French Fry, were on the F train heading to
Delancey Street to get our bargain on. I was feeling good.
Still on a high from my date with Madison. It must've shown
all over my face.

"Randall met a supermodel," Dirk told French Fry as the
train pulled into the West 4th Street station.

"Word? Where she live?"

"Merrick and 244th," I let him know.

"Dude took her out the other night. He ain't wax that ass,
though."

"No?"

"Dang, Dirk. Is sex all you think about? No, Fry. I didn't
'wax that ass.'"

"Kiss her?"

"Didn't do that, either. But I did get a hug."

"A hug?" Dirk scoffed. "Your cheap ass spent some money
on a honey and all you got out of it was a hug?"

"Leave dude alone," French Fry jumped to my defense. "It
ain't *always* got to be about the booty, Dee."

Dirk looked at him incredulously.

"Knee-grow, I know *you* didn't just go there."

The three of us busted out laughing so hard other riders on
the train began staring at us. Fry was one of the most prolific booty bandits in the Jamaica, Queens, area. The only difference between him and Dirk was that Dirk wasn't in a
supposedly committed relationship with anyone. French Fry
had been dating the same girl, Crystal Weaver, since we were
all in tenth grade. (They've got a 3-year-old daughter and live
in the attic of Crystal's parents' house in St. Albans.) Frankly,
I feel sorry for Crystal. French Fry's been promising to marry
that girl since we graduated from high school. I honestly

don't think she knows her baby-daddy's a lying, conniving, serial booty-bandit.

"Anyway, Grasshopper," Dirk continued—talking to me while giving French Fry the hand—"just remember what I told you. Stick and move. Bob and weave."

Dirk sounded like a broken record at times.

"Enough about me, okay? You never said what happened with you and that Puerto Rican chick."

"Dominican, R, *Do-min-i-can*. Her name's Lizette Felix. I took her to a 24-hour diner for some early-morning steak and eggs, then straight to the booty palace afterward. Them Spanish honeys ain't no joke, y'all. Mami damn near had me calling out *her* name in *Español*. She had to go and mess it all up, though. Know what that stunt had the *audacity* to ask me after I finished hittin' that? 'When am I gonna see you again?'"

"Oh, Lawd, not *that,*" French Fry gasped.

"Uh-huh. She's lying there in the bed, butt-naked, looking at me like she's in love. I'm looking back at her and the only thing on my mind is having an ice-cold Heineken and how long it's going to take me to get back home."

"I feel your pain, Dee," French Fry went on. "Right after a honey lets me get those skins all I want her to do for me is disappear, so I can get back home to my two girls."

The two of them found that ridiculously amusing.

I found the two of them ridiculous.

"Wait. I ain't finished. There's more," Dirk said. "She wanted us to exchange numbers. How they say it in Spanish? That bitch is *loco!*"

"Please tell me you didn't give one of your booty kills our home phone number, Dirk."

"Uh . . . *yeah,* Randall. I had to."

"Why?"

"So she'd shut up, get dressed, and let me get home."

Mrs. Francis *must've* been drinking when she was pregnant with Dirk. There's just no other logical explanation.

While Dirk and Fry continued laughing themselves into convulsions over their out cold antics, my thoughts drifted to Madison. I couldn't wait to see her again. If she and I ever had sex, I couldn't fathom ever wanting her to *disappear* afterward.

The train pulled into Delancey Street and the three of us made our way up the stairs and out of the station. As expected, the street was hummin' with a whole lot of other folks looking to get their bargain on, too.

II

DIRK

I was fumbling through a pile of claim forms at my desk trying to stay awake. I'd just come back from lunch and the "blackitis" was beginning to set in. Just then I remembered Rhonda telling me she was staying home from school today to nurse a bad cold. My sister's always been an A student who never got into any trouble or gave my parents any grief. A regular Goody Two-shoes. Amazing, considering we share the same genes. I called Rhonda, hoping doing so would keep me awake. I asked her about her college applications and if she had made up her mind about what school she was going to attend. Howard, Hampton, and Spelman were on her short list. Our conversation concluded with me telling her I planned on stopping by when I got off work today.

Rhonda must've been feeling a lot better by that time because when I got to the house, she had gone food shopping with my mother. With the two of them out, it was the perfect time to follow up on that discussion I was having with my father a few weeks ago. He seemed to be in a much better mood, too. I even managed to pry him out of his recliner with an offer of dinner on me at Red Lobster. He loves their steak-and-shrimp combo.

"You got a steady girlfriend yet, Dirksten?" my father asked, changing the subject from sports to my personal life as we waited for our entrees to arrive.

"Nope."

"Why?"

"There are too many honeys in this city for that one-on-one stuff. You sorry you married Ma?" (Hey, why not, since we were getting personal.)

"She's the mother of my children. How could I be sorry about that?"

"Because it's obvious neither one of you are happy."

The server arrived at our table. "May I get you two anything else?"

"We're good."

"Brenda and I have been married twenty-five years, Dirksten," my father said, getting back to our conversation and getting our grub on. "That's a *long* time. I wasn't much older than you are right now when we got hitched."

"So, what are you saying? People my age shouldn't get married?"

"If you came to me tomorrow and told me you were getting married I'd tell you don't do it."

"Why?"

"Two reasons. One—and no offense—but I don't think you're capable of being monogamous, Dirksten."

Well, if that ain't the pot calling the . . .

"Like father like son?"

He ignored me.

"How many women you done slept with already?" he asked.

"I dunno." I shrugged.

"You don't know?"

"You said there were *two* reasons, Pop."

"Right. I believe you're more apt to have a change of heart about the decisions you make in your twenties than at any other time in your life. Marriage is supposed to be forever. Better or worse. Sickness and health. That's some *heavy* shit, son. When I married your mother no one could tell me I didn't want to be with one woman for the rest of my life. Folks in their twenties ain't got a damn clue about next week, let alone forever. Save those life-altering decisions for your thirties and beyond, Dirksten. You'll be able to live with them the rest of your life."

"What changed your mind?"

He paused to mull that over.

"Brenda was funny, intelligent, and had a wonderful personality when I met her. In addition to all that she was 36-24-36. *Now look at ya mama,*" he grunted.

"Ever think that *you* might've driven her to start drinking?"

He laughed.

"I'm guilty of a lot of things, Dirksten. Causing Brenda to drink ain't one of them. Besides, it wouldn't have made a difference if she hadn't started drinking. Just raising a family took its toll on us. We practically had you right after we said 'I do.' Seems as though we've spent our entire married life chained to one responsibility after another. I was working 24/7 to keep a roof over y'all's head and food in y'all's stomach. Brenda was totally consumed with being a mother. Conversation between us that didn't center around you kids, the house, or bills became as infrequent as the sex between us. We stopped going out socially in part because your mother didn't trust that anyone else could look after you and Rhonda the way she could—even for a few hours. Somewhere in between all of that responsibility, I think we just lost touch with each other. I'm about to turn 50 in a minute, and after spending half my life married with children, I think I deserve to enjoy what remains of it however I please. You got a problem with that?"

"Isn't this the time when couples are supposed to reconnect? Start doing all the things they used to do when life was less complicated and they had fewer responsibilities?"

"I suppose for some. But me and Brenda ain't in love anymore. We're too far apart to whisper. We can only shout at one another these days."

"So, how's your new 'friend' fit in?"

His face lit up like a Christmas tree.

"She makes me feel good, son. She's fun, sexy, younger. Hell, she's *36-24-36*. I'm just more compatible with a woman like . . . a woman like her at this point in my life."

"Why are you still hanging around, then?"

"Beg your pardon?"

"I'm a grown man no longer living under your roof and Rhonda's a self-sufficient 17-year-old who'll be going away to college in a matter of months."

"Your point?"

"My point? My point is, do whatever it is you wanna do with yourself, Pop, but do it somewhere far away from Ma. Stop *flaunting* it in her face. And don't let your pretty, young, Ms. Whatever-Her-Name-Is do it, either. You keep it up, I think you're gonna live to regret it one day."

My father wiped his mouth and took a pause from his steak-and-shrimp combo.

"You done, Dirksten?"

"I'm done."

"Good. Now let me give you a piece of advice, Mr. I Don't Know How Many Women I've Slept With. You better learn how to treat women as something other than a receptacle for your semen before one gives you a lesson you ain't never gonna forget."

12

MADISON

Dining on scrumptious seafood at Sammy's Fish Box on City Island, I peered across the table at Randall. Tried to imagine how he'd look without that Afro and those eyeglasses. Wondered if I could persuade him to stop shopping on Delancey Street.

A nip here, a tuck there . . .

"How long has it been since you were in a relationship?" I asked.

"A while."

"Why is that? I haven't been talking to an undercover playa for the last month, have I?"

"Not at all. I'm strictly a one-woman, one-at-a-time kinda guy."

That was music to my ears.

"Well, good, because I'm a one-man, one-at-a-time kinda woman. Hey, I've been meaning to ask. Is Dirk seeing anyone?" I was entertaining the idea of introducing Fatima to him. She had officially kicked Pine Brotha to the curb and said she was done with married NBA players. She'd dig Dirk. She loves those pretty-boy types. There aren't many of those where Fatima's from. But first things first. I needed to confirm if my suspicions about Dirk were right.

"You interested?"

He sounded disappointed. That was music to my ears, too.

"No. My girlfriend Fatima . . . Well, answer my question first."

"No. Dirk's not seeing anyone. Dirk's strictly into 'slam-bam-thank-you-ma'ams'—'Booty kills,' he calls them."

Booty kills?

I was right. Like Salt-n-Pepa sang, dude was a *t-t-tramp!*

"Forgive me for asking, Randall, but how is it that you're best friends with a guy like that?"

"Dirk? We go way back to elementary school. We're an odd couple. We're friends *in spite* of our differing personalities."

"So, what's your take on his . . . booty kills?"

"He's my best friend, but I don't approve of everything he does, if that's what you're wondering."

"Good answer. I don't typically give guys younger than me the time of day, Randall, but you're already starting to grow on me."

"Like a fungus or something?"

"That was meant as a compliment."

"I know. I'm beginning to feel the same way about you, too, Madison."

This youngster didn't know it yet, but he was categorically getting some tonight.

13

RANDALL

The digital clock on the dashboard of my car read 10:54 PM. I walked Madison to her door, feeling like we had yet another successful date but that our relationship was still in that all-too-familiar-to-me "best-not-to-bust-a-move-yet" window. That said, I was all set to give her a hug, say good night, and be on my way when she beckoned me to follow her inside.

Soon as our feet crossed the threshold of Madison's doorway, she dropped her Chanel bag on the floor, grabbed me by the collar of my shirt, rammed her lips into mine, and began tonguing me down. Unbuttoned my shirt, took it off, leaped into my arms, and locked her ankles around my waist. No small feat considering she was in a miniskirt and heels. I held Madison in one arm and used the other to close the door behind us. Carried her across the room, laid her down on top of her small bed, and got on top of her. Following a few more moments of horizontal face-sucking, I went to work on her neck. The harder I sucked, the louder she moaned. The louder she moaned, the greater my confidence grew.

Madison got out of her blouse and bra. Her tits looked to be about a C cup and perfectly symmetrical. I momentarily paused to behold their splendor as she unbuckled my belt and unzipped my gabardine slacks.

"Take my shoes off," she purred, as she massaged my penis still captive inside of my BVDs. Darn. Her legs looked *so* sexy in those heels.

"How 'bout you leave those shoes on—but let me help you outta that skirt!" I slowly pulled Madison's miniskirt down over her curvaceous hips and tantalizing thighs. (She's five three, 135, with a body as tight as the spandex on a 12th Avenue hooker.) She wasn't wearing any panties.

Lawd! When the saints come marching in.

I grabbed hold of Madison's ass with both my hands. Rubbed that thing so good I thought a genie was going to appear in the room at any moment. As her voice got louder her words grew naughtier—and she got bossy. Started barking orders at me like a drill sergeant. "KISS ME HERE." "LICK ME THERE." "SUCK MY TITS GOOD, YOU SHORT, BLACK, AFRO-HAVIN'—"

"Ssssh, girl!" I said, covering her mouth with my hand. "You're gonna wake up the landlord!"

I shed my BVDs and flung them aside. Then Madison flung me aside—*literally*. From flat on her back, she pulled some kinda World Wrestling Federation maneuver on my ass. Flipped me over, got on top of me, and pinned my arms to the bed with hers. "Sorry," she said. "I can get a little aggressive during sex sometimes."

You don't say.

Madison began making slow, tantalizing circles all over my chest with her tongue. Methodically worked those circles down to my navel and continued downtown until her tongue reached the base of my Johnson standing in salute to her—and stopped.

"You got a condom?" she asked.

"Uh-uh." (Sue me. I was unprepared. Figured *this* moment was at least a few more weeks away.)

"Shit. Neither do I," she lamented.

"What now?" looks blanketed both our faces until Madison came up with what she figured to be a viable solution to the quandary.

"Just pull out before you come, okay?"

She was asking an *awful* lot of me.

"Okay," I promised, though not very confident I was gonna be able to keep that promise. Madison lowered her womanhood onto my manhood. I held her hips tightly as she rode me up and down, back and forth, side to side.

"Oooh . . . aaah . . . sssss . . . yes . . . yes . . . fuck me, Randall," she commanded through clenched teeth.

I obeyed Madison's command until that which made her a woman completely overwhelmed me. Somehow, I managed to pull out in the nick of time.

14

DIRK

I'm a little disappointed that R's met a honey and has folded like an accordion. But I'm not going to try and talk any sense into him. Not *yet* anyway. For one thing, he's got something else to do with himself now, which means I was operating solo tonight—the way I like it. Secondly, he's been spending nearly every weekend at Madison's, which means I've had the apartment to myself nearly every weekend of late. So guess what? I've been bringing my booty kills back to our apartment instead of to a hotel. Can't tell you the dough I've been able to save.

I looked out onto the dance floor and couldn't believe who I saw dancing with a group of other honeys. Lizette Felix. Mami was working the hell out of a pair of Lycra stretch pants and a halter top so small I thought her melons were going to spill out of it at any moment. Lizette had been sweatin' me major league. Calling the crib nearly every other day looking for me. Of course I didn't return any of her calls.

Cut her some slack, Dirk. The punany was all that.

That was my Willy talking to me.

"No can do. She's a rule violator."

I'm telling you, man. You need to cut her some slack. The punany was all that!

That Willy's one persuasive fellow.

Oh, okay. What the hell?

I fought my way through the crowd onto the dance floor as Gwen Guthrie's anthem to no-money-havin' men blasted from Club Savage's ceiling-mounted speakers.

I reached Lizette. She was *very* happy to see me. Grabbed my face in both hands and stuck her tongue down my throat right there on the crowded dance floor.

Surrounding club-goers gawked at us in awe.

". . . Ain't nothin' goin' on but the rent . . ."

I didn't ask her "Would you *like* to dance?" I *made* Lizette dance with me. Planted my left hand on her left hip, and with my right, spanked her right butt cheek like I was spanking a disobedient child.

"SOMEBODY SAY HO-O!!"

Mami was hanging tight with the Black John Travolta. Jigglin' those big melons all in my face and leaving me no choice *but* to bring her back to Queens with me.

When the DJ mixed in a new jam, I left the dance floor with Lizette, copped her drink of choice, Bacardi and Coke, and set the stage to hit those skins again by apologizing profusely for not returning any of her phone calls.

Early the next morning—and I do mean early, I drove Lizette to the nearest subway station. No breakfast, no shower, no nothing. She was *pissed*. On the ride there, she cursed me out in English, then in Spanish, and then vice versa. I found her tirade hilarious. That only made her even more furious with me. I pulled up to the curb at 179th and Hillside, and dropped her like a bad habit. Told her to get out of my car and to lose my number.

"Watch your back, *pendejo!*" she screamed at me.

"Oh, yeah? Why's that?"

"'Cause ju do not know who you fuckin' with!"

Lizette slammed my car door so hard I thought it was going to come off its hinges.

"Adios, stunt!" I shouted back, burning rubber away from the curb I left her standing on.

15

RANDALL

Madison was snifflin' up a storm. It was already 1:00 AM, and I wasn't getting any sleep. I didn't want to catch whatever she was coming down with, so I decided to go home and get in my own bed.

When I entered the apartment, I saw several items of clothing on the living room floor, leaving a trail from the sofa into Dirk's room. I tiptoed across the hardwood floor and put my ear to his door. Heard some faint chatter on the other side.

I know he's not stupid enough to be doing what I think he is . . .

I tapped on his door. No answer. Tapped a little harder. The faint chatter ceased. Dirk cracked open the door slightly and stuck his head out.

"*What* are you doing here, Randall?"

"Mmm, I dunno, Dirk. I *live* here? Whose clothes are those?"

"Keep your voice down."

"Who's in there with you?"

"A honey I met at Bentley's."

"When?"

"A few hours ago."

"*A few hours ago?* HAVE YOU LOST YOUR FREAK-IN'—"

Dirk slapped his hand over my mouth, stepped into the hallway clothed only in the skin God gave him, and closed his bedroom door behind him. "I *said,* keep your voice down, Randall!"

I removed his hand from my mouth. "You picked up some girl in a club a few hours ago and you've got her in our apartment already? What are you *thinking,* Dirk?"

"Dude. I didn't have any money to take her to a hotel and you know I can't be gettin' down on their—"

"That's your *personal* problem, Dirk. You can't be bringing total strangers into our home!"

"Can we talk about this later? You are *seriously* disturbing my groove up in here."

I stormed off to my room, closed the door, lay out across my bed, and stared at the ceiling. I was *hot.* Dirk was taking this shit *too* far now.

It was time for me to draw my line in the sand with Dirk and reel him in once again.

"Help me understand what I walked in on earlier this morning," I asked him as we sat in our usual booth inside of Gaby's Pizzeria in the Franhill strip mall. "You've decided to turn our apartment into your personal booty palace?"

"I was just trying to save a little dough, yow mean? We talked about this, remember?"

"I remember the conversation, Dirk. What I *don't* remember is agreeing that you could use our *apartment* for your lascivious pursuits."

"My luscious what?"

"Never mind."

"What's your problem, Randall? I'm handling *my* business in *my* room. Nobody's up in *your* stuff. And last I checked, my name is on the lease, too."

"That's beside the point."

"What is your point?"

"Beyond tits and ass, you probably don't know shit about that girl you had in our apartment. *That's* my point!"

"How conveniently you forget that you've let a few honeys spend the night in our apartment, too."

"They weren't *one-night stands*."

"Look. It's not like I got 'em lounging, raiding our refrigerator, and whatnot. You didn't have a clue, did you? Know why? Because while you've been spending time over at Madison's getting yours on the regular, I've been busy getting mine, too, and keeping it all crisp and clean in the process."

"Great. So what I walked in on wasn't a one-time occurrence? Look. Since what I'm trying to impress upon you seems too deep for your brain—the one on top of your shoulders— to grasp, as your best friend, and roommate, I'm simply asking you *not* to bring any more of your one-hit wonders back to our apartment. Can you just do that one solid? Please?"

"All right, all right! I won't do it anymore. You satisfied?"

"Yes."

"Good. Now can we finish eating and talk about something else?"

16

RANDALL

I like this job my aunt Ethel got me at United Trust. Really. But my relationship with Madison has got me thinking that it may be time for me to start looking for something else. Not that she's said or done anything to make me suspect as much, but I've got to wonder if Madison's not the slightest bit embarrassed that her new boyfriend doesn't have a college degree, or that he makes a lot less than she does.

I'd love to get a mature woman's perspective as to what if anything Madison might be thinking on the matter. My moms would be ideal except I hadn't told her or PC about Madison yet. Hadn't because I knew doing so was only going to open up a can of worms—particularly with Pastor Crawford. I could just hear his questions: What church does she go to? Is she saved? Y'all ain't fornicating, are y'all?

Wait. I could talk to my aunt Ethel. She'd know if there were any other positions open within this company that I could apply for that would be paying the type of money I'm looking to make. Not only that, she could even give me that female perspective I'm seeking—and keep her mouth shut about it.

I put away the invoices I was processing on my desk and dialed her extension.

"Human Resources, Ethel Crawford-Hanes speaking."

"Hey, Aunt E."

"Hey, Randall, how are you?"

"Good. Listen, there's something I'd like to speak with you about when you have a moment."

"Okay. Want to come by my office around 2:45?"

"I'll be there."

Aunt E thought my timing was odd. That since I had been in accounting five years, she would have envisioned me having this discussion with her maybe two or three years earlier. I explained what was on my mind. That my new girlfriend made more money than me, had a degree from a major university, had her own apartment, shopped in Midtown, etc., etc. She told me to relax. That if what I suspected may have been an issue was really an issue my new girlfriend probably would have kicked me to the curb already. That was reassuring. I think.

Most importantly, though, she said she'd keep her eyes and ears open for me.

17

RANDALL

Me and Dirk were chillin' at the crib watching a bootlegged copy of *Lethal Weapon* when the phone rang. Dirk answered it.

"I'm fine, Mrs. Crawford, and you? That's good. Here's your son."

"Hey, Ma, what's up?"

"Thanksgiving is just a few weeks away and your father and I are planning to do it up big this year at the house. It's been a while. We'd like to have the entire family together for the occasion."

"Sure. Count me in."

"You think Dirk and his family would like to join us?"

Huh?

"Hold on a sec." I told Dirk to pause the movie, went into my bedroom, and closed the door. "What's this, now? You want me to invite the Francis clan to a *Crawford* family Thanksgiving?"

"Yes."

"What for?"

"We don't socialize with the Francises and they live just a

few doors away. Our kids live together. I think we could be more hospitable toward them, don't you?"

"There's a *reason* y'all don't socialize with the Francises, Ma. PC doesn't like 'em."

"You know I hate it when you call your father that."

"Sorry. Was this Dad's idea?"

"It was mine."

"Look, Ma, I can see inviting Dirk. But Dirk *and* his parents? You know those two don't get along. That could get ugly."

"No, it won't."

"If you say so." Part of me thought I might regret what I was about to ask, but what the hell? My folks were bound to find out about my new flame sooner or later anyway. Thanksgiving seemed as good a time as any. "Um . . . can we invite one more person?"

"Who?"

"A friend of mine. A lady friend."

"*Ooooooh*. Wonderful. What's her name?"

"Madison."

"*Suuurre*. You can bring her, too."

"Thanks. Hey, listen. Dirk and I were kinda in the middle of watching a movie."

"We'll talk later. Bye."

I hung up and went back into the living room to deliver the news to Dirk.

"Guess what? You and your folks have been invited to Thanksgiving dinner at my parents' house."

"You kidding? My family and your family sitting down for Thanksgiving dinner?"

"And my girlfriend."

"Oh? You've decided to go public with your special friend over the holiday?"

"You could say that. You gonna come?"

"I don't turn down free meals. I'll be there. But I'm warning you. If your pops starts telling Bible stories over dinner I'm taking my dessert to go."

"That's not funny, Dirk."

"As far as your girl goes . . ."

"What about her?"

". . . I wasn't going to say anything . . . but she be acting kinda stank around me."

"Stank how?"

"The first time she came by the crib to see you, I spoke to her, and she barely pursed her lips to speak. The other day, she called here looking for you. I told her you weren't home, then tried making a little small talk with her. She starts giving me one-word answers to everything I'm asking her. I was just trying to be genial with Madison, yow mean? I'm telling you, R, your girl's got a problem with me. Don't know why 'cause she don't know squat about me."

"Your imagination is running away with you. Just talk to your folks and see if they'll accept my parents' invitation, okay?"

Going on a date with Madison is like going to the airport: arrive early and expect delays. She's slow as molasses. Never ready. But it's too soon for me to start complaining about it. Besides, she's been worth the wait every time thus far.

I slouched down on her couch and started thumbing through an issue of *Trendy* while she was huddled in the bathroom, still doing what I don't know.

"DOES FATIMA HAVE PLANS FOR THANKSGIV-ING?" I hollered to her.

"WHY?" she hollered back.

"I WAS WONDERING IF . . ." I got up from the couch, walked over, and put my face against the door.

". . . I was wondering if you'd like to bring her to dinner

with us. I think it would be kind of nice to have your best friend there. Don't you?"

Madison emerged from the bathroom looking *good*. Her hair was tied in a bun, and she had on some burgundy lipstick that made her perfect lips look even more perfect against her fair skin tone.

"You'd be okay with that?" she asked.

"Sure."

"I don't think she has plans. Her family's down in South Jersey now, and she always goes there. I know she gets bored with making that trip. Let me call her and find out—"

"Do that when we get back from the movie. We're running late."

"It'll only take a second."

Nothing you do takes a second, I wanted to say.

Against my wishes, she dialed Fatima, and then put her on speaker.

"Hey, girl."

"Wassup?"

"You're going to Jersey for Turkey Day, right?"

"That's the plan."

"Well, how would you like to go with me over to Randall's parents' house this year instead?"

"Seriously?"

"Randall wanted me to ask you. He's standing right here."

"Hey, Randall."

"Hi, Fatima."

"That'll work, Maddy. You know just driving down that long, boring-ass turnpike is enough to put me in a foul mood."

"We're on, then. Gotta run, girl. Randall's taking me to the movies and he's giving me that look 'cause we're running late."

"I'm jealous, Maddy."

"Jealous of what?"

"That you've got somebody taking you out. Know what I'm doing right now?"

"What's that?"

"Eating bonbons and watching reruns of *227*. Hey, Randall, you got any cute and available friends you can—"

"Bye, Fatima," Madison cut her off. "C'mon, baby, we're running late."

Ya think?

18

MADISON

Following the movie, Randall drove us over to Gaby's Pizzeria for a late-night snack. "Wanna stay over with me tonight?" he asked.

"I didn't bring any clothes . . . or a toothbrush, for that matter."

"You can sleep in one of my shirts and use my toothbrush. Okay. Just kidding about the toothbrush. I'm sure there's a spare in the crib somewhere."

I did like the idea of sleeping next to Randall in one of his shirts tonight. I was sold. But before I could tell him that, he just as quickly changed his mind.

"On second thought, maybe your staying over isn't a good idea right now."

"Why?"

"You know I read Dirk the riot act when I came home and found that girl in our place."

"I'm your *girlfriend,* Randall."

"Still. I think we should leave that dynamic alone for now."

"Because of what Dirk might say."

"Something like that."

"Have you ever given any thought to getting your own apartment?"

"Now's not the time for that. By the way, Dirk's got it in his head that you don't like him. I told him he was trippin'."

I took a bite of my Sicilian slice without responding.

"He *is* trippin', right?"

"I don't want to say anything negative about your friends. Let's drop it."

"No, speak your mind."

"All right, if you insist. I think he's the consummate D-O-G!"

"That's cold."

"Look, you're the one who told me about his 'booty kills.' Dirk seems to be a shallow, self-centered, immature brotha who doesn't give a shit about a woman's feelings so as long as he gets his. Take that night we met at the Red Parrot. I know you said you were cool with it, but I still think it was a bush move for him to cut out and leave you in the club like that. And for what? So he could get in some girl's pants he knew for all of fifteen minutes? Let me guess. Hit it, split it, then gave you and French Fry the play-by-play like it was all a big game to him." Randall didn't say a word. "That's *so* trashy, Randall."

"Dirk's a good guy, Madison. You just don't know him like I do. He's just going through a phase right now. He's not ready to get serious with anyone yet."

"And that makes his behavior *okay?*"

"Why are *you* getting so wound up over this? Care to share that with me?"

"Not inside of this pizzeria I don't."

* * *

Back at my place, I put on my pajamas and a skin-cleansing mud mask—part of my regimen to stay beautiful. I'm past the point of having to look glamorous for Randall *all* the time. He knows what he's working with. Fixed myself a cup of chamomile tea and cuddled up in bed next to Randall.

"So tell me now. Why's Dirk's behavior such a sore spot with you?"

"I was engaged to a guy back in college, Randall. Star athlete, nice body, real good-looking, campus heartthrob. The first guy I ever had—"

"Uh, that's way more detail than I care to hear. What sport did he play?"

"Football. Starting linebacker."

"What was his name?"

"What difference does that make?"

"I like college football. I might know who he is."

"Graham Browning."

"Never heard of him."

"Anyhow, I was so in love with him. He proposed to me my sophomore year. Got down on one knee and the whole nine. Even gave me a ring—albeit a cubic zirconia. He was the only guy I dated throughout college."

"What happened?"

"What else? Caught him cheating on me—with my roommate, no less. But you know what was more devastating than finding him in bed with another woman? Finding out it wasn't a single indiscretion with one person. He had been hoing around all over campus the entire time we were together. I only *caught* him once. And I only managed to do that because he got sloppy. Sooner or later, cheating dogs always do. You know what that asshole had the nerve to tell me after I busted him? He was *glad* I caught him because he wanted out of the relationship but couldn't bring himself to tell me."

"Graham sounds like an out cold brotha."

"A what kind of brotha?"

"Out cold. Scheming . . . devious . . . scandalous."

"Well, if that's what out cold is, then that's what Graham was. Although a brotha Graham wasn't. He was white."

Randall started laughing like he had just heard a private joke of some sort.

"Guess I shouldn't be too surprised by that. You do have that look white boys love."

"Excuse you?"

"Light skin, green eyes, long hair. You know you could pass as a white girl with a good tan," he said, cracking himself up.

"News flash, honey. *Black* men love my look, too!"

"Touché. Back to this ex-fiancé of yours—"

"I don't want to talk about that fool anymore. Suffice it to say, when I see guys hoing around and taking women's feelings for granted, it reminds me of the time I was on the receiving end of that. It's not a good feeling and I don't *ever* want another man to make me feel like Graham did."

Randall held me in his arms and squeezed me tightly.

"You don't *ever* have to worry about me steppin' out on you like that."

"Say what you mean, and mean what you say, Randall."

"I mean it. Know what else? I'm sorry I told you any of Dirk's business. I just want the two of you to get along, that's all."

"I didn't say I hated him, Randall. It's not that deep. He's your best friend and I'm your woman. For that reason alone I'll find a way to tolerate Dirk."

"Glad to hear you say that 'cause I'm gonna need you to put that tolerance into practice for a couple of hours over Thanksgiving dinner. I forgot to mention that Dirk will be joining us."

"Say what?"

"My folks invited him, too. So, it looks like Dirk and Fatima will get a chance to meet one another. Isn't that great?"

"No, Randall, it's *not*. And furthermore, it's *not* happening!"

19

DIRK

I felt mildly confident that my parents could be civil to one another for a few hours and accept the Crawfords' invite. That mild confidence deserted me two seconds after I entered the house.

From the bottom of the living room steps, I could hear the two of them going at it. Heard Ma tell him she wanted her money. I went into the kitchen looking for Rhonda to find out why she wasn't upstairs refereeing the action. She wasn't there. Thought I heard the hum of the washing machine, so I went downstairs into the laundry room. That's where I found her. Sitting Indian style on the floor, with her back to me, listening to her Walkman, singing that jam by Oran "Juice" Jones about his cheating girlfriend and the "alley cat coat wearing, Punch bucket shoe wearing crumb cake" he busted her with.

". . . I saw you and him walkin' in the rain
You were holding hands . . ."

I tiptoed behind her and stuck my fingers into her sides. She screamed and ripped the headphones from her ears.

"Don't be sneaking up on me like that! You scared the sh . . . mess out of me, Dirk!"

"What's going on upstairs?"

"What?"

"Come listen."

Up the basement stairs we marched. As we reached the living room, Pops had just hit the bottom step. "What's up?" I quizzed him.

"When did you come in?"

"A few minutes ago. Everything all right?"

"Everything's fine, Dirksten. You seen the keys to the garage, Baby Girl?"

"They're on top of the fridge, Daddy."

"You fixin' to go somewhere?" I asked.

"And that's your business because?"

"I need to talk to you about something. In fact, I need to talk to you and Ma."

"What's this about, Dirksten?"

"Chill. HEY, MA, CAN YOU COME DOWNSTAIRS, PLEASE? I NEED TO TALK TO YOU."

Pops sucked his teeth, plopped down in his recliner, grabbed the remote, and flicked on the television. Moms came shuffling downstairs a moment later.

"Hey, baby, I didn't know you were here. Is that laundry done, Rhonda?"

"Not yet, Ma."

"What's this about Dirksten?" Pops grunted impatiently.

"Chill. Sit, Ma. I've got something to tell both of you."

A frantic look came over her face.

"*Laaawd have mercy!*" she gasped. "You done gone and got some heifer pregnant, haven't you?"

"Aaaah, shit," my father fumed. "I know what this is about

now. *Hell, no!* You ain't moving back in here with whomever you done knocked—"

"Would y'all both be quiet and *listen* for a minute? Geez! First of all, I ain't got nobody pregnant!"

"Oh, thank you, Jes—"

"Ma!"

"Sorry."

"The Crawfords have invited me to Thanksgiving dinner."

"That's nice, Dirksten—what the hell does that have to do with Brenda and me?"

"They've invited the two of you also."

"Miles Crawford invited *us?*" my mother asked in disbelief. "Well, Henry?"

My father shifted his body in the recliner so he could get at his ass and scratch it.

"Why?"

"Why? *Why* can't you just be appreciative that he has?" my mother chided him.

"I was talking to *Dirksten,* Brenda."

"Well, I'm talking to you, Henry."

"Oh, shut up!"

"Shut me up!"

"WILL BOTH OF YOU SHUT UP! Geez. Are y'all coming or not?"

"I remember that peach cobbler Eunice made for you and Randall's graduation party," Ma said, ignoring my question. "Ooh-ooh-wee, that was delicious. Is she gon' be making another one of those?"

"I don't know, Ma. You'll have to call Mrs. Crawford and ask her that. *Are you coming . . . or are you not?*" She was working my last nerve.

"Yes, I'll be there."

"Great. Pop?"

He looked over at Rhonda. "Is Baby Girl invited, too?"

"Of course."

"I'll go. But I'm gonna say this right now. Brenda, if you give me any shit between now and then I ain't going nowhere." With that he rose from his recliner and quickly disappeared out the back door of the house.

"I'm going to check on the laundry," Rhonda said. "See me before you leave, Dirk. I have something to tell you."

I was alone with my mother now. Of course I had to get to the bottom of what I walked in on earlier.

"I overheard you and him going at it when I got here."

"I'm beginning to reevaluate my life, Dirksten."

"Meaning?"

"Meaning I need to prepare myself for life after Henry. Maybe start working again 'cause as sure as I'm breathing, your father's going to leave me for that young heifer he's seeing. If not her, it'll be some other young heifer. I ain't about to get caught out here without a safety net when that happens."

"I heard you tell him you wanted your money?"

"I needed to make a run up to Linden Boulevard."

"Oh, I get it. He brings you down, so it's off to the liquor store to uplift yourself—"

WHAM!

She hauled off and smacked the livin' shit out of me.

"Don't you *ever* talk down to me, boy. I'm your *mother!* As for what I do or don't do, it *never* has nor will it *ever* require the approval of one Dirksten Lamar Francis. Do you understand me?"

I didn't say a word. Just rubbed the side of my face that stung like hell as she stormed out of the house on her way to the liquor store, no doubt.

After taking a few moments to compose myself, I went downstairs to find out what Rhonda wanted to tell me.

20

MADISON

"What's the problem?" Randall asked me with a puzzled look.

"Had you already invited Dirk when you asked me to invite Fatima?"

"Yes, but I forgot to tell you."

"How could you forget to mention *that?* Had I known this, I would have let Fatima go on to Jersey like she normally does."

"Am I missing something here? A minute ago you said you'd tolerate Dirk. Or was that just lip service?"

"I say what I mean, and mean what I say, Randall."

"Then I'll ask again. What's the problem? You afraid he's gonna try and hit on your girl or something?"

"What do you think?"

"First of all, it ain't like the four of us are going to a nightclub. We're having dinner at my parents' house. Secondly, Dirk's folks may be joining us, too. And if that happens, I guarantee you he'll be on his best behavior. Now, on the other hand, if Fatima starts making googly eyes at him . . ."

"Wouldn't surprise me. He's certainly her type," I mumbled.

"Excuse me?"

"I'm not feeling this, Randall. Fatima's been bugging me to introduce her to somebody for weeks. You heard her on the phone the other day."

"Actually, I wasn't paying her any mind. I just wanted you to hurry up and get *off* the phone so we could get going."

"Fatima's vulnerable right now. I want the next man in her life to be a quality guy—smart, educated, financially stable."

"Do you hear yourself? How do *you* get to define what a 'quality' guy is for Fatima? Dang. I tell you *one* thing about Dirk and you take it and run. Look, I can't take back the invite, and I'm sure Fatima's looking forward to coming. Besides, those two are the least of my concerns at the moment. And do me a favor, please? Don't bring up Dirk's booty kills anymore. And please don't discuss it with anyone else."

"I won't."

"Promise?"

"I *said,* I won't."

I put Randall to sleep—literally. He awoke a few hours later as the sun began to rise and hurried his clothes back on. Before leaving, he took a cassette tape out of his jacket and handed it to me.

"I recorded this for us. It's our theme song. Listen to the lyrics and imagine me singing it to you every chance you get."

That sounded romantic. (I just love romance.) Randall gave me a kiss and left.

I tried to guess what song he had picked as our theme song. A ballad by Luther? Howard Hewett? Freddie Jackson? I read the label on the cassette. "I Found Lovin'" by the . . . *Fatback Band?* I popped the cassette in the boom box I kept on top of my refrigerator as I scrambled me some eggs and burnt some bacon.

The beat was fresh. It had me shaking my ass as I stood over the stove.

Ah, yeah. I was digging this . . .

  "*. . . I found lovn',*
  Since I found you.
  . . . I'm in love with you babe . . ."

When the song ended, I hit the REWIND button and listened to it again. The second time through it dawned on me that I had indeed heard it before. The DJ was spinnin' it the night Randall and I danced at the Red Parrot.

A WEEK BEFORE
THANKSGIVING DAY
1987 . . .

21

DIRK

My supervisor gave me the okay to leave work early, so I moseyed over to Randall's cube in accounting to see if he was ready to leave, too. We didn't typically commute home together since he got off a half hour earlier than I did. R was staring a hole through his computer screen when I arrived.

"I'm off. Wanna ride home together?"

"Actually, I'm gonna be staying here a little longer."

"Big project?"

"Sit down—and keep your voice down. I'm working on my resume," he said, showing it to me on the computer screen.

"You going somewhere?"

"Maybe."

"You don't like working at United Trust anymore?"

"I've been here five years, Dirk. I can't stay forever."

"Five years is nothing. My pops has been at his job for eighteen."

"Yeah, well, that's what those old heads do. Stay at a job

forever. Don't you ever think about doing something else? Making more money someplace else?"

"Shit, yeah. But I've gotten kinda comfortable here."

"Yeah, well I can't settle for just being comfortable anymore."

"Oh? And when did you come to this conclusion? Wait. Let me guess. Since Madison came along?"

"Don't even go there. I've come to this conclusion on my own."

"Sure you have. Guess the next thing you'll be telling me is that you want to move out and move in with her. *Hmph.* Later, dude, I'm outta here."

I left R to his resume and practically jogged to the Lexington Avenue subway station. Came upon a scene of sheer bedlam once I reached it. Chatter amongst the crowd revealed the cause. Some troubled soul had apparently hurled himself in front of a train at Times Square, resulting in a disruption of service, and massive delays going uptown and downtown. Trains were so packed that when one did arrive there was no room to board. Folks on the platform weren't letting people on the trains get off, and those on the train weren't letting anyone get on. Well-dressed businessmen and businesswomen were behaving like 2-year-olds. Pushing and shoving.

I stayed as far away from the fray as I could 'cause if anyone pushed or shoved me, we was gon' be fighting. That's when my eyes caught sight of something that made all the commotion around me inconsequential for the moment: a supermodel, five foot sevenish, dark-chocolate complexion, with short hair, dressed in a black waist-length leather jacket, white sweater, and black stretch pants tucked inside of her black leather boots.

Turn to the side for me, love. Puh-leeze!

She must've been reading my mind.

PA-DOW!!

Honey dip had a shape like an upside down question mark.

I inched closer to where she was standing. Wanted to get in her field of vision. Stared her down, trying not to be too obvious as another train too crowded to board entered the station.

I might be convinced to give up sticking and moving for this!

She caught me staring at her. I smiled. Mouthed "hello." She smiled back. Couldn't recall ever seeing her at this station before and I remember faces—especially ones attached to a body like that! Wondered if this was her normal time. If so, it wasn't mine, which made me also wonder if this would be the first and last chance I'd get to push up on her.

We made eye contact again and she smiled at me again. That was my proverbial "foot in the door." I moseyed on over toward her.

"Looks like we're going to be here a while, huh?"

"Tell me about it," she said. "What's the deal?"

"Someone committed suicide at Times Square. Jumped in front of a train."

"Oh, my God! That's awful," she shrieked. "You think we can get on the next train?"

"May have to bum-rush our way on."

"Well, you clear a path and I'll follow," she laughed.

We managed to squeeze onto the next train that came into the station. Packed like sardines in a can would be more descriptive.

"So, where do you work?" I inquired.

"I teach second grade at P.S. 143 in Corona, Queens."

"Really? Playing hooky today, are we?"

"Sorta. I took the day off and had lunch with a girlfriend of mine who works on 45th Street. Where do you work?"

"On 47th and Lexington. United Trust. Heard of it?"

"The insurance company?"

"That's the one. I'm Dirk, by the way."

"Fatima."

During the ride into Queens we chatted about her job as a second-grade teacher and about our plans for the upcoming Thanksgiving weekend. Fatima told me she was happy to be staying in town this year.

"Well, this is my stop," she said as the train pulled into the Kew Gardens station. "Nice meeting you, Dirk."

I was nowhere near ready for this encounter to end. Didn't have time to crack for her number before she got off the train, though. Besides, even if I did, there were way too many people in our faces. I didn't want to chump myself in front of all those faces if she *didn't* give me her digits. Had to think fast.

She worked her way off the crowded subway car, and I followed her, managing to push my way out a millisecond before the doors closed in my face.

"Hey, Fatima, wait up. Listen . . . uh, this ain't my stop, but I'd really like to talk to you some more. Are you married? Got a man?

"No and no."

"Good. Can I call you?"

"I . . . don't think so."

Wrong answer, Fatima.

"Why not?"

"Because I don't know you well enough to give you my number. You seem nice, but you could be an ax murderer for all I know."

"That's a joke, right? Do I look like an ax murderer to you?"

"What does an ax murderer look like?"

Geez.

"How 'bout this," she continued. "If we ever meet up again and get to talk a little longer, maybe I'll give you my number then."

"I'll probably never see you again."

"Aren't you the optimist. If it's meant for us to get better acquainted, I'm sure the planets will align themselves and cause our paths to cross again."

"That's another joke, right? Aren't you the *comedian*. Nice meeting you, too, Fatima. Bye."

THANKSGIVING DAY
1987 . . .

22

RANDALL

The girls were looking like all that and then some. Madison wore a white cotton blouse and an ankle-length denim skirt, with a modest slit going up the side of it. Fatima was in a jumpsuit that was hugging her body for dear life.

My mother answered the door and told us to come in. As I gave her a hug, she whispered, "Which one is Madison?" in my ear. I stepped out of our embrace for an introduction.

"Ma, this is Madison and her friend Fatima."

"Hello, ladies, so glad you could make it."

"Thanks for having us, Mrs. Crawford," Madison said.

"Eunice, please. Y'all come on in and meet everyone."

Gathered around the TV in the den watching the Green Bay Packers versus the Detroit Lions were my aunt Ethel, her husband, Billy, my sisters, Stephanie and Mariah, their husbands Curtis and Maceo, and their children, who were rippin' and running all over the house like they didn't have any home training. Lori was there as well with her kids.

I spoke to Mariah and Maceo first. "Which one is your girlfriend?" were the first words out of my sister's mouth.

"The light-skinned one," I said.

"That's *all right,*" Maceo chimed in with a bit too much enthusiasm for my sister's taste.

Mariah rolled her eyes at him.

I went around the house introducing the girls to everyone, then told them to make themselves at home. Went into the kitchen and found PC pacing around in an apron.

"Smells good in here," I said to him. "Can't wait to get my eat on."

"You and everyone else. Any word on whether Henry and Brenda Francis are coming?"

"They'll be here. Dirk's coming with them."

"How about your other friend your mother tells me about?"

"She's in the den socializing. Want to meet her now?"

"Depends."

"On?"

"Do you *really* like this girl?"

"Why?"

"Because all this . . . her coming over for dinner and everything . . . It's probably a *big* deal to her, son. A man should never lead a woman into believing—"

"I *really* like her, Dad."

"In that case, I'm ready to meet her."

I took a deep breath before returning to the kitchen with Madison. Hoped for the best and expected anything.

"Dad, this is Madison. Madison, my father, Miles Crawford."

"Pleased to meet you, Mr. Crawford."

"Miles, young lady, call me Miles. Pleased to meet you, too. *My goodness!* Randall didn't tell me he was dating such a good-looking woman. Come to think of it, he hasn't told his mother or me much of anything about you."

"Well, Randall hasn't told me much about you, either, Miles. But we've got the rest of the evening to get acquainted, now, don't we?"

23

DIRK

Mrs. Crawford greeted us at the front door. Inside, Pops exchanged greetings and a handshake with Pastor Crawford, who promptly fetched him a Heineken and a folding chair, so he could sit in front of the TV and watch the football game. Pastor Crawford also fulfilled my mother's immediate request for a glass of wine.

There was already a nice crowd in the house. Lori was rockin' a tight sweater, spandex pants, and a pair of door-knocker earrings that said "Baby Doll" in the middle. (Is it any wonder she drives the rest of her religious, conservative family up the wall?)

I walked over and gave her a hug.

"What's up, Ms. Thang?"

"I'm fine."

"You look rather um . . ."

"Um?"

"I'm searching for the right adjective."

"Be careful, pretty boy," she laughed. "So, which one of those chicks with my brother is his girlfriend?"

"What do you mean which one?"

"He marched up in here with two girls."

"Two?"

I scanned the room and spotted Madison chillin' on the Crawfords' sectional sofa. She looked . . . scrumptious.

I should have pushed up on you harder that night at the Parrot.

"I don't know who this other girl is, but R's honey is sitting over there."

"The white chick? *Figures.*"

"Geez, Lori. She's not white. She's just light-skinned like me."

"Yeah, okay. She looks white to me. She's attractive, though. How in the world did *Randall*—"

"I've been wondering the same thing myself. But you ain't hear that from me. Excuse me a moment. I'ma go over and say hello."

24

MADISON

Crazy butterflies were in my stomach, but Randall's mom made them disappear soon as we met. (She's sweet. Seems like good mother-in-law material.)

Shortly after we arrived, so did a few other guests. I didn't recognize the man, woman, and teenage girl who entered the house, but I did recognize the individual bringing up the rear behind them: Deputy D-O-G. He did look particularly dapper in a burgundy mock neck and steel-gray slacks, I must say. Okay, I admit it. Dirk's got it going on. It's just a shame he's such a *t-t-tramp.* He was busy chatting it up with a cute but tacky-looking sista dressed more for a nightclub than Thanksgiving dinner.

I took a seat on the sofa while Fatima went to check her makeup in the bathroom. Out my peripheral vision, I could see Dirk excusing himself from that tacky-looking sista and heading my way.

"What's going on, Madison?"

"Hey, Dirk. Is that your family I saw you come in with?"

"Uh-huh."

"Who's the young lady you were just talking to?"

"That's Lori. R's sister."

"Really?"

I peeked over Dirk's shoulder and saw Fatima returning from the bathroom. As soon as she and Dirk caught sight of one another their jaws dropped simultaneously.

"Fatima?"

"Dean?"

"Dirk."

"Right, Dirk. Sorry. Oh, my God. What are you doing here, Dirk?"

"I should ask you the same thing."

"Uh . . . you two know each other?" I interrupted.

"Sorta," Fatima said. "We ran into each other in the subway station last week. The day I came into the city and had lunch with you."

"Uh-huh . . ."

"Where's your man, Madison? Don't y'all have some hob-nobbin' y'all need to do?" Dirk asked.

A sista could take a hint. I'd have to get the details later.

"I'll be back," I said, leaving them alone to search for Randall. "Honey, can I speak to you for a second?" I asked as soon as I found him.

"What's up?"

"In private?"

"Oh. Um . . . let's go upstairs."

Randall took me upstairs into a sloppy bedroom cluttered with toys.

"Whose room is this?" I wondered, surveying the carnage.

"My sister's kids."

"I thought you said your sisters had all moved out?"

"Lori came back home."

"Lori. Right. You've never mentioned her, Randall."

"No?"

"No."

"Sorry. She's the youngest girl."

"How many kids does she have?"

"Three."

"Is she divorced?"

"Never been married . . ."

Whoa.

". . . What did you need to talk to me about?"

I could sense Randall was anxious to get off the subject of Lori.

"You're not going to believe this. Dirk and Fatima have met."

"Great. You knew they would. We're all under the same roof tonight."

"I mean *before* this evening."

"Get outta here."

"Mmm-hmm. Sometime last week, evidently. Fatima just told me they met on a subway train or something like that."

"Hmmm. That's funny. Dirk didn't mention that he met anyone recently."

"Fatima, either."

"So neither of them knew the other would be here tonight?"

"Appears so."

"See that?"

"What?"

"You didn't want them to meet and look what happened. Fate overruled you. Wait here. I gotta use the bathroom. And after that I think we ought to get back downstairs. I don't want PC or anyone else in my family to find us alone in this bedroom."

"PC?"

"Pastor Crawford."

25

DIRK

"Guess the planets aligned themselves after all."

"How 'bout that, Mr. Pessimistic."

"Yeah, right. Like you expected to ever see me again, Ms. Comedian."

"Yes, I'm equally as shocked as you are."

"So, what *are* you doing here?"

"Madison's my best friend. Her boyfriend invited her to have dinner with his family and I was invited to join them. And what are you doing here?"

Best friend? Damn!

"Dirk?"

"I'm sorry. What did you say?"

"I said what are *you* doing here?"

"How's this for coincidence. Your best friend's boyfriend happens to be my best friend, and his family invited me over for dinner as well."

"Small world, ain't it?"

Mr. Crawford entered the room at that moment and asked

everyone to move to the dining area. He was about to bless the huge spread before us. Everyone formed a circle around the dinner table and held hands. I held Fatima's. Peeked at her sexy French manicure. Briefly fantasized how it would feel to have her hands all over my body. Looked up and glanced across the table. Randall and Madison were staring dead at me. He was grinning from ear to ear.

She wasn't smiling at all.

Pastor Crawford bowed his head and began to give grace. *Don't give no long-ass prayer, dude. I'm hungry.*

26

RANDALL

"Amen!"

I was getting full just *looking* at all the food on the table. Turkey, stuffing, ham, duck, chitterlings, candied yams, string beans, corn on the cob, okra, collard greens, turnip greens, mustard greens, potato salad, tossed salad, cornbread, biscuits. And on deck for dessert—amongst a variety of other delectable treats—my mother's peach cobbler.

Food was being passed around the table. Drinks were being poured. Knives, spoons, and forks were clinking and clanging. Multiple conversations were going on.

"So, how did you and my son meet?" PC asked Madison as he reached for the potato salad.

"We met at the Red Parrot in July."

"Oh, okay. Y'all met at a restaurant."

"It's a nightclub, actually."

"You met my son in a *discotheque?*"

I glanced over at Dirk. He was on the verge of busting a gut.

"I didn't know my son went to discotheques. When did you start doing that?" PC asked me.

"Uh, once in a blue moon," I mumbled.

"You got him started on that?" he asked Dirk.

"M-me?" Dirk stuttered.

"That's the Black John Travolta over there, Miles."

That was Mrs. Francis.

"Was it love at first sight, Madison?" That was my mother. As usual being about as subtle as a freight train. Madison's light skin turned beet red in embarrassment.

"Ma!"

"It's okay, Randall. No, Eunice, it wasn't love at first sight. We just got to dancing and talking—"

"*Dancing?* Randall can't dance," my sister Stephanie chimed in.

Everyone found that gut-busting funny. Everyone but me. I looked over at Dirk again. His fool ass was laughing so hard tears were streaming down his face.

"Can we change the subject?" I pleaded.

"Don't mind us, Madison, it's only love," Stephanie assured her.

"So where are you from?" was my mother's next inquiry.

"Upstate New York. Newburgh. Heard of it?"

"Can't say that I have. Do you have any brothers and sisters?"

"One of each. I'm the oldest."

"How old are ya?"

Mrs. Francis again. The nerve of her.

"Now why you all up in that girl's business like that?" Mr. Francis chided his wife.

Cuz her alcoholic ass has had three glasses of wine already, I almost blurted out.

"Oh, I don't mind." Madison was being a real trooper this evening. "I'll be 29 in February."

"Where do you work, Madison?" my aunt Ethel asked.

"I work at the headquarters for *Trendy* magazine on Madison Avenue."

"Do you really? I'm the HR Director at United Trust and I've heard some really good things about their benefits package. What do you do there?"

"Well . . . I was planning on surprising Randall with this later, but I guess now is as good a time as any. I've just been promoted to assistant fashion editor."

"Congratulations!" Aunt E tapped her wineglass with her fork to get everyone's attention. "Hey, folks. In case you didn't just hear, Madison's just received a big promotion at her job. I think that calls for a toast."

Everyone raised their glasses in salute to my girl's accomplishment—which hit me completely out of left field. I didn't know whether to kiss her, hug her, or what. I did nothing—except toss a feeble "Congratulations" her way.

"You're a very lovely young lady, Fatima," PC said, changing the topic of conversation again following the toast to Madison.

"Isn't she," my mother concurred. "Your complexion is beautiful."

"Why, thank you, Mrs. Crawford," Fatima cheesed, revealing a perfectly symmetrical grill.

"Is Dirksten treating you right?"

Fatima nearly spit up on herself.

"Oh, no, no, ma'am. Dirk's not my boyfriend. We just met."

"I think you and Dirksten would make a lovely couple if you don't mind me saying." (My mother just doesn't know when to quit.)

"When you gon' settle down, get married, and raise some chil'ren, Dirksten?" PC wanted to know.

Mrs. Francis swooped in and answered that on behalf of her son.

"My son ain't *even* thinking about settling down, Pastor Miles."

"Oh, shut up, Brenda!" Mr. Francis said.

"Shut me up, Henry!" she said, rolling her eyes at her husband. "Pastor Miles is right, Dirksten. You can't keep chasing hos forever."

Oooooh! No, she didn't.

Dead silence blanketed the dinner table.

Put the wine down, Mrs. Francis. Please!

Dirk's face said it all: he wanted to put his mother under the table—that or crawl under it himself.

"Ain't nothing wrong with Dirksten that a little Jesus won't cure," PC said.

Now *I* was on the verge of bustin' a gut.

Thirty minutes of good eating later, Thanksgiving dinner at the Crawfords' had come to a close. (Which in itself was something to be very thankful for.) I couldn't look at, let alone eat another piece of food. Mom's peach cobbler was going to have to see a doggy bag.

Everyone was saying their good-byes. I was in the kitchen wrapping up a few pieces of peach cobbler in aluminum foil when Aunt E came in.

"I like your friend, nephew. She's very nice—and very attractive. Better hold on to her."

"Oh, I intend to."

"What do you think about her promotion? Couldn't help but notice it surprised you."

"Had no clue about it."

"I'm sure it comes with a good piece of change."

"Meaning?"

"If you had issues before, you're really going to have your work cut out for you now."

"Lucky me, huh?"

"Just be happy for her. If you're smart, you'll figure a way to make her success work for you, too. I'm going to dig around some more for you when I get back in the office on Monday."

"Thanks, Aunt E. Tell Uncle Billy I said good-bye."

Dirk moseyed into the kitchen shortly after Aunt Ethel.

"Dude. Your pops is *out cold*. He tried to embarrass me in front of Fatima. I ask you, is that any way to treat a dinner guest?"

"Forget my pops embarrassing you. What's up with your *moms?*"

"Man, I'm just glad your folks had sense enough to keep the hard liquor in the cabinets tonight."

"I don't think there is any hard liquor in their cabinets. Anyway, what's this I hear? You've met Fatima already? Why didn't you tell me?"

"I struck out. Figured I'd never see that girl again so there was really no point in even telling you about her. But you've got a little explaining to do yourself."

"Me?"

"Yeah, you. You've been seeing Madison for, what, a couple of months? Why were you keeping her fine-ass friend a secret from me? Why didn't you set up a lil som'um-som'um and introduce us?"

"One, I only met Fatima once before tonight. And that was briefly. Two . . . aw, that ain't important. Fatima's got it going on, huh? You feelin' that?"

"Feelin' it. I could see myself getting to know her on an entirely different tip. Felt that way the moment I met her."

"Is there another soul occupying your body? This can't possibly be Mr. Stick and Move talking."

"You got jokes."

"Think she's feelin' you, too?"

"Dunno. We had some good conversation this evening, but

this here wasn't the best setting to find out, yow mean? I got an idea. Let's go to Bentley's tonight. Me, you, and the girls."

"You serious?"

"Very. They're having a special Thanksgiving throwdown tonight. I wanna get that sweet, dark chocolate on the dance floor and see if she can hang with the Black John Travolta. Call it aerobic exercise. Work off all this food we've just ate."

"That does sound like fun. Let me see if Madison's with it."

"Do that. I'll go work on Fatima meanwhile. The *discotheque's* gon' be jumpin' tonight, R."

"Funny, Dirk. Ha, ha, ha."

27

MADISON

The line to get into Bentley's was wrapped nearly around the corner of 43rd Street. I can't believe I let Randall talk me into this. Be that as it may, the guys wanted to party, and so did Fatima, so I couldn't be the proverbial party pooper.

Our theme song, "I Found Lovin'," was playing as soon as we got inside the club. The four of us hit the dance floor immediately. Followed the DJ's instructions to "throw your hands in the air and wave 'em like you just don't care," and sang at the top of our lungs.

> ". . . I found lovin'
> Since I found you . . ."

We danced for what seemed like an hour. Poor Randall. He could barely keep up with me. After working up a sweat, we scooted over to the lounge for a cooldown. I had yet to get up in Fatima's Kool-Aid on her and Dirk's meeting. After catching our breath for a few minutes, me and Fatima excused ourselves so we could talk in private.

"We're going to get a drink. Want anything?" I asked Randall.

"I'm straight."

"Dirk?"

"An Amaretto and OJ, please."

Upon reaching the bar, a pair of brothas relinquished their stools to us.

"How you two fine sistas doing tonight?" asked one of them.

"Very well, thank you."

"I'm Ted and this is my boy, Perry."

"Hi, Ted. Hi, Perry. I'm Tammy and this is my girlfriend, Porsha."

Fatima snickered.

"Y'all *must* be models," Perry said, shaking his head and making strange grunting noises. (This is why I stopped going to nightclubs.)

Perry looked better than Ted—not that that was saying much. Ted had a protruding forehead and was in bad need of dental benefits.

"Haven't I seen you two in *Essence* magazine before?" Perry exclaimed, holding his hands like he was taking pictures of Fatima and me with an imaginary camera.

Knee-grow, please.

The bartender handed us our drinks. As I reached in my purse to pay for them, Ted came to the rescue.

"Let me take care of those, Tammy."

"Oh, that's okay, I—"

Ouch!

Fatima kicked me in the ankle. I rolled my eyes at her.

"All right, I'm tired of waiting. Talk to me. I want the details," I said, taking a sip of my Cosmo, iggin' Bert and Ernie.

"We were standing on the subway platform waiting for the F train at Lexington Avenue. We got to talking on the ride into

Queens. When I got off at my stop, Dirk followed me and
asked for my number."

"You give it to him?"

"Nope. Wanted to, though. That's a pretty boy, Maddy. You
know I love me some pretty boys. But nobody gets my number
that easily. But now that he and I have run into each other
again—especially like *this*—he's getting the digits. And what's
up with you, missy?"

"Me?"

"I've been asking you for weeks if you knew of any guys you
could introduce me to. Why didn't you tell me about Dirk?"

"He's not the right kind of guy—"

"Ladies' night out?" Perry interrupted.

Guess Tom and Jerry weren't about to be ignored after
paying for our drinks.

"Actually, gentlemen, we're here with our boyfriends,"
Fatima exclaimed. "They're waiting for us in the lounge. But
thanks for takin' care of these drinks. That was so sweet."

Fred and Barney got the hint and promptly stepped—not
before calling us "skeezers" under their breath.

"Yeah, whatever, Mutt and Jeff. Did you say *our* boyfriends,
Fatima?"

"Did you say 'not the right kind of guy' for me? *Hello*,
Maddy. Dirk's fine, tall, single, working—"

"You can't be serious."

"Is there some reason you don't want me talking to him?"

"As a matter of fact there is."

"And what is that?"

"He's a D-O-G!"

"Huh?"

"I didn't tell you I met Dirk before I met Randall, did I?
Oh, yeah. First he tries to holla at me. Then he turns his attention to some Hispanic-looking chick sitting at the bar. Next
he ends up waltzing out of the club with her, leaving Randall

there all by himself. He's a serial one-nighter, girl. You know what he calls his conquests? 'Booty kills.'"

"Booty kills?"

"Booty kills!"

Fatima started laughing. "How do you know all this?"

"Trust me. I just do, okay?"

"Dirk seems sweet. You sure you're not trying to run me off 'cause you've got the hots for him?"

"Dirk? Puh-leeze! I've *got* a man, or haven't you noticed?"

"Oh, I've noticed, but let's be honest, Randall's . . ."

"What?" I asked, getting defensive.

"Young, for starters. Short, too. And I'm not trying to be funny, but this is 1987 and the brotha's still sportin' a 'fro, for cryin' out loud."

"Okay, so he's a little . . . *different* from what I'm accustomed to. But so what? He's a good brotha and those are hard to come by these days. You of all people should know that. When was the last time *you* had one?"

"Watch it, heifer. Now you're hitting below the belt."

"All Randall needs is a few strokes of my makeover wand and—"

"Uh-oh. Better be careful, girl. You might create yourself a monster."

28

DIRK

Waiting for the girls to return with my drink, I began having second thoughts about coming here tonight. Five minutes after we got in the club, I spotted Antoinette. My booty kill with the GED. Ten minutes after that, Deanna. My full-figured booty kill—never again. Her fat ass nearly suffocated me. But I digress . . .

I was pretty sure neither of them saw me. Hoped not anyway. The last thing I needed was for some stunt from the past to roll up on me, expose me, and short-circuit my program with Fatima before it had any chance to get off the ground. Fatima knew nothing about my booty killin'—and I intended to keep it that way. Besides, Randall was right. I had been getting careless lately. Like using our apartment for a booty palace. That *was* dumb—and dangerous. I didn't need any more drama. I already had the Dominican Lizette threatening me. I sure hoped her loco ass wasn't in the house tonight, too.

I leaned over to Randall. "Stick a fork in me, dude. I'm

done. No more stick and moves. I'm turning over a new leaf. Call it my early New Year's resolution for 1988."

Randall felt my forehead with the back of his hand.

"You running a fever or something?"

"You got jokes."

"What's brought this on?"

"I'd really like to get better acquainted with Fatima. She just might be the kind of honey I'd wanna get serious with."

"It's about time!"

"I mean, think about it, R. Imagine if some dude treated my sister like a booty kill? Like her new boyfriend."

"Rhonda's got a boyfriend?"

"Yeah, I didn't tell you. She needs one of those right now like I need a hole in my head. Some dude at her high school named Cash. Cash better be that knee-grow's *surname,* yow mean?"

Randall laughed. "Wow, and here I thought all Rhonda was into was getting good grades and getting into college. Bunk boys."

Madison and Fatima finally returned from the bar with my Amaretto and OJ.

"Dang. What took y'all so long?" I asked.

"Girl talk. You got a problem with that?" Fatima replied in a sassy yet sexy tone.

I was officially diggin' this honey something bad.

29

DIRK

*". . . Seen you last night, saw you standin' there,
I couldn't picture the color of your hair . . ."*

Sugar Daddy, Bentley's resident DJ, was rockin' Keith
Sweat's "I Want Her." Fatima was moving her body like a ser-
pent. But she had a brotha in a no-BBFin' zone. (That's like an
invisible fence around the booty.) I hate when honeys do that!

I happened to glance at the couple dancing to the right
of us.

Shit!

It was none other than full-figured Deanna. We made eye
contact. She grinned at me devilishly. *Act like you don't know
me,* I mouthed to her while Fatima's back was turned to me.
Fatima finally backed that thing up on a bruh, giving him a
whiff for a few seconds. Willy got stiff as an Olympic diving
board. Embarrassed by my sudden exuberance, I decided I
better get off the dance floor and calm down.

"LET'S GO SOMEWHERE AND TALK," I suggested.

"OK."

I grabbed Fatima by the hand and pushed my way through the crowd toward the exit at Bentley's. We got our hands stamped so we could get back in later, then headed outside coatless into the chilly November air.

I copped a Snapple Iced Tea and a Diet Pepsi from the cooler inside the 24-hour deli around the corner and slid into an empty booth. Watched as Fatima placed the straw to her full lips and took a sip of soda. I had never seen skin like hers before. So dark. So flawless. She glanced up and caught me staring at her.

"You're staring."

"Maybe I like what I see."

"Maybe?"

Her confidence was a turn-on.

"Okay, I *like* what I see."

"That's better. Figured as much, given the way you were gawking at me on that subway platform last week."

"Gawking? I was hardly—"

"Please. I could *feel* your eyeballs on me, Dirk."

"I was admiring your complexion just now."

"Really? I'm too dark and chocolaty for a lot of guys. I think my body gets most of the attention."

You ain't lying, girl.

"Well, I'm diggin' your chocolaty complexion."

"Thank you. Owe it all to my homeland."

"Homeland?"

"Nigeria."

"Stop."

"True. I didn't come to the United States until I was four-teen."

"I don't hear any accent."

"You haven't heard me around a bunch of other Nigerians, either."

"What's your last name?"

"Ah-coy-yay," she said, sounding out each syllable.

"Spell that."

"O-K-O-Y-E."

"Fatima Okoye. Who knew? So . . . did you like grow up in the ghetto back in Nigeria?"

"No, Dirk. And my family didn't run around butt-naked with spears, killing wild animals so we could eat, either."

"Now see, I wasn't even going there."

"Sure you weren't. My neighborhood in Nigeria is what people in this country would consider middle-class."

"So, what brought you to America?"

"My father worked for the U.N. and his job relocated him to New York in 1974."

"Is that right? Do you know you're the first honey, uh, woman, I've ever met who's actually from the motherland?"

"Are you a native New Yorker?"

"Jamaica, Queens, born and raised," I proudly proclaimed.

"Are you interested in me, Dirk?"

"You don't beat around the bush, do you?"

"Answer the question."

"I am."

"Do you have a girlfriend?"

"Would I be sitting here trying to holla at you if I did?"

"I would hope not. But then we both know some guys are just dogs that way."

"I don't get down like that."

"How do you get down?"

"I was totally bummed when you didn't give me your number last week," I said, sidestepping her question.

Fatima rummaged through her purse, took out a pen, and began scribbling on a napkin.

"I hope this makes up for bummin' you out," she said, sliding the napkin across the table to me.

"This makes up for it quite nicely."

I folded the napkin and stuck it in my back pocket.

"You like basketball?" I asked.

"Do I? I'm a bona fide hoop junkie."

"Great. I get tickets to the Garden from time to time at my job. I'ma see if I can get two for this Monday's Knicks game. Dominique Wilkins and the Atlanta Hawks are in town."

"The Human Highlight Film? Oh, man, I love his vertical game."

"Uh-oh. Let me find out a sista really does know her basketball."

"Word up," she laughed. "But I don't think I want to go to a Knicks game . . . not yet anyway. I was dating . . . never mind. That's way too much information. Look, Dirk, before you and I make plans to do anything together, there's something I need to ask you. This may sound really silly, but, does the phrase 'booty kills' mean anything to you?"

"Booty kills? W-what's that?" I stuttered.

"Madison told me some stuff about you, Dirk."

"Stuff like *what?*"

"She says you're into one-night stands with women you meet in nightclubs. Is that true?"

I could feel the blood in my veins beginning to boil. Only *one* person could have . . .

Damn you, Randall!

I knew it! Knew that green-eyed, high-yellow, long-haired, high-maintenance heifer didn't like me. She saw me and Fatima having a good time at the Crawfords' earlier and decided she was going to put a stop to it quick, fast, and in a hurry. Now I know what took the two of them so long to come back from the bar with my drink. Girl talk, my ass! Madison was at that bar singing like a canary. And here I was paranoid about being exposed by GED Antoinette or full-figured Deanna.

"Yoo-hoo. Earth to Dirk . . ."

"Huh?"

"Are you going to answer my question?"

"No. That's not true and I have no idea why Madison would tell you something like that. She's *so* wrong. Maybe she wants to handpick *her* idea of the perfect guy for you."

Fatima chuckled.

"That thought did cross my mind. That and one other. That maybe she might have a thing for you herself."

"There you go again trying to be funny, Ms. Comedian."

"Women are crazy, Dirk. We can behave in *strange* ways when we've got it bad for someone. I did pose the question to her, though."

"And?"

"She denied it."

"There you go."

"I'm 27 years old, Dirk. Not some giddy teenager. I want an unattached, one-woman kind of guy. Not another 'slam-bam-thank-you-Sam.' If you're lying to me, it's gonna be too late real early for you and me."

"I swear. I don't get down like that, Fatima."

"Okay. You ready to go back to the club?"

Oh, am I, I thought to myself.

30

RANDALL

Dirk and Fatima left for the dance floor. Me and Madison remained seated. Our dogs were barking. Hers from the heels, mine from folks stepping on them all night.

"I had a little heart-to-heart with Dirk while you and Fatima were over at the bar," I told her. "He's really feeling your girl."

"Mmm-hmm. She's feeling him, too. So, naturally, I felt it was my responsibility to warn her . . ."

"Tell me you didn't, Madison."

"Okay, I won't."

"What part of 'Don't discuss Dirk's business with *anybody*' did you not understand?"

"I'm sorry, sweetie, but I had to let Fatima know what she might be getting into if she decides to get involved with that jerk."

"Your timing really sucks."

"What are you talking about?"

"Dirk wants to get to know Fatima on a one-on-one basis."

Madison looked at me like I had just won first prize at the Fool of the Week contest.

"And you fell for that okeydoke?"

"He's sincere."

"Puh-leeze. Where are those two anyway? They've been gone an awful long time. I've got to go to the ladies' room. I'll be right back."

I spotted Dirk and Fatima strolling back into the lounge. She looked pissed and the look on his face wasn't much better. I got up and walked over to them.

"Where y'all been?"

"We went outside to talk for a while," Fatima said.

"In the cold?"

"Inside the deli up the street."

"I'm ready to bust this joint. How 'bout y'all?"

"Sounds good to me," Fatima said. "I'm not in much of a partying mood anymore."

"I need to speak to you, Randall. In private—*now!*" Dirk barked.

"I'm going to the bar to get another drink before we hit the road. Where's Maddy?" Fatima asked.

"Ladies' room."

"Well, tell her where I'm at when she comes back."

When I turned to find out what Dirk wanted to talk to me about—as if I didn't have some clue—he had disappeared that quick. I caught up to Fatima as she was walking away.

"You okay, Fatima?"

"I'm fine, Randall."

"You seem upset. Did something happen between you and Dirk? Y'all get into an argument or something?" She didn't answer. "Madison told you, didn't she? I really wish she hadn't done that. Look, Fatima, Dirk really likes you. I've never heard him this wound up over a woman and I've known him forever. Cut him a little slack, okay?"

"I thought your boy might be man enough to man up. And he did—only after lying to my face twice. Talk about not getting off on the right foot with a girl."

"C'mon. Back a man into a corner and his first instinct is naturally going to be to—"

"Lie? Do you lie to Madison, Randall?"

"I've got nothing to hide."

"If you did?"

That sounded like a trick question.

"I don't plan on putting myself in any predicament that'll make me have to lie to her."

31

MADISON

I left the ladies' room to find Dirk standing right outside the door. He grabbed me by my arm forcefully.

"Why you all in my fuckin' business?"

"Excuse me?"

"You heard me."

"You need to let go of my arm."

"Answer me, bitch!"

Uh-uh . . .

"*BOY, LOOK!* You best take two muthafuckin' steps back from me before I—"

"What? Tell Randall? Go ahead. *Do it.* 'Cause right about now, I'm tempted to kick *his* ass on general principle. What is your fuckin' problem anyway?"

"I wasn't aware I had a problem. You on the other hand obviously do. Can't keep your dick in your pants for one," I mumbled under my breath.

"Speak up if you got something to say."

"Kiss my ass, Dirk."

"Ever since you hooked up with Randall you've been acting funky towards me. What have I done to *you?*"

I took a deep breath. This was getting ugly. We were beginning to attract the attention of other patrons in Bentley's.

"You haven't done anything to me. It's what you do to *other* people that I have a problem with."

"*Other people?* WHAT THE FUCK ARE YOU TALKING ABOUT, MADISON?"

My eyes began welling up. He was scaring me.

"STOP YELLING AT ME! I AM NOT YOUR CHILD!" I screamed back at him. "Fatima's my best friend and that's *one* girl you won't get to jerk around."

"Is *that* what this is about? You think I'm gonna . . . I would never treat Fatima like a . . ."

"What, Dirk? *Booty kill?*"

"That's it. I'm done talking to you. Let's you and me get something straight right now, Madison. One, I don't give a shit if you are Randall's girlfriend. Two, I *really* don't give a shit whether or not you like me. But you better not *ever* shoot your fuckin' mouth off about me to anybody else again."

We had definitely drawn an audience at this point—an all-female one. (After all, we were arguing right outside of the ladies' room.) One of those onlookers decided to come to my defense.

"Girl, don't let him talk to you like that. He cute . . . but he ain't *all that*."

Dirk diverted his attention away from me to collectively acknowledge the spectators his uncouth conduct had attracted.

"You hos need to mind your fuckin' business, too."

I was balling now. My mascara was running and I had a healthy accumulation of snot in my nose.

"You brought this on yourself, Dirk. Don't blame me. You ain't *good* enough for a woman like Fatima!"

"FUCK YOU, MADISON."

"No, FUCK *YOU,* DIRK!"

I shoved him out of my way with all the strength I could muster and ran off to find Randall.

32

RANDALL

"What the *hell* happened to your face?" Madison's eyes were all puffy and her makeup was a mess. "You left for the ladies' room fifteen minutes ago looking *fly*. You've come back to me looking straight *busted*."

"Gee, thanks, Randall. You really know the right things to say to a woman. You want to know what happened?"

"Yes, I want to know—"

"I'm coming out of the bathroom and guess who's standing outside of the door waiting for me? Starts going off on me."

"Dirk?"

"*Yeah.* That fool cursed me out—in front of other people."

Tell me this isn't happening.

"He and Fatima came back in the club shortly after you took off. It's all out in the open now and she doesn't want to talk to him anymore. Do you get it now? This is the reason I told you to drop it. To stop talking about—"

"Oh, *shut up,* Randall! No matter what you think, I think I did the right thing. Anyway, *my* actions are hardly at issue right now. Are you going to let him get away with talking to me like that?"

"No. I'm not. Where is he?"

"Try the *ladies'* room!"

I combed the Bentley's crowd in search of Dirk, ready to throw blows. I eventually caught up to him on the dance floor freakin' some honey. I stepped right in between the two of them.

"Dude? Can't you see we're dancing?" he asked.

"Ask me if I care. What did you say to Madison? She's in tears."

"You're out cold, R. You told her my business. I told you that chick didn't like me, didn't I? You failed to keep your woman in check, so I did it for you."

"Do you mind?" Dirk's dance partner chimed in "We're trying to get our freak on."

"Not anymore y'all ain't. Bounce, bitch!"

As ready as I was to defend my boo's honor, I knew I was partly at fault. All this drama could have been avoided had I let business between boys remain business between boys. So, I had to take the high road. Pour water on this fire rather than add fuel to it. We stepped off the dance floor.

"The girls are ready to go. Why don't we all just cool off and talk about this tomorrow or something," I said.

"I'm not riding home in any car that has Madison in it."

"She's not going to say anything else to you."

"She best not."

"Look, I know you're angry, but I'm not letting you get in her face again. You wanna be mad at somebody, be mad at me, Dirk."

"I *am* mad at you. I don't want to be around *either* one of you. There are mad honeys up in this joint tonight. I'm staying. Maybe I'll get lucky."

"I thought you said you were done with that?"

"*Was.* Past tense."

"Fatima's just a little disappointed in you at the moment. She'll get over it—"

"Fuck her, too! I sweats no chick. What was I thinking anyway? Being exclusive is whack. Monogamy ain't even *natural* for a man—especially not one in his twenties."

"I'm gonna get the girls so we can get out of here. Know what I think?"

"Ask me if I care."

"You really ought to come home with us before you hang around here and do something stupid."

"See you when I see you."

"Suit yourself. Do me a favor, Dirk. Grow up!" I turned to walk away.

"Yo, R."

"What do you want?"

"You watch. That chick's gonna have you married and pushing a baby stroller before you're 25."

Following some early-morning sex, and an additional forty winks, I got dressed and left Madison's place. The apartment was empty when I arrived home. Everything was undisturbed from the previous night. I looked in Dirk's room and could tell he hadn't come home yet. There was a message on the answering machine. I hit the PLAY button. It was a man with a heavy Hindu accent.

"Hello. This is Dr. Fareed Mataraji. I am calling from Lincoln Hospital in the Bronx. A patient by the name of Dirksten Francis was admitted to our facility earlier this morning. This number I am calling was found on his person. If you are a relative or friend of Mr. Francis, it is of the utmost urgency that you call the hospital back immediately at the following number . . ."

My hands started shaking so bad I had trouble holding them steady enough to dial. After being transferred several times I finally got Dr. Mataraji on the line. He told me a cleaning woman had found Dirk severely beaten inside of a hotel room in the South Bronx and that he had slipped into a coma.

The phone fell from my shaky grip, hit the floor, and broke into several pieces.

CONSEQUENCE

33

RANDALL

Rhonda and I had been waiting nervously for two hours in the visitors' waiting room. Neither of Dirk's parents was home when I called, leaving me to give the bad news to Rhonda. She didn't have her license yet, so I picked her up, and we rode to the hospital together. En route, she was full of questions. Like what was Dirk doing in a hotel in the South Bronx? There was no way I could tell her what I suspected he may have been doing.

I was having horrible thoughts of Dirk dying before his parents could get here. Given my apathy toward religion, I hadn't been the type of guy to pray much. But that's all I had been doing for the past few hours. Praying to the Lord not to let Dirk die. I didn't want Mr. and Mrs. Francis to lose their only son. Didn't want Rhonda to lose her big brother who she adored. I didn't want to lose my best friend.

Rhonda took charge once we got inside the hospital. Her parents hadn't arrived yet, so she stepped up and calmly gave the doctors and nurses all the information they needed. While she huddled with the medical staff, I spoke with the two officers that were called to the hotel where Dirk was found. I asked them if it was a robbery gone bad. They said it didn't look that way. Dirk's wallet, watch, and beeper were left behind.

"Looks like whoever did this to your friend was more concerned with settling a personal score," said Officer McKinnon. I read his nametag as he spoke to me. The other cop, a thick-necked Italian dude named Vinchezzi, asked if Dirk was into drug dealing or drug use. What a surprise *that* question was. I set Vinchezzi straight. "I know he's a young black male, but, no, Dirk doesn't use or sell drugs!"

The officers scribbled in their little notepads and told me if they found any evidence or leads on suspects they'd contact me immediately. I gave them Mr. and Mrs. Francis's number and address, and told them to contact them with any news before calling me.

Dr. Mataraji gave me and Rhonda permission to look in on Dirk but warned us he was still unresponsive. Beyond that the doctor wasn't saying much. I got the feeling he was saving the in-depth stuff for Dirk's folks if and when they ever got here. Rhonda went in. I passed. I didn't want to see my buddy in his current state. I hated being here. I *hated* hospitals. The smell of them made me nauseous.

When Rhonda returned, I asked her how he looked.

"They've got a bandage covering his head, both his eyes are swollen shut, and his mouth is all busted up." She seemed remarkably composed given the circumstances. Myself? I was beginning to feel queasy. Thought I might hurl at any moment.

I asked Rhonda to try calling her house again. She left to find a pay phone. A few seconds later I got up to do the same. I hadn't called Madison yet to tell her what had happened. Hadn't called my parents, either. By the time I found a pay phone, I decided against calling any of them. Used my loose change to call French Fry instead. Crystal answered.

"Hey, Crystal, it's Randall. Is Fry . . . um, Raymond, home?"

"Hold on a sec."

"Ray, git the phone!" I heard her yell.

French Fry picked up. "Who dis?"

"It's me, Randall. Dirk's in the hospital, man. Somebody beat him up in the South Bronx last night. He's in a coma."

"*What! What* was he doing in the South Bronx?"

"Don't know exactly . . . though I have a theory. But never mind that right now. I'm here at the hospital with Rhonda. We can't reach either of his parents."

"What hospital? I'm on my way. I'm bringing Crystal with me."

"We're at Lincoln in the Bronx. Know where it is?"

"I'll find it. Be there as soon as I can. It's gon' be all right, R. Dirk ain't going nowhere 'cept home when he comes out of that coma."

"I hope you're right, man. I hope you're right."

When I returned to the waiting area, Rhonda had already returned as well.

"Did you reach your parents?"

"Uh-uh. I left a message, though. Told them exactly what's happened and that they need to get here ASAP."

"Damn! Where could they be? Did anything happen at your house last night?"

"Why?"

"You don't find it odd that it's the middle of the afternoon on Black Friday and you have no clue where either of your parents are?"

"When we got back from dinner last night, my father's girl-friend called."

"Your house?"

"Yep."

"No, she didn't."

"*Yes, she did.* My father was in the kitchen talking to her.

Now, I didn't hear him call her by name, but who else would he be telling how sorry he was that he couldn't be there for Thanksgiving? As soon as he got off the phone, he took a shower, put on some fresh clothes, got all cologned-up, and was out the door again."

"Your pops is out cold!"

"What?"

"Nothing. You left a message, so maybe they'll get it and get here. I called Raymond. He and Crystal are on their way." I tried changing the subject to take our minds off the current state of things. "How's school? Have you decided what college you're going to?"

"Hampton University. But I haven't told anyone of my decision, so keep that under wraps for now."

"Cool. So I hear you've got a boyfriend now."

"Dirk told you?"

"Mmm-hmm. You and him ain't knocking boots, are you?" Rhonda's pale cheeks turned beet red.

"Raan-daall."

"Just kidding. Are y'all?"

"Next question."

"What's his name?"

"Cash."

"First or last name?"

"Neither."

"Better not let your brother hear that."

The smile covering Rhonda's face disappeared and the cool, calm disposition she had been exhibiting vanished. She lost it. Broke down sobbing uncontrollably.

"Dirk's not going to die, is he, Randall?"

"No! Absolutely not. I promise."

I wrapped my arms around Rhonda and squeezed her as tight as I could while silently praying to God to let me keep that promise.

* * *

I must have dozed off. Awoke with that sticky, nasty feeling in my mouth. Had an incredible urge to brush my teeth but couldn't. Rhonda's head was in my lap. She was out like a light. I glanced at my watch. We had been here nearly four hours now and still no sign of either Mr. or Mrs. Francis. I gently woke Rhonda.

"What time is it?" she asked, rubbing her eyes.

"Almost six."

"Are my parents here?"

"Not yet. I gotta go to the bathroom. Sit tight."

As I returned from the bathroom, I saw a man and woman standing at the reception desk. The man looked like Mr. Francis from behind. The woman didn't look anything like Mrs. Francis. I moved in a little closer to get a better identification.

Finally!

It was him. And the woman with him was no joke. She didn't appear to be much older than me.

"Mr. Francis?"

He turned and saw me. He was frantic.

"Where's Dirk? Where's my daughter? What happened, Randall?"

"Slow down, Mr.—"

"Dammit, don't tell me to slow down. *What happened to my son!*"

"Let's step over here and talk," I told him. "I don't know how much Rhonda told you in her message, but Dirk's been in an accident and now he's in a coma. We've been here for hours waiting for an update on his condition. Rhonda's been with me the whole time."

"What kind of accident?"

"I'm going to let the doctors fill you in on everything. You need to let them know you're here ASAP." I turned to the mystery woman. "And you are?"

"This is Amel," Mr. Francis said, answering for her. "I gotta get in there and see my son."

He bolted. Amel took off after him. I intercepted her.

"Hold on. Hope you don't think I'm out of line for asking, but what's your relationship to Mr. Francis?"

"I'm his . . . friend."

Oh, snap. This is her?

Amel had it going on.

What are you doing with an old fart like Hank?

"I don't think your being here right now is such a good idea, Amel."

"Why not?"

"Because *Mrs. Francis* may be here at any moment."

"Oooh. I hear you. Sorry, I didn't get your name."

"Randall."

"Nice to meet you, Randall. Me and Henry were together when he got his daughter's message. I just want to be here to offer my support in any way I can."

"That's beautiful, Amel. Beautiful. But I think the best way you can help is to take a seat and *not* move until I get back with you. Just chill for a while. I'll let Henry know where you're at. Okay?"

"Okay. I'll be in the waiting area reading a magazine. Don't forget about me, Randall."

Little chance of that happening.

"I won't, Amel. I promise."

34

RANDALL

Me, Rhonda, and Mr. Francis stood outside of Dirk's hospital room waiting for Dr. Mataraji to give us an update. Mr. Francis looked shaken, to say the least, after seeing the condition of his son. He pulled me aside and asked about Amel. I told him where she was and why. He asked me to go check on her.

That's when I saw Mrs. Francis. I was so happy she finally made it to the hospital that I practically ran over to greet her.

"Mrs. Francis . . ."

"Randall? Chile, what's going on?"

Something wasn't right about her. There wasn't any anguish in her voice. She appeared *too* calm under the circumstances. I smelt whiskey on her breath.

Incredible. He shows up with his mistress and she waltzes in here inebriated.

I waited for her to sign in and get a visitor's pass. While she was taking care of that, I remembered what I had originally come out to do: check on Amel. Maybe even convince her to get lost altogether before Mrs. F showed up.

Too late.

My first instinct was to go over to Amel and remind her again of what I had asked her to do: *stay put.* Instead, I played it cool in front of Mrs. Francis and didn't even acknowledge Amel's presence.

She ain't hard of hearing.

Rhonda was so relieved to finally see her mother that I don't think she even noticed the whiskey on her breath. Or maybe she did. Anyway, they hugged tightly. Mrs. Francis barely acknowledged her husband, however. The tension between those two was thick enough to cut with a knife.

Dr. Mataraji began to brief us by breaking down Dirk's situation in a bunch of medicalese. Among some of what we could understand was that the prognosis of a coma patient depended on the type and extent of the brain injury.

"Amazingly, there are no skull fractures," he said. "There is a very deep laceration in his scalp, and his jaw was dislocated. We've reset his jaw. The good news is that I've seen patients make a full recovery from trauma much worse than Dirk has sustained." Dr. Mataraji followed up by cautioning everyone to remain guarded, though. Told us Dirk's progress or lack of would be measured by reactivity and perceptivity to external stimuli—whatever that meant. The bottom line was this: if Dirk survived the first seven to ten days of this coma and came out of it, his chances for a full recovery were very good. That had us all feeling much more optimistic.

"How's he doing, Henry? Any news?" a female's voice asked out of nowhere.

No "excuse me" or anything. The voice sounded like . . . like . . .

Oh, hell, no!

"Who are you?" Rhonda asked.

"I'm Amel. A friend of Henry's," she said, extending her hand to Rhonda.

Didn't I tell you to sit your ass down and not move?

Evidently, I was wrong about Amel. She *was* hard of hearing. That or just *hardheaded.*

Rhonda looked at me.

I looked up into space.

"Daddy?" she asked.

"Henry?" Mrs. Francis asked. "Is this—"

"We're in a hospital full of sick people, Brenda. *Do not* make a scene."

"You b-b-brought *her* in front of my son? My daughter? *Me?*"

Mr. Francis got a whiff of his wife's breath.

"You been drinking, Brenda?"

She ignored his inquiry and instead turned her attention to Amel. Got right up in her face. So close their lips were no more than an inch apart.

"So! *You're* the young whore who's been sleeping with my husband of twenty-four years."

Mr. Francis quickly stepped in between his wife and girlfriend.

"Brenda, I *said,* We're in a hospital. Randall, get her out of here."

He wasn't referring to his girlfriend.

Before anyone could blink twice, Amel and Mrs. Francis had come out of their shoes and earrings and were rolling around on the hospital floor. The rest of us stood frozen in shock at what was taking place before our eyes. A scene right out of *Black Buffoonery Illustrated.*

Mrs. Francis was on top of Amel, pepperin' her pretty face with lefts and rights.

Poor Dr. Mataraji was so horrified I thought he was going to pee on himself. He was hopping up and down on one leg like a kangaroo, screaming in his thick Hindu accent, "Se-cu-ri-tee, se-cu-ri-tee! Sumbuddy, call se-cu-ri-tee!"

A guard and two orderlies came flying out of nowhere and attempted to separate the ladies, who were still on the hospital floor trying to gouge each other's eyes and pull each other's hair out. I grabbed Rhonda, who was screaming hysterically, and got the hell out of their way.

When the dust settled, Amel's clothes, hairdo, and makeup were things of the past. Mrs. Francis didn't look any better. One orderly had a hold on Mrs. Francis, the other, Amel. But both ladies (and I use that term loosely at the moment) were still struggling to break free and get at each other for another round of fisticuffs. Amel was poppin' major shit. Spewing serious venom in Mrs. Francis's direction.

"That's right, you old-pussy-havin' alcoholic be-yatch! I *am* fuckin' your husband! What chu gon' do, huh?"

Why did Amel have to take it *there?*

Mrs. Francis broke free from her captors, rushed Amel, and landed a picture-perfect right cross to her nose. Amel's shoeless feet went straight up in the air, leaving nothing but her shapely ass to break her fall.

It took hospital personnel—with the help of smelling salts—about a good seven minutes to bring Amel back to life. Her nose was a bloody mess. Needless to say, she wasn't poppin' any more shit.

Mrs. Francis wasn't quite done, though. Next in line to feel her wrath was none other than her philandering husband. She walked up to him, reared back, and slapped him so hard across his face that the sound reverberated off the corridor walls.

"You have flaunted your relationship with that young bitch in my face for the last time, Henry. Now you've pushed me too far."

"Pushed *you* too far?" he fired back. "Our son is in the hospital and you have the audacity to show up here drunk *and* assault my friend? No, Brenda, you've pushed *me* too far this time!"

35

MADISON

Serves his trifling ass right!

That was my initial reaction when Randall called me from the hospital with the news. It came from a place of anger. When my anger subsided, I felt horrible for Dirk. I hung up the phone and prayed that he'd pull through. I even wanted to come to the hospital, but Randall begged me to stay away. Said things had turned into a complete mess and that he'd explain it all when he got to my house.

I began to wonder if what happened to Dirk was in any way my fault, or if Randall would eventually blame me. Had I just kept my mouth shut . . .

What was Dirk doing in the South Bronx anyway?

Probably chasin' another piece of ass whose name he wouldn't even bother to remember was my presumption.

No. This isn't my fault.

I wasn't going to feel responsible. Even if this were to end in the worst possible way. I pissed Dirk off warning Fatima about his foul ways, but I didn't make him act in a reckless manner the way I suspected he may have. He was doing that long before he met me.

Knowing a hot meal would soothe my man's tired body when he came through the door, I put some chicken breasts in the oven and a pot of vegetables on the stove. Tidied up a bit, lit some coconut incense, and put a Phyllis Hyman tape in my boom box to create a nice mood. Today was a reminder of how things can change in the blink of an eye. Randall and I had only been dating less than six months, but I felt like the time was right. What was I waiting for? Twenty-nine was just around the corner and I had 2.5 babies to birth in six years or less.

36

RANDALL

I drove the Clearview Expressway in complete silence. Didn't want to hear any music. Didn't want to hear anybody's yackin'.

I was mentally and emotionally drained. After calling Madison from the hospital, I decided to go by my parents' house first and give them the bad news. Moms was heartbroken. In part because she was imagining me being in the hospital in a coma. I didn't even mention the brawl to her. That would have simply been *too* much to digest in one day.

PC came in the door shortly after I had already run everything down to my mother and Lori. I reiterated the bad news to him.

"He was probably in that sleazy place fornicating," was his matter-of-fact response. He didn't stop there. Next, he reminded us that the "Lord didn't like ugly" and quoted Galatians 6:7: "Whatever a man is sowing, this he will also reap."

"This is what happens when one is a slave to the flesh rather than a slave to Jesus," he said.

PC's moralizing was the last thing any of us needed or

wanted to hear right now. Lori—in typical Lori fashion—
rolled her eyes at him and stormed out the room calling PC an
asshole under her breath. Not sure why, but I asked Pastor
Crawford if he would say a prayer for Dirk. As if a prayer from
him would hold more weight with the Lord than one from me.

"His head is so far up his ass it's unreal," I angrily said to
my mother as soon as he was out of sight.

She gasped.

"You show some respect—"

"Does he *ever* see the world in anything other than the
black and white pages of the Bible? Do you think the Lord is
looking down on Dirk right now saying, *'Serves you right.
Told you to leave them ho's alone'?*"

"Randall Isaac Crawford!"

"You ever think that maybe Dad's part of the reason Lori is
such a mess? She's been a pain in the butt from the get-go. No
one's disputing that. But all she ever got from Dad after
having an out-of-wedlock baby was criticism and Scriptures.
I think Lori had the next two on *purpose,* Ma. Just to get
under Dad's skin further. To embarrass him in front of the
congregation at First Savior—"

"THAT'S ENOUGH!" my mother hollered at me. "You
watch your mouth when you're under my roof, Randall Isaac.
You ain't too big for me to lay the rod to your narrow ass. Secondly, don't you *dare* go blaming Miles for Lori's problems.
That girl was given everything. No one's made her make the
choices she has. Remember I've raised two other daughters by
the same man who've turned out nothing like her."

"None of your children have had *everything,* Ma."

"What didn't you kids have, Randall?"

"We all had *Pastor* Crawford when what we really could
have used from time to time was simply *Dad.*"

* * *

Madison had dinner waiting for me when I got to her crib. I could sense there was something specific she wanted to talk to me about. I told her about the rumble at Lincoln Hospital between Mrs. Francis and Amel. She was speechless. So much so that I think she forgot all about whatever it was that was on her mind. Good. I wasn't up for a lot of conversation anyway.

I looked over at her lovely face as she lay next to me. We had just finished making love and she was sound asleep. I couldn't sleep. I was still thinking about the ramblings of Pastor Crawford earlier, which made lying here this way with my woman conflicting for me. It was another example of me living contrary to my father's expectations.

37

MADISON

We got the news from Lincoln Hospital two days ago . . .

Good news! Dirk was alert and responsive. The worst was over and he was expected to make a full recovery.

I literally dropped to my knees, thanked God, and broke down crying when I heard. I know I said I wasn't going to shoulder any blame no matter how the situation ultimately turned out, but I felt like a weight had been lifted off my shoulders. But the news about Dirk wasn't the only good news to come. There was even better news.

Randall proposed.

Okay. So the "moment" wasn't exactly as romantic a moment I always dreamed it would be. He didn't get down on one knee and pull a ring out of his pocket like my (jerk) ex-fiancé did. He woke up the following morning after spending the night with me, rolled over in bed, looked me in the face and asked, with cold in his eyes and stinky morning breath, "Will you marry me, Madison Mya Jones?" Twice I had to ask Randall to repeat himself. I needed to make certain I wasn't asleep and dreaming and that he wasn't merely talking in his sleep.

I am *soooo* happy right now. Randall's proposal couldn't have come at a better time. With Christmas just weeks away, I didn't care if he got me a single gift—except my engagement ring, of course. One karat at least. (Anything less is unacceptable.) Everything was happening just as I planned.

Of course the first person I called with news of my impending nuptials was my mother. She was shocked—but ecstatic. She got to boo-hooin', which in turn got me to boo-hooin', and I really didn't want to start boo-hooin'. Dad? Unlike Randall's, mine has never been one to get into my personal affairs, so I wasn't expecting too much of a response from him. Boy, was I wrong. He hit me up with the "21 Questions" immediately. "How old is he?" "What kind of family is he from?" "What does he do for a living?" "When are you bringing him to Newburgh?" He sounded less than thrilled when I told him my fiancé was six years my junior and earned considerably less than I did. Though my parents both have full-time careers, my dad still holds fast to the old-fashioned notion that a husband—if not being the sole breadwinner—should at least be able to support his wife.

My parents wed way back in 1956. Attitudes have changed a lot since then and so has the financial landscape of America. Don't misunderstand me. I'd love to marry a man as financially successful as my dad. What woman wouldn't? I'd relish the option of raising the 2.5 kids Randall and I are going to have as a stay-at-home wife. That's just not this reality right now. Not to say it couldn't be, though.

I got Fatima on the line next. She started hoopin' and hollerin' like a crazy woman. When she came back down to earth, she began tossing her various concerns at me. Randall and I had been dating less than six months, so how was I sure he was "The One?" My answer? It just *felt* right.

I also let Fatima in on something I had been keeping from her: Dirk's accident. She had been in the dark since that evening we all went clubbin' at Bentley's. That was Randall's idea. He didn't want anyone outside of close friends and family knowing anything until we knew more details. This time, I did exactly what my man asked me to do and kept my mouth shut. But enough with all that. I'm getting married. Nothing but happy, happy, thoughts from this point forward. Now, where's my calendar? I've got a wedding to plan.

Late again. I was supposed to meet Randall at Gaby's for lunch at noon to discuss plans for our wedding. It was now 12:20. My lack of promptness drives him crazy, but I swear I try. Found him sitting in a booth with his face scrunched up.

"Hey, honey—"

"You're late."

"I know, I'm sorry. If I'm not on time for anything else, I promise I'll be on time for our wedding."

"You better be. My aunt E called the other day. She said to tell you hello and congratulations. She also told me there's a position in payroll opening up at United Trust that she thinks I should interview for."

"Great."

"There's a catch. It's in our downtown office on Vesey Street."

"Would you want to work in Lower Manhattan?"

"Not particularly. But then I did ask Aunt E to look out for me and that's what she's trying to do. And now that we're getting married, I guess I need to consider any and all options if it means putting us in a better financial position."

Randall went on to tell me what the position was paying.

"Not bad. We'll be able to get a decent house on our combined incomes if you get the job."

"House?"

"Yes, Randall. A house."

"I was kinda thinking you could move into the apartment."

"The apartment you're sharing with Dirk?"

"At least for a little while. You know, maybe the first year or two of our marriage."

"And where's Dirk supposed to live, Randall? With us, too?"

"Nooo. Rhonda and I have been talking. She's going to ask Dirk to move back home when he's discharged from the hospital."

"Because?"

"Remember how Mrs. Francis got into that fight with that Amel chick, right? Well, to add insult to injury, she also got busted for DUI later that same evening. There's more. Dirk's father has officially moved out of the house and in with Amel. So needless to say, Mrs. Francis is a mess right now. Rhonda and I both agree that Dirk should move back home and keep an eye on things. When we're done here, I'd like to drive out to the hospital and pay Dirk a visit. Give him the news about us and tell him he's going to have to move out 'cause we'll need the apartment. He'll understand."

Silence.

"Randall."

"Yes?"

"Are you out of your freakin' mind?"

"What?"

"First of all, you're going to go over to the hospital *today* and tell Dirk he needs to move out of an apartment you two have shared for the past three years? He's just come out of a *coma,* for crying out loud. What are you trying to do, send him *back* into another one? Second of all, I am *not* moving into any apartment—especially not one you've shared with Dirk. I want us to have a place of our own when we get married. I want a *house.* And we don't need to wait another year or two to buy one. I've already saved enough for one by myself."

"And where do you suppose we buy this . . . house? Laurelton, St. Albans, Cambria Heights?"

"I wasn't thinking Queens."

"No?"

"Long Island."

"Long Island?"

"Amityville."

"Amityville? Are you out of *your* freakin' mind? That's Suffolk County, Madison. A hundred miles from here."

"Oh, stop. It's not that far."

"And how are we supposed to get to and from work if we're living in Amityville?"

"The Long Island Railroad."

"Suppose I get this gig downtown? Do you realize my commute—"

"Oh, okay, okay. How about somewhere a little closer? Nassau County. Uniondale, Hempstead . . ."

"How 'bout we just stay in Queens? I like it here."

Getting Randall to do this my way was going to require a little more effort than I originally thought. We put the discussion on the back burner for the time being, finished lunch, then jumped on the Clearview Expressway and headed over to Lincoln Hospital to see Dirk. Today would be the first time Dirk and I saw each other since our confrontation in Bentley's.

BORN AGAIN

38

DIRK

My head was pounding. My mouth felt stiff and sore. Couldn't see that well, either . . . just well enough to see that she was a cutie pie. The nurse standing at my bedside, that is.

"How are you feeling, Mr. Francis?"

"Where am I?" I mumbled, not able to open my mouth fully. My jaws felt like they were clamped together.

"You're in Lincoln Hospital."

"W-why?"

"You were in an accident."

"Accident?"

I sat up in the bed and felt my face. It was swollen and puffy. Felt around the top of my head. It was covered with a gauze bandage.

"What happened to my face, nurse?"

"Relax, Mr. Francis. I'm Nurse Benitez."

"Look here, Nurse Bentez . . ."

"Be-ni-tez."

"What-ev-a!"

"Your physician is Dr. Mataraji. He'll be in shortly to discuss your condition with you."

I eased back into the bed. Had no recollection of any accident. A few moments later, this Dr. Mataraji dude came in.

"How do you feel today?"

"Like shit, Doc. I got a headache, my mouth hurts, I can barely see . . . Is somebody gonna tell me what I'm doing in here?"

"He was definitely more pleasant when he was in a coma," the nurse said.

Coma?

"What the fuck are y'all—"

"Mr. Francis, please, watch your language. There's another patient on the other side of this curtain."

"Sorry. Would somebody *please* tell me why I'm in this hospital? Nurse *Be-ni-tez* over there wouldn't. Did I get your name right this time?"

"Your headache, sore mouth, and vision problems will dissipate in due time. In regard to why you're here, you were found by a hotel housekeeper in pretty bad shape a few days ago. Someone had beaten you up. You were comatose for three days. Fortunately, you suffered no skull fractures. There were, however, several lacerations to your face and head. The most serious of which is right here," he said, pointing to the spot on his own head. "That one took twenty-four stitches to close . . ."

Twenty-four stitches?

". . . Your jaw was dislocated, but it's been reset. Thus the reason for the stiffness and discomfort in your mouth. As for your vision, your eyes are still badly swollen. All that said, however, you're a very lucky young man, Mr. Francis. Your prognosis could have been much worse. You should be back to your old self in no time."

"Who did this to me?"

"I was hoping you'd be able to tell me that. Do you remember how you ended up in that hotel room or what you were doing there?"

"Where was this hotel?"

"In the South Bronx."

My memory was fuzzy, and trying to remember anything only made my head hurt more.

"Don't remember."

"That's okay. Don't worry about it right now. Some aspects of your memory are going to take longer to return than others. What's important now is for you to get plenty of rest so you can regain your strength. You're going to be on soft foods for a while until your jaw completely heals. I have to go and look in on another patient. Nurse Benitez is going to change the bandage on your head. Let her know if you need anything, okay?"

"Okay, Doc."

Nurse Benitez was *Spanish fly*. She'd probably look even better to me if I could see straight. I needed a mirror. I was beginning to feel self-conscious.

"Sorry for being so rude to you earlier."

"Apology accepted."

"You're very attractive, Nurse Benitez. On top of that you look good."

She laughed. "Are you flirting with me, Mr. Francis?"

"Please. Call me Dirk. And, yes, I am flirting with you. Have you been taking care of me this entire time?"

"I've been taking shifts with other nurses."

"Bet those other nurses ain't as fine as you."

Nurse Benitez was laughing even harder now. The Francis charm was starting to get to her. That coma might've zapped my memory but not my mackin' skills, obviously.

"Mr. Francis—"

"Dirk."

"Excuse, me. Mr. Dirk. You really ought to give your mouth a rest. It needs to heal."

"Aw-aight. I know I'm looking all busted and whatnot right now, but just give me a few weeks, and I'll—"

"I have a boyfriend."

"Oh? And how long have you had that problem, may I ask?"

"You're too funny, Mr. Dirk. Tilt your head a little more this way for me," she said in her Spanish accent as she finished wrapping a fresh piece of gauze bandage around my head.

"What's your first name, Nurse Benitez?"

"It's Daisy."

"Daisy Benitez. You're Puerto Rican, right?"

"Dominican. Is the bandage too tight? Mr. Dirk . . . ?"

Dominican . . . South Bronx . . .

" . . . Mr. Dirk?"

"Huh?"

"The bandage. Is it too tight?"

"N-no. It's . . . fine. I remember, Daisy."

"Pardon me?"

"I remember what happened to me now."

"Do you want me to find Dr. Mataraji?"

"No. I um . . . do you mind? I'd like to be alone for a little while."

"Sure."

"Daisy?"

"Yes, Mr. Dirk?"

"Would you bring me a mirror, please?"

39

DIRK

I'd gotten sloppy. Violated my own rule. It's that simple. I should have known that night was only going to get worse for me.

Check it out.

I stick a piece of Juicy Fruit in my mouth and roll up on her as the crowd in Bentley's is going berserk to Lisa Lisa & the Cult Jam.

I grab her by the hand and ask a question I *never* ask a honey.

"Would you like to dance?"

"Fuck you!" she says, snatching her hand back.

"You don't mean that. Let me buy you a drink. Damn, you look good tonight." A dose of flattery seems to chill her out a bit.

We make our way over to the bar. Bacardi and Coke for

her and another Amaretto and OJ for me. My third. Two more than I can safely handle. I'm feeling dizzier than a blonde.

> *" . . . I wonder if I take you home*
> *Would you still be in love, baby*
> *Because I need you tonight . . ."*

As we drink, Madison's words echo in my subconscious: *"'You ain't good enough for a woman like Fatima!'"*

"Let's bust this joint," I tell her.

"Where are we going?"

"Where you wanna go?"

"I wanna go dance. This song is the bomb!"

"That's not exactly what I had in mind."

"Let me guess. You wanna take me somewhere and fuck me again, right? Maybe back to your apartment, then discard me like I'm your personal stunt, right?"

I summon up all the (fake) sincerity I can muster and gaze into her eyes.

"I feel *awful* about that. I won't do you like that again. I'ma take you to IHOP in the morning for some pancakes. Promise."

"Mmm-hmm. You gonna have to come around my way this time," she says.

I call her bluff.

"Sorry. I don't get down like that."

"You must not want this bad enough, then."

She places her empty drink glass down on the bar. Tugs at her halter top in an effort to get those big jugs of hers firmly back inside of it. Gets up to leave.

"Wait," I say, grabbing her by the arm. "What chu got in mind?"

"I know a spot in Mott Haven."

"The *South Bronx*?"

"Gotta problem with that?"

That right there should have been the soundest reason for me to cancel this ill-advised plan of mine and take my ass home. But then everyone's a genius *after* the fact.

"Let's do this," I give in.

Lizette hands me her coat-check ticket.

"Get my coat for me, please? I gotta make a quick phone call."

"Who you gotta call at 2:00 AM in the morning? Your Papi?"

"Yeah. I gotta call my Papi. Just get my coat, please?"

Can't tell you the name of the street, but it's definitely the *Barrio*. Three burly-looking dudes are sitting outside of a bodega on the corner, listening to salsa music on a boom box. It's too early in the morning and too cold outside for all that. They're staring me down as I exit the cab. Probably wondering what this fly black kid is doing with this Dominican honey in this hood at this hour.

Hombres better recognize.

I enter the joint Lizette's chosen. Slide the desk clerk the damage, then check my wallet to see how much I've got left. Cool. Enough to catch a cab back to Queens right after I hit this. Damn. Had I been thinking, I would have told that same cabbie to circle back in thirty minutes. The clerk hands me a key and directs us to a room up one flight of stairs.

Granted, I wasn't expecting the Waldorf-Astoria. (A booty palace need only be a notch above fleabag status, remember?)

But, geez. This joint is falling short of even booty palace standards. I'm *really* in a hurry to hit this and be out.

As soon as I get inside the room, I strip down to my drawers and jump on the bed. I left my socks on. God only knows what might be crawling around in the nasty-ass carpet under my feet. I don't bother pulling back the bed covers, either. Too afraid of what I might find under there. Bunk foreplay. Her ass is gonna be lucky to get *two-play* for bringing me to a repugnant shit hole like this.

Mami's moving awfully slow. She's still in that halter top and spandex pants.

"Yo, Lizette. Get out of them clothes. You got me here. Let's get this party started, yow mean?"

"Wait a minute," she says. "I gotta go pee first."

Geez.

"You better be butt-naked when you come out of that bathroom, girl."

"Oh, I will be, *Papi Chulo,*" she purrs.

I lie back on the bed. Close my eyes. Reach into my drawers and kid around with Willy while I wait for Lizette to—

BANG! BANG! BANG!

What the . . .

Somebody's banging on the door like they've lost their friggin' mind. I'm not expecting company.

Lizette bolts out of the bathroom—still fully dressed—opens the door, and runs out of the room. Three burly-looking dudes come barreling in. Those same three I saw in front of the Bodega outside. It's just them and me now—in nothing but my drawers and socks.

I suddenly remember that phone call Lizette said she had to make before we left Bentley's.

I'm fucked.

One dude grabs me in a headlock, yanks me off the bed, and throws me headfirst into the dirty, nasty carpet that's probably infested with God only knows what. The other two join in and begin pummeling me with their hands and feet. They're screaming at me, but I can't understand what they're screaming at me 'cause they're screaming at me in Spanish.

"... *ESTO ES PAGO, HIJO DE PUTA! TE ESCOGISTE EQUIVOCADA LA MUJER* ..." (This is payback, you son-of-a-bitch! You picked the wrong one.)

They're kicking me in my stomach and back simultaneously. I've never been in so much pain in my life. They scoop me up off the floor. Two straighten me up while the third cold-clocks me in the face. I feel my jaw shift in a way that isn't natural.

"... *NO TE DIJO QUE CUIDATE LA ESPALDA? NO ESCUCHASTE, AHORA TE JODISTE, PENDEJO* ... !!"

(Didn't she tell you to watch your back? You didn't listen, now you're fucked, asshole!)

A warm liquid covers my face. It's blood. Mine. Lots of it. The two holding me up release me. I have no strength in my legs and crumple back to the floor. My attackers take a brief recess from their assault to admire their handiwork thus far.

"... *QUIENE CARAJO TE CREES, JODIENDO CON DOMINICANAS? ERES LOCO* ... ?"

(Who do you think you are, fuckin' with Dominican girls, huh? Are you crazy?")

As I lie on my back writhing in pain, they resume their assault—this time stomping me in the face and head with their Timberland boots. I can't see out of my eyes anymore. The pain in my head is excruciating.

"*. . . VAS A NECESITAR UNA AMBULANCIA CUANDO TERMINAMOS CONTIGO . . .*"

(You're gonna need an ambulance when we're done with you.)

Soon the room goes quiet. The pain in my body ceases, and a weird, wonderful feeling of tranquility overtakes me.

I am dead.

40

DIRK

"You've got two visitors," Dr. Mataraji said, entering my room.

"Who?"

"Randall and Madison."

I could really have used a visit from Randall right about now. I had no desire to see Madison, on the other hand. And I definitely didn't want her to see me like this.

"Send Randall in, Doc. But just him, okay? Not the girl."

"Any reason why?"

"It's personal."

"As you wish."

"Thanks. Oh . . ."

"Yes?"

"I remember now. Everything. I know why I'm in here."

"Fantastic. Let's talk about that when your visitors have gone."

I barely recognized Randall. And not because my eyes were still swollen. He came over to my bedside and gave me a hug.

"How you feeling? The doctor told me it's a little hard for you to talk. Just don't start slobbering on yourself 'cause I ain't wiping your mouth for you," he said, cracking himself up in the process.

I had to laugh myself.

"Stop, dude. You're making my ribs hurt."

Ouch!

"You know you look fucked up, don't you?"

"This is the face of a dude who got his ass whupped, R. Not only that, I got the shit beat out of me."

"I see you haven't lost your sense of humor. That's good."

"Enough about my face. What the hell happened to *yours?*"

Randall's Afro and eyeglasses were missing. His head was shaved nearly bald. He looked like a five-foot eight-inch Milk Dud with a mustache.

"It was time for the fro to go."

"And your glasses?"

"I'm wearing contacts."

"Mmm-hmm. And whose idea was all this . . . or do I even have to ask?"

"Have you heard from your folks?" he asked, ignoring my comment.

"They've both called, but neither has been by to visit me since I came out of the coma. Unbelievable. Did they come to see me when I was comatose?"

"Of course. They were here as soon as they got word of what happened. Lots of folks have been through here to see you. My moms, Aunt Ethel, Lori, Fry, Crystal . . ."

"Rhonda called me earlier this morning. She was acting awfully funny on the phone. Like there was something she was trying to keep from me."

"A lot's gone down that you don't know about."

"Like?"

"Let's save that discussion for when you've got your strength back."

"Don't do that. Tell me now."

"Your moms got arrested for DUI. She's had her license suspended. Luckily, it was her first offense or it could have been much worse. So, I suspect she's having a little trouble getting over here to see you now that she can't drive herself."

"She was drinking and driving again?"

"There's more. Your pops moved out. I think for good, too. I suspect he's with his lady friend. Her name's Amel. I met her. She's no joke, Dee."

"Let me see if I've got this straight. My moms gets arrested for drunk driving and my pops moves in with his girlfriend? And this all happens while their only son is lying comatose in a hospital? Don't they have any respect for the dead?"

"Dirk."

"What?"

"You're not dead. Look, I'm giving you the Cliffs Notes version. Believe me, there were a lot of circumstances that led up to everything I just mentioned. Not the least of which is your being here in the first place. You've put everyone who knows and loves you through a lot of unnecessary stress. What in the *hell* were you doing in the South Bronx?"

"I couldn't remember myself until a few hours ago. I got ho-jacked, R. The bitch set me up."

"I knew it! Who?"

"Lizette Felix."

"That Puerto Rican . . . I mean, Dominican chick you met at the Red Parrot the night I met Madison."

"The night *we* met Madison. Yeah. *That* bitch! But I don't want to get into it right now. Do like Rufus and tell me something good instead. Have I missed anything on a positive note?"

"Actually, you have. I'm getting married."

Silence.

"I don't think I heard you correctly."

"Yes, you did. Madison and I are getting married, Dirk."

"Why?"

"*Why?* Because she's the one for me and it's the right thing to do."

"The right thing to . . . She's your first real girlfriend, dude. The only honey you've ever slept with. Not counting Shavonda, a.k.a. Kat-the-Stripper."

"Your point?"

"Ever since you met that chick you've been going 100 miles per hour. *Slow down.* Play the field. Sow some oats before you put yourself on lockdown for the rest of your life. You're 23 years old, Randall. Geez! Enjoy your youth."

"Sorta the way you've been enjoying yours? Just look where all that enjoyment has landed you."

"That's a low blow. But since I'm in no condition to get out of this bed and kick your ass, I'ma let that slide. No, Randall. I'm not telling you to do what I've been doing. This has been the most humbling experience of my life."

"I don't have to sleep with a bunch of women to know I've already found the one I want to spend the rest of my life with."

"What are you going to do when you run into some cutie on Jamaica Avenue and she starts giving you play? Like that one you were trying to push up on over in the Queensbridge houses a while back."

"Myesha?"

"Dude. She was bowlegged *and* pigeon-toed!"

"I haven't seen or heard from Myesha in over a year. Ain't been looking for her, either."

"Answer the question, R."

"I'm not a chick magnet like you, Dirk, so I doubt marriage is going to be that difficult of an adjustment for me."

"You know what my father told me about marriage, Randall?"

"Stop. Marital advice from *your* pops? No thanks."

"Okay. It's your life. If this is what you truly want to do, congratulations. I wish you the best."

"You mean that?"

"Mmm-hmm. Truthfully, I'm really not all that surprised by this news. I've always thought you were a love TKO waiting to happen. What do your folks have to say about all this?"

"I haven't told them yet. You're the first."

"Don't I feel special. Have you gotten her an engagement ring?"

"We're going to the Diamond District to price some as soon as we leave here. You know this means I'll be moving out of the apartment. You may want to give some thought as to whether you can afford to stay there by yourself or if you need to find another roommate. Rhonda thinks you should move back home. But I'll let her discuss that with you. Another thing. Me and Madison aren't having a long engagement, so you need to get well, get back on your feet, and get your face fixed soon. You're going to be my best man and I can't have you effin' up my wedding pictures looking like you do right now."

"Stop making me laugh, dude. I told you my ribs hurt!"

"Seriously, Dirk. I need you to put your animosity towards Madison behind you. I mean it. She's my fiancée now. Pretty soon, my wife. All this that's happened to you . . . it's not *her* fault. Now I know you don't want to see her, but she came all the way out here with me to see how you were doing, too."

"She can come in."

"Great. I'll go get her. In fact, I'll get lost so you two can clear the air alone."

Randall reached over and gave me another hug.

"Glad to have you back. We all would have been devastated if you hadn't pulled through."

"I'm glad to be back."

41

MADISON

Dirk's once-handsome face was a complete mess. He looked like he had been hit by a train.

"I'm really glad you came out of that coma. Everyone was very worried about you."

"Especially you, I'll bet. I didn't die. You don't have to feel guilty now . . . That wasn't very nice was it? I'm sorry," he said.

"I'm sorry you think this is all my fault, but—"

"How's Fatima?"

"She's well."

"Does she know what happened to me?"

"Yes. She says get well soon. This is for you." I handed Dirk a get-well card from Randall and me. "About Fatima—"

"I understand congratulations are in order?"

"Yes. Randall and I are getting married."

"Mission accomplished?"

"Excuse me?"

"You were looking to snag yourself a husband from the jump, weren't you? Thing is, I don't even think Randall's your type."

I didn't give a damn what kind of condition Dirk was in. I was two seconds away from cursing his ass out again.

"Is that right? Why don't you tell me what my type is, then?"

"Me."

You conceited son of a . . .

"I think the doctor needs to adjust your medication, Dirk. You *must* be high."

"Don't front, Madison. Think back to last year. The night you tapped me on the shoulder in the Red Parrot. You gon' tell me there was absolutely no attraction there?"

I couldn't believe we were having this conversation.

"Please. You were foaming at the mouth when you got a glimpse of me. Aaaah. I know what this is about. In order to massage that colossal ego of yours, you're fishin' to find out if the feeling was mutual. Know what your problem is, Dirk?"

"No, but I'm sure you're fixin' to tell me."

"You're so used to those young, brainless chicks you mess with falling for you and your fake-ass, mack-daddy-wantin'-to-be charm. *I'm a grown woman,* Dirk. Trust me when I tell you. You had *no* shot. Not being cruel, just being honest. (Boy, did that feel good.) Now that we've cleared that up, what do you say, Dirk? Let's me and you call a truce, okay?"

"Maybe I can do that. For *Randall's* sake anyway."

"Great."

"Are you gonna tell him we had this conversation?"

I mulled that over.

"No. Nothing said in this room is leaving this room. Now sit up, please?"

"Huh?"

"You're slouching. Sit up!"

"What for?"

"Because I'm about to leave and I'd like to give you a hug before I go."

I gave Dirk a hug and a bonus peck on the cheek.

THREE YEARS LATER
1990 . . .

42

RANDALL

The news that I had decided to get married was met with a positive response—mostly. Moms was happy, but cautiously concerned that I might've been moving too fast. My sisters were onboard with it—except for Lori. Not surprising, being the wet blanket she is. She claimed the only reason I was getting married was because that's what PC expected me to do. In regard to the latter, he was extremely pleased and for all the reasons I knew he would be. I would no longer be living with Dirk—a cohabitation he was dead set against from the get-go—and Madison and I wouldn't be "living in sin."

Shortly after our engagement, I took a trip over the Christmas holidays to Newburgh to meet my future in-laws for the first time. That house of theirs was large. And I don't mean just in square footage, either. Mr. and Mrs. Jones were really cool and down-to-earth. So were Madison's brother and sister, Hamilton and Kennedy. They all had me feeling like part of the family.

Madison's parents wanted to throw us a *big* wedding.

"Madison's our oldest daughter and first child to wed, so whatever you kids want," they said.

We decided we didn't want a Broadway production. If her parents were willing to throw a lot of dough into a wedding we figured why not get them to *give* us that dough as a wedding present instead. Her folks bought the idea. In fact, they did one better. They bought our house for us . . . well, gave us much more than the standard 20 percent down payment, and paid all our closing costs.

Married life was off on a good foot.

Our wedding ceremony took place at First Savior on Friday night, September 16, 1988. God, did Madison look beautiful. When her father walked her down the aisle and gave her hand to me it brought tears to my eyes. It was the happiest day of my life thus far.

We kept the wedding party simple. Two groomsmen, two bridesmaids. Dirk was my best man. (His face had completely healed by then so he didn't eff up our wedding photos.) French Fry served as the other groomsmen. Speaking of French Fry, I felt bad for bro on my wedding day. My getting hitched had him catching heat from Crystal like never before. I guess after five years or so of his shuckin', jivin', and empty promises, she had reached the end of her rope with him.

At one point during the reception, Crystal calmly approached the bridal table and gave Fry this final ultimatum: "Raymond Walker, you better throw *me* a party like this one in six months or less, or we're through!"

French Fry missed the deadline for that "party." So, despite an eight-year relationship that began in the tenth grade, and having a child together, I'm sorry to say those two are history now.

Madison and I spent our wedding night at the Plaza Hotel in Manhattan, courtesy of my aunt E and uncle Billy, drinking lots of champagne, counting our gift money, and making passionate love to one another for the first time as husband and wife after months of self-imposed celibacy—her idea, not mine. We added a different twist and had the reception the following afternoon in Newburgh at her parents' house. Three-quarters of the way into our reception, my new wife and I bid adieu to our guests, and a limo whisked us to the airport for our honeymoon destination: a five-day stay on the island of St. Lucia. A wedding gift from my collective family.

We didn't move to Amityville like Madison wanted. We reached a compromise and got a place in Nassau County. A single-family house located between Sunrise Highway and the Southern State Parkway in Lynbrook. Three bedrooms, two baths, a finished basement, and a two-car garage.

I got that job downtown in payroll, too. I'm feeling a lot less insecure these days now that the earnings gap between me and Madison isn't quite as wide anymore. On the downside, I hate my commute. I still say we would have been better off staying in Queens.

Madison and I didn't get around to discussing how children would or wouldn't fit into our life until some three months or so prior to the wedding, believe it or not. The only feasible explanation I can come up with is that we had just gotten so wrapped up in making wedding arrangements, house-hunting, and the like, that we overlooked that important discussion.

I was down for *a* kid. Just not any time soon. Maybe five years down the road. I wanted Madison and me to enjoy life as a young married couple for as long as possible and do all the things young, childless couples do. She was feeling my sentiment about that as much as I was the thought of us living in Amityville. Her argument was that she'd be 34 in five years and wasn't trying to have her first child that late. *First?*

We were definitely on opposite sides of the page on this one. In fact, things got pretty heated there for a while. So much so that I actually thought about calling off the wedding.

Think I would have, too, if not for the fact that so many plans had already been made. Plus, I knew doing so would have broken Madison's heart. *We'll work this matter out,* I kept re-assuring myself in private. And we did. We agreed to put off starting a family for three years instead of the five I lobbied for. Madison was on the pill, so we weren't concerned about any mishaps before our mutually agreed-upon time.

Noah Julius Crawford was born September 14, 1989, weighing in at seven pounds, three ounces. We named him after one of PC's favorite people in the Bible and Madison's late grandfather. His complexion's a perfect blend of my chocolate brown and Madison's high yellow. Everyone says he looks more like me than Madison. (But don't let her hear you say that.) Noah's eight months old now. Madison and I haven't even been married two years yet.

Do the math.

How in the *hell* did this happen? I marry Madison, and three months later she's puking every morning. I take her to see her doctor. He says, "Congratulations. You two are having a baby." Want to know the first thing that crossed my mind? It wasn't how much I loved my wife, our baby on the way, or the won-derful life we were all going to have together. Not even close. It's what Dirk said to me that Thanksgiving night at Bentley's: *"'That chick's gonna have you married and pushing a baby stroller before you're 25.'"*

Don't get me wrong. I adore my son. Adore my wife. But being a husband *and* a father at 25? That just wasn't part of my plan. I figured we'd be spending the first several years of our marriage chillin'. Taking trips. Throwing parties for friends and family at our house in Lynbrook. And when we weren't doing any of that stuff, I figured I'd be hangin' with the fellows. Not losing sleep to a teething baby. Running back and forth to Duane Reade at odd hours of the day and night for baby formula. Playing second-string to a toddler.

Madison never seemed quite as shocked by her pregnancy as I was. She explained it away as "shit happens." I read those articles over and over inside the pages of those *Trendy* magazines she brought home from work. That Ortho whatchamacallit was supposed to be 99 percent effective. C'mon. What were the odds of she and I being the unlucky 1 percent? I'll tell you. Right up there with us winning the lottery!

Betcha *that shit* won't happen.

I ain't gon' lie. I'm a little disillusioned with this marriage thing already. But maybe it won't be that bad. After all, I've got a beautiful wife, son, home, good friends, family, and a good job.

What more could a nice guy ask for, right?

43

DIRK

New York's finest never did capture my attackers. I haven't set foot inside of another nightclub since. The Black John Travolta has retired his dancing shoes.

Aside from saving a little bit of dough (Pops is still footing the mortgage, utilities, etc.), I see no upside to being back on the old block in St. Albans. And now that R's living out on the Island and working downtown, we don't see much of each other. I still can't believe the dude went out like a jellyfish and actually married that chick. The wedding was classy, though. She'll probably never be one of my favorite people, but Madison made a beautiful bride. Fatima looked stunning at the wedding, too. We hadn't seen or spoken to each other since *that* night. She was pretty icy toward me during the rehearsals, the wedding, and the reception, but it was good seeing her just the same.

I hope R's happy working downtown around all those conservative, stuffy, Wall Street types. Happy living in the burbs of Long Island. Happy shopping in Midtown. Says he is, but I doubt it. Can't tell me he doesn't miss working in Midtown, living in Queens, shopping on Delancey Street, and even clubbin' every now and then with his main man. And now that he's got a child . . . I was *floored* with that news. Noah's a cutie, though. Doesn't look a thing like Madison or Randall. (But don't let either of them hear that.) Little man's going to be calling me Uncle Dirk when he gets old enough.

My sister graduated from Julia Richman High School with honors and was accepted to Hampton University. I was so proud of her. This year would have been her sophomore year except she didn't enroll. She hasn't enrolled in any college to date. She's working at United Trust. Randall's aunt E came through once again.

"Cash" got my sister pregnant—on prom night. Her maiden voyage. I don't believe Rhonda set out to have sex with him that night, but she fell for the classic male okeydoke. Cash told her he wanted to make her feel "special." Wanted to be her first. Told her it was okay because the two of them were going to be together forever. At *eighteen*.

My sister hasn't seen or heard from that piece of shit since he spilled his semen into her. Worse, rumor has it *he's* still pursuing his college dream somewhere deep in the state of Texas. No one even knows if he knows my sister had his child.

Cash better stay in Texas.

My niece's name is Rochelle Ameeka Francis. Rhonda's keeping her head up and doing all right for a 20-year-old single mother. When Rochelle's a little older Rhonda's hoping she can attend college like she had planned. If not at Hampton, somewhere. Ironic, isn't it? My mother always feared it would be me—her womanizing son—who'd bring her an illegitimate grandchild. Never her straightlaced, Goody Two-shoes daughter.

Speaking of moms, she finally divorced my father after

twenty-six years of marriage. Only after I convinced her that he wasn't leaving Amel to come back to her. Why she even entertained the idea of taking him back was beyond me.

But that's a woman for you.

She's still got Johnnie Walker, though. In fact, since my pops left and Rhonda made her a grandma, those two seem closer than ever.

As for my father, the situation with Rhonda really tore him up. Don't know what hurt him more—the fact that his baby girl had a baby girl, or that he wasn't around to maybe stop his baby girl from messing up her potentially bright future.

44

Madison Crawford

The past three years have been a blur. I'm just catching my breath. My wedding was simple, classy, and very well done. Exactly the way I've always envisioned my wedding being. And, yes, I kept my promise to Randall and got to the church on time.

About two hundred family and friends came out to see us take our vows. Even more attended the reception that followed the next evening at my parents' home in Newburgh. We did things that way so that guests who couldn't make it to the wedding could attend the reception and vice versa. The guys looked so handsome in their black and gray tuxedos. My hubby being the stud of the group. Maybe I'm a bit biased, but Randall's gone from Average Joe to hot boy overnight. (I'll take most of the credit for that.)

Of course my girls and I were saying som'um, too. Our color scheme was burgundy and pink, and I looked nothing short of stunning in my bridal gown if I say so myself. Our hair and makeup was hooked to a tee. We looked like four Ebony Fashion Fair models walking the runway. Everyone said ours was one of the most beautiful weddings they'd ever attended.

Our honeymoon was equally awesome. I got a killer tan and came back to New York *looking* like a black girl. Between the sun and waves, Randall and I made love, toured the island, made love, snorkeled, made love, ate and drank like there was no tomorrow, and made love. My only regret is that we couldn't stay longer and make more love.

My promotion and new position at Trendy is going quite well. A lot more responsibility, but the pay is great, and I think I'm on the right track to my ultimate career goals.

I haven't done much recreationally since getting married and having the baby. Fatima and I haven't seen much of each other lately, either. Mostly because of the geographical distance between us now.

Wish that I could say everything's been peachy since Randall and I became husband and wife, but that would hardly be true. Whoever said the first year of marriage is the toughest wasn't lying. I think we could have seriously benefited from a little premarital cohabitation. That would have gone over real well with the ultrareligious Crawfords, ya think? Now most of our issues are minor, although one in particular could become *major*.

But first the minor. I've learned my new husband's a compulsive neat freak. While I rarely leave home without my hair, nails, toes, and makeup on point, I confess to not being nearly as meticulous to detail when it comes to housework. Cleaning my tiny basement apartment in Laurelton was a breeze. This house? Whoa, Nelly! Randall tries to keep it clean, though. Vacuums the entire house about every other day. Sometimes he doesn't get started until 10:00 PM or later. Is it just me, or is this so friggin' necessary? I swear there are times when I'm tempted to sneak up behind him when he's running that damn vacuum cleaner, grab the power cord, wrap it around his

neck, and choke the livin' shit out of him with it. And don't let
my dirty clothes miss the hamper or a dirty plate miss the dish-
washer. You'd think Randall came home and found me in bed
with the mailman. Last but not least, he's got this completely
anal obsession with arranging things with labels in alphabet-
ical order. LPs in the stereo rack, canned goods in the pantry,
spices in the spice rack. *Aaarrgh!!!*

I hope to have one or two more kids before I have my tubes
tied five years from now. Everyone says Noah looks more
like me than his dad. (But don't let his dad hear you say that.)
While I know my little Noah's a blessing from the Lord, I've
been praying for His forgiveness ever since he was born.

You see, my son's entry into the world came as a shock.

Sort of.

It all began roughly six months prior to our wedding. Far
from a virgin, a sista still wanted to feel like one on her wedding
day. In order to bring some semblance of chastity to our union,
if you will, I told Randall I wanted to refrain from intercourse
until after we were officially husband and wife. He was totally
bummed by my decision at first, but got over it. Given his up-
bringing, the concept of no sex before marriage wasn't totally
foreign to Randall. Now, I suppose we could have explored
"alternatives" in the interim, but the only "downtown" Randall's
ever gone is to the office. And well, I'm just too prissy a girl
to . . . you know. Yuck!

Anyway, around the time we were on this sexual hiatus the
subject of children came up. It's hard for me to believe we
hadn't discussed the subject sooner, but I suppose we got
caught up in *everything else* regarding the wedding. Nevertheless, I made my preference on the subject crystal clear: 2.5 by
my thirty-fifth birthday. Randall didn't agree with that number

or my timing. He thought we should wait at least five years to start a family. *Five years?* He was trippin'.

On numerous occasions I tried explaining my objections to this proposed five-year delay. He wasn't hearing me. Just kept coming up with one reason after another why *his* idea made more sense. Which brings me to one more thing I've learned about my new husband that irritates the hell out of me. *He's* always making sense.

I felt Randall was being incredibly selfish, so I called my mom to get her take.

"Make sure the two of you are on the same page *before* y'all get married," she said. "If y'all can't get there and this particular issue is that important to you, *don't* marry him."

I thought about taking her advice and calling off the wedding. Really. But I knew doing so would break Randall's heart. I couldn't bring myself to break his heart. *He'll come around to seeing this my way,* I kept telling myself. Well, shortly before the wedding, Randall came to me with a compromise. What *he* thought was a compromise. He told me he'd be willing to wait three years instead of five to start a family. As the saying goes, timing is everything, and by then, I had become so frustrated at Randall's weeks of not hearing me that I had stopped *hearing him. I* had done all the compromising I was going to do for the sake of our relationship.

Look, Randall wasn't even my type—from a physical standpoint, I mean. He wasn't on the same economic level as me or in a position to upgrade my standard of living. I was bringing home the majority of the money. Paying more than half the mortgage on a house in a town that wasn't even my first choice to live in. A house my husband didn't have to contribute one red cent of his own to obtain. Furthermore, if Randall had had his way, we'd still be living in the same tiny, two-bedroom rental apartment he shared with Dirk for years. The way I saw it, it was time for *him* to make a sacrifice or two for *me. My* biological clock was ticking—not his. I decided I was going to have a child when I wanted to have one. Not when my *husband* wanted me to. So I merely pretended to go along with his compromise. Now I think I may have gone too far.

To borrow a phrase my husband loves to use, I did something *out cold*. I stopped taking my birth control pills.

I opted instead to let nature take its course. Gambled on my presumption that upon resuming sexual relations following the wedding, if I happened to come up pregnant sooner rather than later, Randall would be as happy about it as me once he got a glimpse of our beautiful son or daughter. My pregnancy was no accident. No fluke result of the 1 percent failure rate of oral contraceptives, which I've led Randall to believe was the cause.

Have I gotten this marriage off on the wrong foot or what?

My mother and Fatima are the only ones I've told. Both are extremely disappointed in me, as you might imagine. But what's done is done. I can't change a thing about it now. And truth is, when I look at my precious little Noah, I'm not sure I would if I could.

THE REAL LIFE

45

RANDALL

I hovered near the bar, with a Long Island Iced Tea in hand. To my right stood Dirk in the ear of a honey with thick, full lips, bedroom brown eyes, and a dope hairdo. And to my left was French Fry getting his mack on with a different honey.

Dirk had been trying to get me to come to his "new spot" for a while. A bar called Honeysuckles, on Columbus Avenue between 84th and 85th streets. Now I see why. There weren't enough ashtrays in the city of New York to contain the amount of butt in this joint. This was definitely more to my liking. A more sophisticated crowd. No DJ or dancing, but that was fine by me. (I can't dance anyway, remember?) There was music, however. Live music. A group calling themselves the Gordon Dukes Band was onstage performing a cover of Maxi Priest's "Close To You."

I glanced around at all the beautiful people eating, drinking, and mingling. Surmised that 98 percent of them must've been single. I took my left thumb and felt the band of gold circling my ring finger. Doing so reminded me of how different my life is now. In fact, at the moment I was feeling like a bit of an outsider looking in.

I wondered if any honeys in here noticed that I was married. Like the light-skinned one who'd been clockin' me for the past seven minutes.

"Day-um!" French Fry whispered to me, breaking my train of thought. "A brotha could sit his Grand Marnier on that right there!"

I nearly spit out my drink. French Fry ain't got a bit of sense. I wanted to laugh, but "that" was standing no more than a foot in front of us. She didn't have to know her gi-normous (a cross between gigantic and enormous) ass was the subject of our attention.

Dirk took a time-out from his banter and asked how I was enjoying myself.

"I'm feeling this place a lot more than Bentley's, that's for sure."

"Make sure you have another of whatever it is you're drinking. It's spring again. A brand-new decade and the boys are back!"

That called for a toast. I quickly swallowed what was left in my glass and signaled the bartender for another.

"It's about time Madison let you out of the house," Dirk joked.

"What-eva. Who's the girl? She's cute."

"I'll introduce you. Candice . . . Camille . . . Carolina?"

"It's *Carmella!*" she snapped, clearly annoyed that Dirk had been in her ear for ten minutes and couldn't even remember her name. A new decade, but some things never change.

"Yeah. Mmm-hmm. I'd like you to meet my man, Randall."

"Hi, Randall."

"Hi, Carmella."

"This is Randall's first night out with the fellas since getting married."

Dang, Dirk. Tell her all my business why don't you.

"Congratulations," she said.

"Thanks."

Carmella had a small diamond stud in her nose. I think that's so sexy.

The three of us made small talk until she excused herself to go holla at someone she saw.

"Is Carmella your booty kill for the night?" I asked.

"You know I don't get down like that no more."

"Just checking. Hey, see that honey over there in the plaid mini?"

"The redbone?"

"Uh-huh."

"She looks like Madison."

"Ya think?"

"She's clockin' you."

"For the past eleven minutes and counting."

"So you're over here talking to *me* because?"

"Because I'm married now."

"*So?* Know like I know, you better have some fun tonight. No telling when Madison's gonna let you out of the house again. What you ought to do is grab one of those roving barmaids and send that honey dip a drink."

"I've already bought two drinks tonight."

"Geez, R. *I'll* pay for the damn drink. You are one cheap ass . . . How in the world did you get Madison to marry you?"

"Oh, shut up! What should I send her?"

"Something with a message. Send her a screwdriver."

Not.

I flagged down a waitress, pointed out the young lady, and sent her a glass of red Zinfandel. She smiled, mouthed "thank you," and motioned me to come over. I reluctantly obliged—after Dirk placed a sharp elbow in my ribs. Before making my way over, however, I did something else with my left thumb—

and pinky. Used both to slip my wedding band off my finger and into my pocket.

I got home at 10:00 PM feeling horny but not very confident anything would be happening in our bedroom to address my horniness. Madison and I used to go at it like rabbits. Nearly two years of marriage and a baby later, that already seems like a distant memory.

I tossed my keys on the kitchen table, grabbed the container of Tropicana out of the fridge, took a swig, then headed upstairs to my son's room to check on him. He was out like a light. I kissed him gently on the forehead, being careful not to wake him. I fully expected to find Madison sound asleep as well. To my surprise, she was wide-awake under the covers, reading *Jet* magazine. I immediately jumped in bed next to her.

"What's up, babe?"

"How was happy hour?" she asked, giving me a peck on the lips.

"Okay."

"Just okay?"

I had an absolute ball. Saw so many honeys tonight it almost made me wish I wasn't married with a child. I want to go to happy hour every Friday night with my friends. Which would be a lot more feasible if I wasn't stuck all the way out here in Long Island.

"Yep. Just okay." I snuggled up close to Madison and began sucking on her neck. Watched her fair skin rapidly turn red. "It's been a while you know. Whadda you say we—"

"Pew! You smell like cigarettes."

"May I finish?"

"I'm sorry. Go ahead."

"How 'bout you and me doing a little som'um?"

"Not before you get out of those stinky clothes and take a shower."

I peeled back the covers to see what she was wearing. A pair of sex-repellent pj's. Those weren't going to do the trick.

"Cool. I'ma hit the shower right quick. While I'm in there, why don't you slip into something sexy for your husband."

"I'll see what I can do," she said, giving me a wink of her green eyes.

Yes!

I made a beeline to the bathroom so fast I tripped and fell on the way.

As the soap and hot water erased the scent of cigarette smoke from my body, I fantasized about how I was going to put it on Madison. The thought alone of her waiting for me under the covers in some sexy dental floss—no, sitting on the edge of the bed butt-naked in nothing but red pumps—had my Johnson harder than it was to get an Afro pick through my nappy head as a child.

I was done showering in ten minutes flat, dried off, cocoa-buttered up, and ready for action.

"Ready for me, baby?" I shouted from behind the bathroom door. Complete silence greeted my enthusiasm. I cracked open the bathroom door and stuck my head out. Didn't see Madison sitting on the edge of the bed, butt-naked in nothing but red pumps.

Okay. She's under the sheets in some sexy dental floss.

I crept over to the lump under the covers. Peeled them back to discover my wife still in those sex-repellent pj's *and* as sound asleep as our son was in the next room.

This was some bullshit.

I moped back into the bathroom and gently closed the door behind me. (What I really wanted to do was slam it hard enough to wake up her slumbering ass.) Flipped down the toilet lid, sat, and stared blankly at the wallpaper trying to count how many different geometric shapes I could find in the pattern.

Pissed at being a married man still having to make love to himself more often than not, I closed my eyes tight and got busy. Felt one part satisfied, and one part like a young, dirty old man. When the deed was done, I snatched my smoky-smelling clothes up off the floor, reached into the front pocket of my pants, and pulled out the tiny piece of paper I had almost forgotten I'd stuck in there.

Beverly (718) 555-4463.

46

MADISON

I was in a hurry to leave the office and didn't want to answer my phone. Had exactly five minutes to walk three blocks to Grand Central Station, where I was to meet Fatima. She had won two tickets from WBLS radio station to see Brian McKnight in concert tonight at the Garden. Before the show, though, we planned on having dinner at B. Smith's on West 46th Street. I was really looking forward to the evening. It had been a good minute since Fatima and I got to hang out like this. Best of all, I didn't have to rush back home after the concert because Randall's folks had Noah for the next few days.

My better judgment told me I'd better answer the phone. Good thing I did because it was Fatima calling from a pay phone at the Queensboro Plaza subway station to say she was running twenty minutes late. I swear that girl's worse than me when it comes to being somewhere on time.

Soon as I got off the phone with her, it rang again. This time it was my boss, Melanie Hamlin, calling.

"Hey, Melanie."

"Hi, Madison. Sounds like you're on your way out."

"I am. Meeting someone for dinner. What's up?"

"Would you swing by my office on your way out, please? It'll only take a few minutes."

I grabbed my jacket and pocketbook, and hightailed it down the hallway to see what my boss wanted, hoping it wasn't any bad news.

I took a seat in Melanie's office. An office that was bigger than my entire basement apartment in Laurelton.

"I want to run something by you real quick, Madison," she said, pulling her glasses down on the bridge of her nose and rummaging through some paperwork on her desk. "First, though, I want to commend you. I think you're doing a fabulous job thus far as our new assistant fashion editor. Now, to the reason I called you in. How would you like to represent our department at the FMPA conference this year? It's in Las Vegas. Following the daytime sessions, your evenings would be free to do as you please."

"When is it?" I asked.

"Starts two weeks from today. Maybe you and your husband can go together. Of course, you won't be able to expense his airline ticket or his meals."

"Of course. But that's a great idea, Melanie. My husband and I could use a getaway. When do I have to let you know?"

"By the end of this week."

"Not a problem."

I hurried out of Melanie's office and ran for the elevator.

"Can I get you ladies anything else?" our server at B. Smith's asked as he brought out the Apple-Roasted BBQ Ribs for Fatima, and the Barbequed Red Snapper for me. Our very *cute* server.

"Your phone number would be nice," Fatima told him.

"Ignore my friend, please. She's only kidding."

"Enjoy your meal, then," he said.

"I swear, Fatima. I can't take you anywhere! He was cute, though," I said, giving her a high five. "I've missed your black ass."

"I've missed your high yellow ass more," she laughed.

"I hope Brian McKnight sings his ass off tonight."

"Who cares? I'd be satisfied just gazing at his chocolate scrumptiousness for a few hours."

"Mmm . . . don't think we're going to be close enough to the stage for mere stargazing. Those tickets were *free,* remember?"

"This is true. So, how was your day today at one of New York's leading fashion magazines?"

"Funny you should ask. Right before I left to meet you, Melanie called me into her office and asked if I'd like to attend an industry conference out in Las Vegas."

"That sounds nice. Gonna go?"

"I think I am, Fatima. I think it would be a good career move for me. I'd get to meet some movers and shakers, do a bit of networking. What do you think about this? I'm going to ask Randall to join me. Make a minivacation out of it. You know we haven't gone anywhere since St. Lucia and the baby. Who knows, maybe five days in Vegas will rejuvenate our sex life."

"What's wrong with your sex life?"

"It's been about as irregular as your periods."

"That's so not funny."

"Just the other night, I fell asleep on Randall right after promising to break him off a lil som'um-som'um. We used to do it twice a day, four times a week."

"And now?"

"About once every other week."

"Yikes. What's the problem?"

"This motherhood thing is turning out to be a lot more difficult than I imagined it would be. Five days a week I'm up at 5:30 in the morning getting Noah ready and myself ready for work. I'm out the house by 6:30 to get him over to the sitter's by 6:45. From there, it's off to the Lynbrook Centre station to catch the LIRR to work. At the end of every day, I'm breaking my neck to get out the door by five on the dot just so I can make it to the sitter's before 6:30, when she starts charging overtime. I get home, get Noah situated, then it's straight into the kitchen to get dinner started so it'll be ready by the time Randall gets home from work. By 8:00, I'm completely out of gas. At which point, putting on some Victoria's Secret and sexin' my husband just feels like another damn *task* I've got to perform."

"Question. Why can't Randall take Noah to the sitter in the morning, or pick him up after work, or cook dinner?"

"Because he's got even less time to get ready in the morning than I do. He's commuting all the way to Wall Street these days. Besides, Randall *can't* cook, Fatima. Ten minutes alone in the kitchen and that man's liable to burn our house down."

"How did he feed himself all those years he lived with Dirk?"

"Girl, please. All those two did was eat TV dinners and Gaby's pizza."

"Well . . . this *is* the life you wanted, isn't it? A husband, babies, and a house out on the Island."

"I watched my mother raise three kids while pursuing her career as a psychiatrist. Watched my dad support her every effort along the way while pursuing his own as a surgeon. They made it look so easy. Ever since I was a little girl I've wanted my life as an adult to emulate theirs."

"That's commendable, Maddy. But you're going about it in the worst possible way. Talk about keeping up with the Joneses—

no pun intended. This idealistic picture of the successful husband, the 2.5 kids, and the house with the white picket—"

"What's wrong with it?"

"It's not something you can go into your laboratory and *manufacture*. You've got to *arrive* at all that, girl. You're not your mother. And, let's face it, Randall's nothing like your dad. He may already be about as ambitious as he's going to be."

"Don't say that."

"What if he is? You can't make him into something he's not . . . though you sure have tried."

"What's that supposed to mean?"

"Well, a) you gave him a physical makeover—but kudos on that 'cause you've turned him into somewhat of a hot boy; b) you made him find a higher paying job—which isn't necessarily a bad thing, either; and c) you purposely, without his knowledge, made him a father when you knew darn well he wasn't ready for that level of responsibility. That was just *inexcusable*."

I stopped eating, put down my knife and fork, and wiped my mouth with my napkin. "I must be a really bad person, huh?"

"No. You're not a *bad* person, Madison. You're my best friend in the whole wide world. My best friend who wants what she wants, when she wants it, by any means necessary, and damn anyone who tries to stop her from getting it—including herself."

"I always thought that made me a go-getter."

"Wrong."

"Then what does that make me, Fatima?"

"A spoiled bitch."

47

RANDALL

"Dude. Who the hell is *Beverly?*"

"Let me call you back."

Click.

"Who was that?" Madison asked.

"Dirk."

"What's he want?"

"Nothing that can't wait til you finish telling me about this business trip."

"It's the FMPA—Fashion Magazine Publishers Association—conference, and it's held in different cities annually. My boss asked if I'd like to attend it this year. It's going to be in Las Vegas."

"Vegas? You going?"

"Uh-huh."

"How long will you be gone?"

"A week."

Great. With all the trouble we had connecting of late, now she was going to jet all the way across the country and be gone for an entire week.

"When do you have to leave?"

"Next week."

"Next week? What about Noah?" I asked, perturbed. "You know it would be awfully difficult for me to get him to and from the sitter on time. And, honestly, Madison, I'm really not yet comfortable taking care of him by myself."

"I know, honey. I'm thinking we could leave Noah with your folks. Think they'd mind?"

"Of course not. They can't get enough of their new grandson."

"So, you're okay with that?"

"Yeah. I'll bring him over there and pick him up before you return from your trip."

"Sounds good. Hey, how much vacation do you have?"

"Two weeks. Why?"

"Why don't you come with me?"

"To Vegas?"

"We haven't been anywhere since our honeymoon, Randall. We can spend a carefree week together, just the two of us. It'll be fun. My evenings are going to be free. Think of all the stuff we can do in Las Vegas together. I hear it's like Disney World for adults. Your plane ticket will be my treat. Just pay for your meals."

Madison got up from her chair at the kitchen table, came over to me, and sat in my lap. I had almost forgotten how good it felt to have her in my lap. Action immediately began stirring in my BVDs.

"I know I haven't been as attentive to you as I'd like to be. Let me make up for some of that," she said. "Take this trip with me. Please. You'll have me all to yourself every night. No distractions of any kind."

I didn't know what to make of Madison's sudden realization

that in addition to a new job, house, and baby, she had a *husband,* too.

"I-I—"

"Shut up and kiss me," she said. Madison forced her tongue deep inside my mouth, then retrieved it. "So it's settled, then. You're coming, right?"

I couldn't answer that.

"Oh, okay. You need a little more convincing, is that it?"

Madison removed the belt to her bathrobe, allowing it to open and expose her C cups. Her nipples were already fat and hard. "Well? Don't just stare at 'em. Put 'em in your mouth and suck 'em like a newborn," she commanded.

Wow. If going on a business trip is what it takes to turn you on these days, maybe you should go away more often.

I went to work on my wife's titties so good Noah would have been jealous. I simultaneously cleared a spot on the kitchen table, picked her up, and placed her on top of it. Removed her robe completely and spread her legs apart. Knew what I wanted to do next, just didn't exactly know *how* to do it. Though I had seen a tutorial on it in one of those *Better Sex* instructional videos Dirk ordered through the mail a few years back. *Here goes nothing . . .*

I dove in, cleared the forest, and went to work. Judging by the way she began moaning, groaning, and squirming, I must've been doing something right.

"Eeeww, aaah, mmmm, do that shit, baby," she purred, palming my head in both her hands.

"Whose kitty-cat is this?" I paused to ask.

"Yours, you short, black, bald-headed, mustache-having, Average Joe-turned-hot boy, carpet-munchin' Mandingo!"

"Better recognize!"

Madison climaxed within minutes. Clamped her thighs together with a degree of strength I didn't know she possessed.

Thing is, my head was still in between her thighs. It felt like she was going to squeeze my brain right out the top of my skull.

"M-M-Madison . . . b-baby . . . r-raise up, girl . . . I c-can't breathe."

"Oops. Sorry."

Let me find out I need to wear a helmet the next time I try this.

Having successfully gone "downtown" for the first time, and brimming with newfound sexual confidence, I backed two feet away from the kitchen table, unloosened my belt, dropped my pants and BVDs, and looked my wife straight in the eyes.

It was time for a husband to get some reciprocity.

Madison got down off the table, walked over to me, stuck her index finger into my chest, and ordered me to sit like I was Fido the dog. I grabbed a chair. She grabbed onto my thighs and dropped to her knees.

They say it's better to give than to receive.

Hmph. I'll be the judge of that.

Madison lowered her head s-l-o-w-l-y . . . I heard orchestral music playing . . . a fifty-member choir singing . . . and then I heard . . . "WAAAH! WAAAH! WAAAH!" Our son screaming at the top of his goddamn lungs.

Oh, hell no!

Madison stopped what she was doing. Correction—*about* to do—and sprung to her feet with quickness.

"Hold on. Let me go see—"

"Noooo," I said, grabbing her by the arm and pulling her back. "He's fine."

Let's do this!

She reassumed the position. Began to lower her head again s-l-o-w-l-y . . .

"WAAAH! WAAAH! WAAAH!"

Shut up, Noah!

"I can't concentrate with the baby crying, honey. Wait." Madison raced upstairs to check on our son.

My Johnson went south like black folks to a family reunion. This was some bullshit.

I slipped my limp biscuit back into my BVDs, grabbed the cordless, and called Dirk back.

48

DIRK

I double-parked my Cutlass outside of the convenience store on Linden and put on my hazards. Needed to duck inside and grab a couple of Lotto tickets for my moms. Saw Lori coming out of it. She was sucking on a lollipop and dressed in a Puma sweat suit that I recall used to cling to her tight body. It looked about a size too big on her now. She was with some big, swole, just-got-out-of-the-pen-looking knee-grow with a perm in his head.

"Hey, Dirksten."

"Hey, yourself."

Dude had a "Who's this punk?" expression on his face. I chose to ignore him. Lori chose to introduce us.

"This is my friend, Nero, Dirksten."

"Waddup, dog?" Nero grunted.

"Waddup?" I grunted back. "What chu doing here, Lori?"

"I got the munchies."

"Yo, L, meet me in the car," Nero said. "I'ma go rap to my man over here for a minute."

"Who is that big, greasy-looking muthafucka?" I asked her.

"Why don't you say that a little louder so Nero can hear you?"

"Naw. I don't want to wind up in another coma. It's nine o'clock on a school night, girl. Why you ain't home with your kids? You know ain't nothing good happening on this boulevard after a certain hour."

"Aw-aight, pretty boy," she said, licking her lollipop in a suggestive manner.

"So, who is he?"

"Dang, Dirksten. Mind your business."

"Stop calling me, *Dirksten*. You losing weight?"

"I've been on a diet," she exclaimed, biting into her lollipop. I didn't believe her.

"Mmm-hmm. I'm double-parked. Let me get in this store and buy this Lotto ticket before I *get* a ticket. Don't get caught up in no nonsense on this boulevard, Lori."

Soon as I got back in the house, Rhonda told me Randall was on the phone. I ran upstairs to my room, picked up the extension, and closed the door.

"I got it, Rhonda. Hang up. Yo?"

"Whassup?"

"Whassup? Who's this Beverly chick calling my *moms'* house, looking for you?"

"I had to think fast at the time and that was the only number I could think of. I couldn't give her my number."

"So?"

"So?"

"Who is she?"

"Just some girl I met."

"That's it? That's all you're gonna tell me?"

"If you *must* know, she's that honey you told me to send a drink to at Honeysuckles."

"Get outta here. You didn't even want to talk to her if I recall correctly. Where's your wife?"

"I dunno. Upstairs changing Noah's diaper, I guess."

I sensed a trace of annoyance in Randall's voice.

"Make sure she's not eavesdropping."

"I'm way downstairs in the basement, Dirk."

"You've got telephones all up and through that house. Humor me."

"Hold on," Randall sighed.

He came back on the line a few seconds later.

"Coast is clear. She's in the bathroom."

"Why you ain't tell me you were rappin' to that honey?"

"You're my boy, Dirk, but I don't tell you *everything*. Sound familiar?"

"If you expect me to be covering for your ass you *better* start telling me everything. *You hittin' that?*"

"No. Hell, no! We're just . . . kickin' it."

"Yeah, well you need to find another way for her to reach you 'cause she can't be calling my mama's house no more."

"Forget about her. I'll handle that. Let me ask you something. Madison just told me she's going on a business trip to Las Vegas in a few days. She wants me to go with her. Think I should?"

"Wow. I'd love to go to Las Vegas. Depends."

"On?"

"What would you be doing while she's conducting business?"

"Doing my own thing, I guess. Her days are going to be full, but she says her nights will be free."

"What about your son?"

"We'll leave him with my parents."

"Why not? Sounds like you might have a good time. Although . . ."

"What?"

"Nothing."

"Spit it out."

"If Madison's going to be all the way across the country for an entire week, and your son's going to be at your parents', that's an entire week you and I could be hanging. A week of some serious man-bonding, yow mean? We can hit all kinds of spots in the city."

"In other words, instead of going away with my wife for a week, I can *get away* from her for a week."

"Your words, not mine."

"Wish it were that cut-and-dry, Dirk. Madison and I have been having some issues lately."

"Like?"

"Like I ain't been getting any for one."

"Makes two of us."

"What's your problem?"

"Another time. We're talking about you right now."

"I'm not cheating on Madison if that's what you're thinking. It's just that ever since she had the baby . . . never mind. Let me get off this phone and figure out what I'm going to do."

"Before I forget. I ran into Lori on Linden a minute ago. She ain't looking too tough."

"How so?"

"No disrespect, but your sister's body is beginning to zag in places it once zigged. Plus she's socializing with some big, black knee-grow I've never seen before. Ugly as homemade sin. Dude was spewing some unsavory ions in my direction, R. I'ma have to get French Fry to sniff around on Linden and find out what the dilly is with this cat."

"I've got my own stuff to deal with. I can't be concerned with Lori's, too. My sister needs to get a life. If you notice anything else you think is a cause for concern, ring the bell and tell PC. I'm out."

49

MADISON

The view from my window seat was simply spectacular: a piercing orange sun against the backdrop of a bright blue sky and a sea of clouds. It all looked so peaceful out there. Made me wish I could've taken a seat on the wing of the plane.

Randall opted not to join me. Gave me some excuse about pressing matters he had to attend to at work. Sure, if he'd told me the real reason my feelings would have been hurt—as if they aren't already—but I would have preferred him simply being honest with me: he'd rather be in New York hanging out with his friends than in Las Vegas with his wife. *Is he crazy?*

I'd bet anything Dirk put him up to this. Bet that scoundrel was all up and through my husband's ears persuading him not to join me. Why did I even bother trying to make amends? Trying to get our relationship back on good footing? Trying to show my husband the attention he says he hasn't been getting of late? I said *please*. Hell, I was even down on my knees ready to . . . by the way, thank you, my sweet, darling little Noah. You saved Mommy from doing something to Daddy she really didn't want to do anyway. (But boy did Mommy enjoy what Daddy did to her.)

What I ought to do when this plane lands is pull out the sexiest outfit I've packed in my suitcase—yes, I did pack a few hot numbers for the road—go to the Mirage—no, Caesars Palace—and find me the handsomest . . . Oh, what am I saying? That would just bring on a whole new set of problems. Nope, nope, nope!

Look, all that stuff I said before about Randall . . . about him not being my type physically, not being financially able to take care of me on his own, etc, etc. Well, here's the thing. I *still* love him in spite of all of that. I'm married to the only guy I've ever dated who I know sees me as more than a shapely, light-skinned, long-haired, green-eyed trophy. The quintessential "It girl" he can show off to his friends.

Who knows? Maybe we didn't need to take this trip together. Maybe a week apart will give both of us some time and space to gain a better appreciation for each other, our marriage, and what we could be building together.

"This is your captain speaking. We've caught a tailwind and should be landing in Las Vegas in less than an hour. So, sit back and enjoy the remainder of your flight. And thank you for flying . . ."

I'm going to enjoy myself while I'm out here. But when this conference is over, and I get back home to New York, I plan to get to work. Personally speaking. I'm not going to leave dirty dishes in the sink overnight anymore. I'm going to help Randall with the vacuuming. Get butt-naked more often in nothing but red pumps like he likes me to get. I'm going to be a complete 180 from that spoiled bitch who wants what she wants, when she wants it, and damns anyone who gets in her way.

50

RANDALL

"How's my favorite grandson?" PC asked, with my mother standing by his side.

Lori just happened to be passing through the room at that precise moment.

"Your *favorite* grandson? What? *My* son don't rate up in this camp no more?"

Dirk was right. She looked unusually thin.

"Oh, stop it, Lori," my mother rebuked her. "Give me the baby, Randall."

"Why is it every time I turn around you and Madison are bringing that kid over here?" Lori snapped at me.

Uh-uh.

"That *kid* has a name," I snapped back.

"Take the baby upstairs, Eunice," PC ordered my mother, sensing it was about to jump off in his living room.

"If you must know, your *nephew's* going to be over here all this week because his mother's away on a business trip." I was immediately pissed with myself for even giving Lori an explanation.

"*So?* That kid is yours, too. Why can't you watch him in that big ol' house of y'all's on Long Island?"

She had *one* more time to refer to my child as "that kid."

"I'll be back," my mother said, taking Noah upstairs like my father asked her to.

"You ain't need to get married, Randall," Lori kept on talking. "I knew you only did it to appease *him,*" she said, referring to our father, no doubt.

PC threw a look of disdain at Lori I had never witnessed before.

"Get out of here," he told her.

"Gladly!" She stormed out of the room.

"Excuse me. I have a conference call I need to get on," PC said, exiting the room next.

"I put Noah down," Moms said upon returning.

"What the hell is Lori's problem?"

"You know I don't like that kind of language in my house, Randall. I don't know what your sister's problem is. She's been like a fuse ready to ignite 'round here lately."

"We both know Dad doesn't want her here. Why doesn't he just—"

"Because she's got three young children. Our grandkids. Why punish them?"

"I think she's smoking crack, Ma."

She slapped her hand over my mouth.

"That's a terrible thing to say about your sister. She ain't smoking no dope."

I removed her hand from my mouth.

"How would you know? I bet you don't even know the kind of people she's been . . . Never mind. Not my problem. Madison will be back in a week. I'll get Noah before then.

I'm going to be staying at the Francises' for a few days while she's gone."

"Why don't you stay here with us?"

"No offense, Ma, but any thought I had of doing that went out the window five minutes ago. Besides, I already told Dirk I'd stay over there. With Mr. Francis gone, I won't find myself in the middle of any drama."

She laughed.

"That Henry Francis is a mess, ain't he? There aren't too many things in this life lower than an adulterous husband, Randall."

I sat in my cubicle, barely able to keep my eyes open. Had only managed about three hours of sleep last night at the Francises'. Just couldn't get comfortable for some reason.

Before my nocturnal misadventures, however, I spent the early part of the evening catching up with Rhonda. She seemed to be handling her unexpected bout with parenthood a whole lot better than I was. Much the way she handled her brother's stint in a coma better than I did.

Mrs. Francis was nice enough to let me make a long-distance call to Madison's hotel room in Vegas. I purposely didn't tell her I planned on staying at Dirk's while she was away. As I expected, she wasn't too happy to hear that, but to my surprise didn't put up much of a fuss about it, either. She seemed to be having a good time, but I couldn't let her go into any detail because I didn't want to run up Mrs. Francis's phone bill. She did tell me she had met another sista at the conference who happened to live in Queens, too, and that the two of them planned to hang out together.

I got up and made my way into the office kitchen for a second cup of coffee. Atypical for me, but I needed something to keep my eyelids open, and toothpicks would've been too painful. Dirk and I were going to Honeysuckles after work and I needed to find some energy between now and five. I could hardly wait. I needed to see if pulling that Bev chick was a mere fluke, or if matrimony, of all things, had really begun to transform me from a "nice guy" into the chick magnet I always wished I could be.

51

RANDALL

Ten City's "Devotion" was blastin' on the stereo of my SX as Dirk and I cruised the Van Wyck Expressway on our way to Honeysuckles.

"This is my jam," he exclaimed, head steadily bobbin'. "Who mixed the tape for you?"

"Jean Pierre, this Haitian kid at work. Reminds you of Bentley's, doesn't it? Sugar Daddy used to cut this to pieces."

". . . Devotion, someone by your side.
Devotion, when things aren't going right . . ."

"Man, did I big-booty-freak me some honeys to this!"

"You miss it, don't you?"

"Hell yeah, I miss BBFin'."

"I meant clubbin', Dirk."

"Oh. Yeah, that too. But I can't revisit that scene anymore. Not in this city, at least. Too afraid I might run into people I don't need to run into."

"Like Lizette Felix?"

"Dude, every time I see a chick on the street who just *looks* like that stunt I wanna haul ass running. I feel like Jesse Owens Monday through Wednesday and Carl Lewis the rest of the week."

"Stop it, man, I need to see where I'm going," I said, trying to drive with tears of laughter pouring down my face. I turned the music up louder.

Dirk started to say something, but I couldn't hear him anymore.

"WHAT CHU SAY?"

He reached over and turned the music back down to a volume conducive for conversation.

"I said, I need to move outta my mama's house."

"Why?"

"You and Rhonda were right—at the time. Moving back home was the smart thing for me to do. I was in bad physical shape, you and Madison had gotten engaged, my father was leaving my mother for a woman half his age, and my pure, virginal younger sister got knocked up. But it's been three years since all that and I really think the worst is over."

"How so?"

"For one thing, my moms is starting to get her act together. I haven't told you, but she's gone and gotten herself a part-time job at the Grand Union in Hollis. Secondly, my pops has committed to keeping up the mortgage payments on the house until it's paid off. That'll be in a few short months. Things will be financially manageable for my mother and Rhonda since I'm certain she's not leaving to go anywhere anytime soon with the baby and all."

"So your moms is working at the supermarket? Way to go, Mrs. Francis! What's she gonna be doing?"

"Checkout clerk."

"Good for her. But how's that job gonna work out with her—"

"Drinking problem? I've got some more news for you. She hasn't been drinking lately."

"Get out."

"Word, R. She hasn't imbibed in weeks. Perhaps not coincidentally, she seems to have developed a new fixation with playing Lotto. But, hey. That's a much better vice, yow mean?"

"Think your father's absence has got anything to do with her turnaround?"

"Ironically, yeah. He's not around to set her off anymore. Maybe she's figured out that she only has one demon to fight now—herself. That fight might actually be winnable."

"Well, let's keep our fingers crossed that your pops doesn't come back around and do anything to mess up your mother's progress."

"I don't think he will. So, you see, now's the perfect time for me to move out again and get my groove back. I can't bring honeys to my mama's crib, and I'm scared to death to take one to a hotel now."

"Living at home with your mama ain't got nothing to do with why you ain't been getting any."

"Oh? What's your theory, please tell."

"It's the nineties now."

"And?"

"And you light-skinned pretty boys, with good hair expired with the eighties. Honeys ain't feelin' y'all no more, Dee. They want those Michael Jordans now; cocoa-flavored brothas, with little or no hair like me."

"Yeah, aw-aight, Dark Gable. You got jokes. Fuck you!"

Woo Lawdy! I hadn't been able to laugh this hard in a while. It felt good.

"Anyway," Dirk went on, showing me his middle finger, "I've been kickin' around the idea of asking French Fry to room with me. Dude's got to be as pressed as I am. Since he and Crystal broke up, he's gone from living in the attic of her parents' house to back into the attic of his."

"We've got to come up with a new nickname for Ray."

"How 'bout Attic Boy?"

We hooped it up big-time to that.

"That's not a bad idea. Fry moving in with you, I mean. Where are you thinking about getting an apartment?"

"I'd like to get another in Cunningham Heights, where we used to live."

"Sometimes I wish we were still living in that old phone booth."

"You live on Long Island, with your beautiful wife and baby boy, in a three-bedroom house, with a basement, back-yard, and a two-car garage. No, you don't."

"Beautiful wife? Wow. Haven't heard you refer to Madison in such glowing terms in a long while."

"I've never said she wasn't beautiful—I just can't stand her ass."

Dirk got to view my middle finger this time.

"We enjoyed our youth, didn't we, R? At least I did."

"I enjoyed mine, too. Even if it wasn't to the degree of las-civiousness you did."

"Luscious what?"

"Never mind. You never know how good being single and carefree is until at 25, you have a wife instead of a girlfriend, get stuck with a big house and mortgage to manage, a whole host of other expenses you've never had to consider, and become an unexpected father to a child you're partly responsible to feed, clothe, and shelter for at least the next eighteen years."

"Sounds like somebody regrets getting married."

"Not in totality. I'm mostly regretting all the extra stuff that's come along with it that I didn't anticipate. We would have been so much better off staying in Queens and getting a small, cheap apartment to start off with like I suggested. Not to mention, waiting a few years before having any kids like I suggested, too. *That* alone changed everything for me, Dirk."

"Noah was an accident, R. I won't say an unfortunate accident because he's a living, breathing thing whom the two of you love, but an accident nonetheless. Madison was on the pill. It wasn't like she was *trying* to get pregnant. Shit happens."

"If I hear 'shit happens' out of somebody's mouth one more time, I swear I'm going to lose my will to live!"

"Geez. Sorry. So . . . like what are you guys doing to make sure there aren't any more 'surprises,' shall we say? She's still on the pill, right?"

"And I'm on Ramses."

"No."

"Yes!"

"You're taking showers with a raincoat on?"

"Each and every time."

"What's Madison think about that?"

"Ask me if I care. I'm only getting some twice a month anyhow."

"You're out cold, R. Can't say I blame you, though. I'd probably be doing the same thing if I were in your shoes."

"Probably?"

"Look, forget all your issues and problems right now, 'cause here's the good part. Tonight, Dirk Francis is bringing light-skin brothas back, your wife's nearly three thousand miles away, and your folks are watching Noah. That said, I want you to act like you ain't got a damn bit of sense when we get to Honeysuckles. I want you to act like you're single again, R."

"Act like I'm single again, Dee?"

"Act like you're single again!"

We laughed until both of us had tears filling our eyes this time.

MGM GRAND
HOTEL & CASINO,
LAS VEGAS, NEVADA . . .

52

MADISON

"Always bet on black!" she shouted over my shoulder as the dealer gave the roulette wheel another spin.

I told myself I might venture into a casino or two, but only to watch other people win and lose money. At most, I might throw a few coins in a slot machine. But she managed to talk me into this, and so far, I had already won one hundred dollars.

I was racing to get in line yesterday to register and receive my conference badge, when I literally bumped into her. A petite, brown-skinned sista, no more than five feet tall, working enough T&A for somebody twice her size. I think we were both equally pleased to see another black woman at this conference.

Following an apology, I discreetly peeped out her outfit: a striped faux-wrap jersey dress, with a pair of slings on her feet that really set off the dress. But Yours Truly wasn't bringing up the rear in the fashion department by any means. I was representin' in a khaki twill shirtdress, with a pair of boxed-toed Fitzwells on my feet. We engaged in a bit of small talk. Mostly about the heat in Vegas—and the heat in Vegas.

(Damn is it hot in Vegas!) She asked what company I worked for, and went on to tell me that she worked in Manhattan and lived in Queens. She handed me her business card.

```
Myesha Coffey
Public Relations Assistant
McCann Publishing
750 Third Avenue
New York, NY 10017
```

I tossed it into my Fendi bag. That is, my Fendi knockoff, which I copped on Jamaica Avenue. My designer handbag fetish is so bad, I would never have been able to save for a house if it weren't restricted to knockoffs. One day soon, though, I'm going to Bloomingdale's and treat myself to the real deal.

After getting registered and receiving our canvas bags full of handouts we'd be required to lug around over the next couple of days, Myesha and I learned that we had both made the trek to Las Vegas alone and were staying at the Treasure Island. Right then and there we decided to partner for the duration of the conference and explore the strip together.

"Aw, shit!" I sighed. My streak of luck had come to an abrupt halt. The little ball didn't land on black this time. Just like that, I had to give the house back half of my winnings.

"What time is it?" I looked over my shoulder and asked Myesha.

"Ten fifteen. One more spin, one more spin," she egged me on.

Easy for her to say. I noticed she hadn't gambled another dime of the one hundred and fifty dollars she won at the blackjack table.

"I need to call it a night, Myesha. My first session's at nine in the morning. I quit. I'm going to cash these chips in and collect my money."

"Mine is, too. But, hey, let's go have a quick drink before

heading back to the hotel. I want to soak up the atmosphere of this place a little longer. This hotel is the bomb, Madison. Besides, I'm not ready to go back to my room yet. It's not like I've got some hot brotha waiting for me," she whined.

"This *is* Sin City, remember? You never know."

We busted out laughing.

"One more drink? My treat?"

I gave in. "Oh, okay."

We left the casino and moseyed into the first bar we found in the hotel lobby. I got a Cosmopolitan and she got an apple martini.

"There's like zero chance of meeting any men at these conferences," she informed me. "Although, I did meet this one guy a few years back when the FMPA was in Los Angeles. His name was Eric. One of the few men at this thing who wasn't 'flamboyant,'" she chuckled. "He lived in L.A., though."

"The long-distance thing wouldn't have worked, huh?"

"Probably not. But that's not the reason things didn't work. He did come all the way cross-country to visit me one winter. Girl, I went out and bought a whole bunch of sexy lingerie in anticipation of Eric's visit. It was worth it, too. After that he sent me a plane ticket and flew me out to L.A. to see him. Next thing I knew, I was going back and forth to L.A. to see him at least twice a month over the next three months. It cost me a fortune, too, since Eric only picked up the tab on my first visit."

"So what happened?" I asked, suddenly engrossed in Myesha's tale of a bicoastal FMPA love connection gone awry.

"He was cheating on me. When I was with him in L.A. he pretended I was the only girl in the world for him. When I was back home in New York, he was busy getting it on with some hoodrat from Inglewood named Sha-tiffany. He hurt me, girl. I was really diggin' him."

"I can relate. My ex-fiancé cheated on me, too. Caught him in the act."

"Aw, see. Now that's just nasty. I've come to the conclusion that no man is capable of being faithful or monogamous and for us to expect monogamy is just a setup for disappointment."

"I used to believe that. But I don't anymore. You've just got to find the right guy, Myesha. The one-woman kinda guy."

"There's no such thing as a one-woman kinda guy, Madison. When presented with motive and opportunity all guys cheat."

"I'm gonna have to disagree with your assessment of all men. I happen to be married to a one-woman kinda guy."

"You're married?"

"Sure am."

"Where's your ring?"

"Oh," I said, noticing my naked ring finger. "I heard Vegas is full of seedy characters who prey on tourists, so I decided to play it safe and leave my jewelry in the room safe."

"How long have you been married?"

"Two years."

"Any kids?"

"A beautiful baby boy." I reached into my pocketbook, took out my wallet, and started showing her photos of Noah.

"Ooooh, he's adorable. How old is he?"

"Nine months. And this is my husband." I pulled out a photo of Randall. One I took of him during our honeymoon in St. Lucia. Myesha stared at it. Moved it closer to her face and stared a little harder.

"What's your husband's name?"

"Randall."

"Randall Crawford?"

"Mmm-hmm."

"What a coincidence. I used to kick it with a guy by the same name."

"Not my husband," I joked.

"Naw, the guy I'm talking about had a . . . and a . . . oh, never mind. Your Randall is much cuter," she said, still staring intently at the photo.

Okay. Stop drooling and gimme back my picture.

She handed the pictures back to me and I put them away in my wallet.

"If what you say about every man is true, if given the opportunity that means my husband would cheat on me. Nope. Won't happen. He knows what I've been through and would never inflict that type of hurt on me again."

"Well, I don't know your husband, Madison, but I know *men.* Often I've had husbands and boyfriends try to get with me despite being spoken for and despite me knowing they were spoken for. And I've gotten with a few of them a time or two or three just to see how far they'd go. Not that I'm proud of that, mind you. I'm not exactly a saint, either. I can be a bit of a tease."

"How old are you, Myesha?"

"Twenty-three."

Thought so. Give me your theories on men when you're a little more grown-up.

"You're still young and green."

"Young and green? Is that what you think? How old are you?"

"Thirty-one."

"Okay. Well, you don't have to agree with me, Madison, but I'm sticking by what I said. For your sake, I hope your husband's that lone miraculous exception to the rule."

Myesha's negative ions were trying to infiltrate my positive universe. I wasn't having it. "I'm ready to head back," I said.

"Me, too."

We knocked out our drinks, left the bar, and started our trek back to the Treasure Island.

"What do you want to do tomorrow night?" I asked, noticing for the first time that Myesha was bowlegged *and* pigeon-toed.

"Hitting another casino out of the question?"

"Is for me—but don't let me stop you," I laughed.

"How 'bout a Wayne Newton concert?"

"Again. Don't let me stop you."

53

DIRK

Last night was a bust—for me anyway. I lost my pager for one, and, two, it was as if Randall was right: light-skinned brothas were out of style. Don't get me wrong. I gotta few seductive glances, even a "Can I buy you a drink?" But they were all *two-baggers*. Why is it every time I go out only the *ugly* chicks wanna step to me now? What do they think? I'm ugly, too? *Shyyyt!*

I'm fresh out of paper bags.

Fine. It's taken a quarter century, but the consummate mack is finally ready for a "special friend." Someone I can make plans with. I'm done stickin' and movin'. Bobbin' and weaving. Yeah, I know I said that very same thing when I met Fatima, but this time, I meant it. I was staying the course no matter *what* happened.

Anyway, Randall's evening turned out to be everything mine wasn't. Had I not seen him in action with my own eyes, I wouldn't have believed it. Dark Gable was mackin' his ass off. This honey, that honey. Even saw dude buy one a drink—and that's the cheapest bastard I know! Randall was doing a *remarkable* job of following my advice.

Until . . .

Who shows up in the spot but his new friend, Beverly. At first, I thought her presence was going to upset him and that nice groove he had going. Instead, he lit up at the sight of her like Times Square on New Year's Eve. On some level, I can't say I blamed him. Ms. Thang strutted into Honeysuckles in a pair of black each-and-every-curve-huggin' leggings that quit at her ankles, stilettos, and a blouse so sheer her lace bra was clearly visible underneath it. Things got real interesting following her arrival. The two of them vanished. Couldn't find either for an hour and a half, and Honeysuckles ain't even that big of a place. When R finally reappeared—minus Beverly—he had a silly grin on his face. The same silly grin I saw on his face the night I walked into our apartment after he lost his virginity to Shavonda.

54

RANDALL

I swear I only intended to show her my whip. Maybe let her drive it around the block once or twice. Didn't intend to drive over to a Park-N-Ride garage on 79th and Riverside, or put my tongue down her throat once we got inside it, or undo the lace bra she wore under that sheer blouse she had on, or do to her breasts what I did to them after getting her out of that bra, and I damn sure wasn't expecting her to give me that special treat I'd been waiting for my wife to give me for the longest time.

It happened, though. All of it.

It's not your fault stuff like this never happened to you when you were single.

Bev was flapping her gums about anything and everything on the way back to Honeysuckles. What I needed more than anything was silence. For her to just shut the eff up for five minutes so I could hear myself think. Had I just betrayed the woman who I loved deeper and harder than any woman I've ever known? The woman who ended my years of frustration with being seen by most women as nothing more than a "nice guy"? The woman who brought tears of joy to my eyes on our wedding day? The woman who caused me to fall in love with an old song by the Fatback Band?

It's not your fault you were only getting it twice a month.

Finally discerning that I wasn't in the mood for a lot of conversation, Beverly shut her mouth, flipped down the vanity mirror in the sun visor, and began applying a fresh coat of lip gloss. I watched her do so as I waited for the light to change on 86th Street. Dirk was right. Same complexion, same build, same long, honey-blondish hair as Madison. She didn't have baby's green eyes, though.

It's not your fault Madison's been more preoccupied with the needs of her little man than the needs of her big man.

"That was pretty risky, huh?"

"What?" she asked.

"What just went down in that public parking garage, Bev."

"More like exciting. Did you like how I went down on you? You don't have to answer that. I know you did. I kept peeking at you. You probably couldn't tell 'cause your eyes were rolling back into your head. Your wife must not be anything like me. What's her name anyway?"

True. Madison was too prissy to . . .

"Let's leave my wife out of this discussion."

I pulled up next to Bev's car. She decided to call it an evening and head back to Brooklyn.

It's not your fault you've had to make love to yourself most of the time.

"Call me. Since I can't call you anymore," she groaned, then leaned over and fed me her tongue one more time before exiting my car.

I didn't even feel guilty.

55

MADISON

I got out of bed, brushed my teeth, washed my face, then got back in bed. Stared at the back of Randall's head, thinking about how bummed he had been over our sex life of late—or lack thereof. How he felt I had been neglecting him of late in favor of our son.

"What time is it?" he rolled over and asked.

"Time to brush your teeth and wash the cold out your eyes."

He swung the covers off himself and shuffled off to the bathroom, scratching his head with one hand and his genitals with the other. I grabbed the remote and turned on the television to check the weather forecast. Bright sunshine, with highs in the mid- to upper 80s. I slipped out of the peekaboo teddy I had worn to bed.

My husband crawled back into bed. I crawled on top of him.

"You're naked," he said.

"You noticed!" I began to suck on his neck. Reached for his manhood and began to play with it. It didn't respond to me. "What? I don't turn you on anymore?" I asked, one part jokingly and one part wondering just what in the hell was going on with his lack of desire for me lately.

"You're being silly, Madison."

I slipped my tongue into his mouth and continued to stroke his manhood. It continued to behave uninterested.

It had been like this since I got back from Las Vegas. Randall didn't seem nearly as happy to see me as I was to see him. Oh, I got an "I miss you," but it seemed forced. He asked me a few general questions about the conference, but seemed totally uninterested in anything I did on a personal note.

Randall moved my hand away from his penis. I sat up and stared intently into his blank eyes without saying a word.

"Whassup, Madison?"

"It certainly isn't your dick."

"I'm not in the mood right now. I just woke up," he grunted.

First thing in the morning used to be my husband's *favorite* time of the day.

"You still love me, Randall?"

"You're being silly again. Don't ask questions you already know the answer to."

"Well, sometimes I need to *hear* answers you *think* I already know. What did you do while I was in Vegas?"

"Didn't we have this discussion already?"

"Let's have it again."

He sighed.

"Friday after work, Dirk and I went to happy hour at Honeysuckles. Saturday afternoon we went to Jamaica Avenue and later that same evening, stuck our heads in the Shark Bar on Amsterdam for a minute. Sunday, we went to Delancey Street."

"That's it?"

"That's it."

"You realize you never asked me what I did for fun in Las Vegas?"

"Did, too. You told me you went to a casino, saw a Chippendales show—which I still can't believe—and went to a nightclub."

"Details, Randall. You never asked for any *details*."

"Such as?"

"Like *who* I did all that stuff with."

"You told me you were going to hang with that sista you met."

"You never asked me her name, what she looked like—"

"Okay, okay. Tell me. What's her name? What does she look like?" he questioned in a patronizing tone.

"Never mind. I don't want to talk about it."

"Now you've got an attitude? I'm going back to sleep," he said, burying his head into his pillow.

"Sit up, Randall. I want to talk to you about something."

"You just said you didn't want to talk. Make up your mind."

"I don't want to talk about *Las Vegas*."

"What do you want to talk about, Madison?"

"I think we should sell this house and move back to Queens."

Randall yanked his head up from the pillow so fast it's a wonder he didn't get whiplash. That idea got him more excited than anything of a sexual nature I had tried on him in weeks. I had a good mind to feel his dick again. Bet it was hard *now*.

"*Really?* Why?"

"Your commute could be simpler. Mine, too. And, frankly, I can't keep rushing out of work at five on the dot to get Noah from the sitter. I need some flexibility to stay as long as necessary to accomplish what I need to accomplish. If we were back in Queens we'd be closer to both our jobs. And we need to be closer to family who can pitch in and help us out whenever we need it. My family's in Newburgh, so that leaves yours by default. And, last, I know you'd be happier back in Queens."

"Wow. I don't know what to say, honey. You sure you're okay with doing this?"

"Mmm-hmm. Under one condition."

"What's that?"

"I want us to get another house. I'm not living in an apartment, Randall."

56

MADISON

I damn sure hope I'm not living in this apartment long.

I wasn't anticipating this move happening just six weeks later. Neither of us were. Because we hadn't been in our house long and the previous owners had kept it in immaculate condition, there wasn't much to do to get it sale-ready. So, we listed it with an agent right away, never imagining we'd get an offer just two weeks later and make a nice profit on it at that. The buyers, a couple in their mid-thirties, said they had been searching in our neighborhood for months with no luck. Expecting their third child shortly, they offered us $10,000 above our asking price in return for a quick settlement. What were we going to say to that? *We're not ready?*

Of course the only downside to our coup is that we hadn't even started looking for *our* new house yet. Which explains why we're currently renting a cramped two-bedroom apartment in Hollis. (Why are the words "spacious" and "apartment" mutually exclusive words in New York City?) I can't wait to get the hell out of here. *I better not see a roach!*

Our move back to Queens hasn't been the only significant change of late. Dirk's moved as well. Out of his parents' house and into an apartment in Queens Village with French Fry. And Fatima seems to have had a change of heart about him. Said she had done some thinking since that awful night at Bentley's and came to the conclusion that she may have overreacted. She agrees with Randall now. As disgusting as Dirk's antics were, it was all stuff that he did before he met *her.* That any D-O-G can be trained to behave properly with the help of the right trainer. "Haven't we *all* stooped to lows we aren't proud of, Maddy?" she asked me.

Hmph. Haven't we, though.

So as of today, Fatima's giving that heathen another chance if he's still interested. Who knows? If I could turn Randall into a hot boy, maybe Fatima can make an honest man out of Dirk. Besides, that's what we women do when it comes to the men in our lives, right? Forgive 'em, forget all the shit they put us through, then hope and pray they'll get better at whatever it is they're currently not very good at. It's a model as American as apple pie.

I will say this. Fatima's on her own now. I'm going to keep an open mind about this, but I'm staying out of it no matter what. I mean it this time.

"Dirk's looking good, ain't he, Maddy?" Fatima commented as we waited in the refreshment line at Sunrise Cinema. The guys had gone ahead to find seats for Eddie Murphy's *Another 48 Hours.* Yes, strange as it may seem, me and Randall were on a double date with Fatima and Dirk. (I said I was going to keep an open mind. Believe me now?)

"He always *looks* good, Fatima. Spend every bit of that ten dollars he gave us for snacks. Get some Dots and Milk Duds, too, while you're at it."

"You're wrong."

"What-eva."

"Have I told you how glad I am that you guys are back in Queens?"

"Only about a ga-jillion times."

"Well, make it a ga-jillion and one times."

"Listen, I need your opinion on something." I lowered my voice. Looked around to make sure there wasn't anyone within earshot of us that we knew. "Remember how I told you our sex life was practically in the toilet before I left on my business trip?"

"Y'all rockin' and rollin' again?"

"Hardly. Get this. All of a sudden Randall doesn't seem interested in having sex with *me* now."

"Yikes."

"Check this out. The few times that we have, he's barely been able to perform, if you get my drift."

"Let me get this straight, Maddy. Randall wanted it morning, noon, and night before you left for Vegas. Now that you're back, he's totally gone in reverse?"

"Bingo."

"Think he's trying to punish you?"

"Punish me?"

"Teach you a lesson for all those times he wanted some and you had that endless headache."

"Randall's not capable of 'punishing' me like that. Even if he was, I couldn't see him trying that for more than a week—two, tops. This crap's been going on for several. Randall couldn't hold out that long if he wanted to."

"He did when you had that beaver on padlock before the wedding."

"That was different, Fatima. He wasn't lying in bed next to me every night, either."

"What can I get you?" asked the guy behind the refreshment counter.

"Two medium buttered popcorns, two medium Cokes, a box of Milk Duds, and a box of Dots," she told him. "Here's a thought, Maddy. Actually, never mind. It might upset you."

"Nine dollars even."

"Just say it, Fatima. I'm not going to get upset."

"You sure?"

"Girl, don't make me have to pimp slap you inside this theater. Spit it out!"

"Don't get colored with me, little red girl. Think Randall might be getting it somewhere else? Have you given that any thought?"

"*Excuse you?* What do you mean he's getting it *somewhere else?*"

"I didn't say that. I *said* . . . have you given any *thought* to that possibility? Do you know who he was with or what he was doing while you were in Vegas?"

"He was with Dirk . . . oh, no. *Dammit!* I swear Fatima. If I find out Dirk—"

"Stop. I'm sure Dirk made sure Randall kept his nose clean while you were gone."

"Are you kidding me? As much as he dislikes me?"

"You're such a drama queen. Dirk doesn't dislike you. He probably *likes* you more than he realizes—and vice versa. Look, I'm sure I'm off base about Randall. Just get your antenna up, girl. His behavior of late is definitely not kosher. Now, c'mon. Grab some of this food, put some pep in your step, and let's go find our dates."

57

DIRK

Randall and I grabbed four seats ten rows from the movie screen and settled in.

"I'ma patch things up with Fatima. Make her want me again, you watch," I told him. "I can't believe your wife ain't trippin' about this double date."

"If she is, she's doing it silently. Madison's been a model citizen of late. I'm impressed."

I looked around to make sure I didn't see anyone we knew sitting close by. Lowered my voice.

"French Fry did some sniffing around on Linden. That Nero cat your sister's been hanging with just finished doing a bid at Fishkill. Knew that cat ain't smell right. No one seems to know what he was in for, though. That or nobody's saying."

"I bet it was drug dealing. I think he's got my sister on crack."

"What? You serious?"

"Yep. Just can't prove it. Next subject."

"Okay. Well, you've been real *incog-Negro* since you came back to Queens. You still messin' with that Beverly chick? Has she slobbed the knob lately?" I laughed.

"It's gone *way* beyond that."

"YOU *HITTIN'* THAT, R?"

"Sssh, you dummy. Lower your voice!"

"Sorry," I said, lowering my voice to a whisper and surveying the area around us once more. "You *fuckin'* her?"

"Gol-lee, Dirk. Do you have to make it sound so crass?"

"Excuuuuse me! I'm sorry. Are you icing her cake? Sautéing
her onion? *Flipping her burger?"*

"This is funny to you, huh? All I intended to do was talk a
little stuff to her—like *you* do when you meet a honey. Flat-
ter her a little. Let her stroke my ego a little. Pretend I was
single again for a minute—like *you* told me to. Somehow I've
gone too far. I think I may have really messed up, Dirk."

"She's PREGNANT?"

"Will you *puh-leeze* stop talking so loud! No!"

"Well, good. Then you just went too far, but you didn't
mess up."

"Say what?"

"Nothing. She catchin' feelings for you?"

"No."

"You catchin' feelings for her?"

"No, Dirk. Nobody's catching feelings for anybody. We're
just . . . knockin' boots. No strings attached."

"Daaay-umm. So what *is* the problem?"

"Messin' with Bev is affecting my ability to . . . you know . . .
with Madison."

"No, Randall, I don't . . . *ooooh."*

"Yeesss."

"Chick-on-the-side is wearing your little pecker out?"

"You are absolutely no help, you know that?"

"Quiet. Here they come."

I saw the girls with their hands full, scanning the theater in
search of us. "Over here," I said as I waved to get their attention.

58

RANDALL

Act like you're single again. Thanks for nothing, Dirk.

I kind of sensed things had gone too far with Bev the last time I was intimate with Madison. I wanted her to do something I could never have imagined wanting her to do. *Disappear*. I didn't want to kiss, cuddle, or talk. All the things I normally enjoyed doing after a session of lovemaking with my wife.

Sue me. I got caught up. Took a page out of Dirk's book and began writing an entire chapter. Found excuses to rationalize my irrational behavior. Now I'm barely able to make love to my wife. Not because I don't want to, but because *now* I'm feeling guilty. Guilty because Madison's been a changed woman since she got back from her trip. Guilty because she's been going all out for me lately. Butt-naked-in-nothing-but-red-pumps all out for me lately. When we were dating she poured her heart out to me. Told me how crushed she was over her ex-fiancé's betrayal. What did I do? Looked straight into her beautiful green eyes and assured her I'd never do likewise.

Worse, I know Madison would *never* deceive me in any way, shape, or form.

"There aren't too many things in this life lower than an adulterous husband, Randall."

You're right, Ma. You raised me better than this.

Lord Jesus, I know I don't pray to you like I'm supposed to and I know I'm a hypocrite—but that's beside the point. Madison doesn't need to know about this. Really. I will never cheat on her again. No matter how fine the honey is or how much play she—

"Hold on a second, Lord. My work phone's ringing."

I hoped it was Beverly calling so I could tell her right now that I wouldn't be "kickin' it" with her anymore. It was my mother.

"We've been robbed!" she screamed into the phone. "They came right through the front door."

"Who?"

"I don't know *who.*"

"Was anyone home at the time?"

"No."

"What'd they steal?"

"Just your father's stuff. His computer, stereo system, television—"

"They take his rifle?"

"No, thank you, Jesus. Miles brought it upstairs and was cleaning it just the night before. Is that some divine intervention or what? That's all we need is for that gun to get into the hands of the wrong person. I've been telling your father to get rid of that damn thing for years! He don't hunt anymore."

Damn thing?

"Have y'all called the police?"

"They're here now. They don't see any sign of forced entry. They think whoever did this had a key to the house."

"You're kidding."

"No, I'm not."

"How's Dad taking it?"

"He's livid, Randall. We're just glad they didn't ransack the entire house or take any other valuables. It appears they knew exactly what they were after."

"You need me to do anything?"

"No. We're getting the locks changed on the entire house and getting a security system installed. Where in the hell would somebody have gotten a set of keys to this house?"

Hell?

"I dunno, Ma. Bad guys know all kinds of means to do that. Saw it on *60 Minutes.* The main thing is nobody got hurt, Ma. Everything taken of Dad's can be replaced. I have to get off the phone. It's almost five and I have to wrap up my work. I'll call back when I get home, okay?"

I left work at five on the dot and headed to Chambers Street to catch the E train, still feeling the aftershock of my mother's news. Put on my Walkman and tuned it to KISS FM. LeVert's "Casanova" was playing.

". . . I ain't much on Casanova
Me and Romeo ain't never been friends . . ."

Hmph. How apropos, I thought to myself.

I pulled a token out of my pocket, went through the turnstile, and headed down to the platform below. Crowded as usual. Saw a honey about twenty feet ahead of me that looked somewhat familiar from a distance. It looked like . . . like . . . *naw.*

Got a little closer. Viewed her from a better angle. It *was* her. She had put on a little weight—good weight—but that's about it.

I'll be damned. How long has it been? Four years since we last saw or talked to one another?

I snatched off my headphones and stuffed my Walkman into my knapsack as the train came barreling into the station. I was still about four folks deep, fighting to make my way on, too, when she boarded.

C'mon people. Move it. I cannot miss this train!

I pushed forward, simultaneously using my thumb and pinky to slip off my wedding band. Got it off, had it in my fingertips, and was about to stuff it in my front pocket when I got jostled from behind by another person pushing his way onto the train, too. Fool knocked it right out of my hand. I watched helplessly as the symbol of my lifelong commitment to one woman hit the ground, took a short bounce, and disappeared into the narrow black space between the train door and the subway platform.

Oh, SHIT!!!

I tried backing out of the door of the train, but my 155-pound frame was no match for the contingent behind me who literally forced me onboard. The train doors closed and that was that.

I cursed the fat fuck (under my breath) who caused me to lose my wedding band, then turned my attention back to the reason I had taken it off in the first place. Spotted her hanging on to a pole in the center of the car. Slithered through and around other passengers to reach her.

"Pardon me . . . Excuse me . . . Pardon me . . ."

Grabbed hold of the same pole she held. Her head was down as she read a folded section of the *Daily News*. I cleared my throat. She looked up. Our eyes met.

"Myesha?"

She stared at me blankly.

"And you are?" she asked with a lot of "What's it to you?" in her voice.

"It's me. Randall."

"Randall? Oh, my God. It *is* you!"

59

DIRK

My sweet tooth was kickin' in, so I ducked into Grand Union to satisfy it. Saw my mother holding it down at the 10 Items or Less register. I was so proud of her. She'd been sober for weeks. And what this job was doing for her was far more important than money. It was giving her a sense of independence she'd been without since marrying my father.

I grabbed the biggest bag of nacho chips they had along with a container of crab dip, and got in her line to pay for it. To my surprise, I saw Madison in front of me in the line. She didn't see me, however.

"How're you, Mrs. Crawford?" my mother greeted her as she began ringing up her stuff.

"Hey, Ma," I chimed in.

"Oh, hey, Dirksten. I didn't even see you standing there."

"Whassup, Madison?" I asked, full of cheer.

She turned around and said, "Oh, hey, Dirk," about as dry as that ginger ale from Canada.

Madison looked sad. My mother noticed likewise.

"What's the matter, chile?" my mother asked.

"Nothing."

"Madison?" I butted in.

"*What,* Dirk?"

"You all right?"

"DO I *LOOK* ALL RIGHT TO YOU?" she snapped at me.

A hush came over the entire supermarket. Felt every eyeball inside of it on the back of my neck.

"Leave that woman alone!" some blue-haired lady scolded me from her position over in the adjacent checkout lane.

"Mind your business, Grandma," I shot back at the wrinkled prune.

"Stop it, Dirk! That's not nice," my mother scolded me.

"She started it."

"I WISH *ALL* OF YOU WOULD SHUT THE FUCK UP!!" Madison screamed, then bolted out the store leaving her groceries behind.

What the . . .

"I'll pay for her stuff, Ma. Just add mine to her total."

"Hurry up and go after her, Dirk," she said as I paid. "Find out what's wrong with that chile."

I grabbed the grocery bag and hurried out of the store. Spotted Madison's car in the parking lot and ran toward it, hoping to catch her before she pulled off. She was sitting in it, engine running, and balling when I reached her. I rapped on the window motioning for her to roll it down.

"WHAT!!" she screamed at me yet again.

"Okay. Like first of all, you need to take some of that bass outta your voice. You just embarrassed the shit out of me in that store. Secondly, I paid for your groceries you left back in there."

"Put the bag on the backseat," she barked.

I did as she asked, then went around to the passenger side. "Let me in."

"I apologize," she said, as I slid into the seat. "I didn't mean for what happened in there to happen. I'm just having an emotional moment right now."

I used my hand to wipe away the tears that were streaming down her perfect cheekbones.

"You wanna tell me about it?"

"I can't talk to you about this."

"Why?"

"Because it involves Randall."

"Then I am the best person for you to talk to."

"Okay, but not in this parking lot."

"Let's go in Gaby's. I'll buy you a slice."

"Not there, either."

"Then you pick a spot, but I'm driving. You're not in a good frame of mind. Let's get in my car."

Madison turned off the engine, removed the keys from the ignition, and handed them to me.

"Drive my car. Wait . . ."

"What?"

". . . There's ice cream in that grocery bag."

"My apartment's right up the hill. Let's go put it in my freezer until we're done."

60

MADISON

"Go wash your face," Dirk said, handing me a washcloth. "Use my bathroom."

Dirk's bathroom was sparsely decorated but clean. Curiosity made me want to peek inside of his medicine cabinet, but I refrained. (He may have had it booby-trapped for all I know.) I soaked the washcloth in cold water and applied it to my face.

"Much better," he said when I came out. "You look like a supermodel again."

"Supermodel? Is that what you think I am?"

He didn't answer me.

"How's it feel being back in Queens again?"

"Ask me that when we've found a house."

"Where do you want to go to talk?"

"I haven't given it any thought."

"I have. Let's stay here."

"In your apartment?"

"No, Madison, in my *neighbor's* apartment. Is that a problem?"

"No, but I don't want French Fry coming home and finding us alone in here. I don't need anybody jumping to the wrong conclusions."

"He won't be back until late tonight."

"And what if Randall drops by?"

"He won't be coming by here, either."

"Oh? Do you know where he is today? Because I don't."

"Nope. But Randall wouldn't come over without calling to see if I'm home first. I haven't heard from him all day."

Sure you haven't.

"Look, Madison, the sooner we chat the sooner you can get your ice cream out of my freezer and be on your way."

"Fatima said something to me recently. I thought she was trippin' at first, but now I'm not so sure, and it's bothering the hell out of me."

"What was that?"

"That Randall might be messin' around on me."

Dirk's jaw hit the floor.

"She actually said that?"

"Didn't say she *knew.* Said it was a possibility. You haven't noticed how un-Randall-like his behavior has been of late?"

"Mmm, no."

Sure you haven't.

"Well, in addition to his odd behavior—which you claim not to have noticed—he claims to have lost his wedding band to add to it."

"Did he tell you how?"

"Said someone knocked it out of his hand and that it fell onto the subway tracks and disappeared."

"You believe him?"

"No, I don't. And what he has yet to explain to my satisfaction is why it was in his *hand* and not on his *finger*."

"You don't really think Randall's capable of cheating on you, do you?"

"No, but then I didn't think I was capable of . . . my marriage is important to me, Dirk. Randall and I have a child together. We're about to invest in another home together. I know you haven't been my biggest supporter—"

"Nor have you been mine—"

"But I *do* love him. I'm with Randall because I want to be with him. Not because he's the first guy I could get to scratch my itch to be married, as you believe." Dirk rubbed his temples as if he was feeling a migraine coming on. "You know exactly what's going on with Randall, don't you?"

"What I know is that your marriage is very important to Randall, too. And that maybe I've misjudged you, Madison. You've got nothing to worry about. Trust me. Randall's just got some things he needs to sort out for himself right now. I don't know if he's ever let on, but he was completely blindsided by your pregnancy. He was barely a husband before he became a daddy, too. It all happened too fast for him. Don't ever tell him I told you that, though."

Dirk chuckled.

"What's so funny?"

"You realize this is the first time you and I have had anything close to a civil conversation?"

I chuckled.

"Scary, ain't it? You know, I can sorta see just a *little* bit why Fatima likes you."

"Oh, my God! Did you just pay me a *compliment?*"

He got the hand for that. "I'd prefer this conversation stay between us."

"Nothing said in this room leaves this room. May I walk you back to your car?"

"After you get my ice cream out of your refrigerator, yes. I'd like that."

61

DIRK

I'd been looking forward to seeing Madison get her come-uppance. You know, like I got mine. I'd been too thrilled that R was waxin' that Bev chick behind her back. Too thrilled to learn that he had reconnected with Myesha, and hoping that he'd be waxin' that ass real soon, too.

Until I bore witness to Madison's meltdown.

Fatima and I were dating now and Madison wasn't trying to interfere in that any longer. That said it was time for me to bury the hatchet with her for real this time. Let bygones be bygones, and assume a role I'd never had to before when it came to my relationship with Randall: the voice of reason. Somehow, I was going to have to find a way to reel *him* in this time.

I stared at the phone on my nightstand wondering if I should initiate this conversation with him over the phone or in person. Before I could decide which approach was better, I had already dialed and the phone was ringing.

Madison answered.

"Hello?"

"Hey, Madison, it's Dirk."

"Your ears must be burning. Fatima's on the other line. Randall's not home."

"Okay, well . . . tell him I—"

"Hold on, okay?"

Madison came back on the line a few seconds later. I let her know she didn't have to end her call on my account.

"It's cool. We'd been on the phone for over an hour. How are you?"

"I should ask you that."

"I'm okay."

"Telling me the truth?"

"Mmm-hmm."

"Have you guys talked?"

"Not really. Not yet anyway."

"So where is Mr. Man?"

"He drove downtown late this morning. Said he wanted to do some suit-shopping at Century 21. Fatima was just telling me about the private picnic you two had," she followed up, laughing.

"What's so funny?"

"Trying to picture *you* eating cheese, crackers, and fruit on a grassy knoll in Central Park."

"Sippin' fine wine, too."

"For goodness' sake, Dirk. Fatima asks you to bring a bottle of wine and you bring a bottle of three-dollar Canai?"

"What-eva. I'm not a wine drinker, yow mean?"

"Obviously. You stick with my girl, okay? She'll teach you some class. Anyway, she did say the picnic was your idea, so I guess you get a few brownie points for romantic creativity. I'm impressed. Hey, did Randall tell you?"

"Tell me what?"

"Our realtor's showing us a house on 226th Street in Cambria Heights this evening at six o'clock."

"Naw, he didn't."

"It just came on the market and she doesn't think it's going to last long. I've got to get out of this apartment. I'm too high-maintenance for this soup can. You know I found a damn cockroach in here the other day?"

"Hope it was a male."

"That's not funny."

"I know. I'm sorry. Well, let me let you go, Madison."

"Hey, Dirk . . ."

"Yeah?"

"Thanks for checking on me. And you know . . . the other day. I'll let Randall know you called when he gets home."

62

RANDALL

This was like déjà vu all over again. Me and Myesha spending an afternoon together while she got her shop on. Except we weren't sashaying up, down, and around 34th Street in the sub-freezing cold this time. We were on West 4th Street, in the heart of Greenwich Village, and the temperature was a comfortable 70 degrees.

Look, I know I asked the Lord to forgive me for my extra-marital indiscretions with Beverly—but that was *before* I ran into Myesha again. C'mon. It's not like I went *looking* for this girl. Doesn't the Bible say that the "soul is willing, but the flesh is weak"? Therefore, would not the Lord understand if I maybe, just so happened to, you know, one last time?

Strange, but Myesha had yet to inquire about my status since we reconnected. Uncharacteristic of the chick I knew previously, but then I hadn't bothered asking about hers, either, so maybe we were both playing a game of "don't ask, don't tell."

Worked for me.

After a few 50-cent franks at Gray's Papaya, Myesha and

I headed over to Washington Square Park, where we copped two ice-cream cones, commandeered a bench, and watched various street performers entertain the afternoon crowd.

"I didn't think I could ever get you to hang out with me like this again," she quipped.

"Well, at least I know today isn't about you buying sexy lingerie to impress another guy with."

"Is *that* why you left my apartment in such a huff back when? You were jealous, Randall?"

"Girl, you trippin'."

"Mmm-hmm. Right. Hey, know what would be a great way for us to cap off this afternoon?"

Now you're talking, girl.

"What's that?"

"Seeing a movie."

Not what I had in mind.

"A movie?"

"Yeah. We've never gone to the movies together."

It was already four o'clock and I had been cavorting around Lower Manhattan with Myesha much, much longer than I had planned. This was turning into an all-day thing. I had only given Madison a half-day's excuse.

"It's too nice outside to be cooped up in a movie theater."

"Oh, don't be such a poo-putt, Randall," Myesha said, sticking out her tongue and taking a tantalizing lick of *my* ice-cream cone.

Halfway through *Goodfellas* it hit me like a sledgehammer: I had totally forgotten about the appointment with the real estate agent this evening.

Was I in trouble now.

I nudged Myesha's head off my shoulder and I told her I'd be back in a second. Raced up the aisle and out of the theater in search of a pay phone. I found one on the side of the building and quickly dialed home. The answering machine came on.

Think, Randall, think . . .

Beeeep.

"Uh, hey, baby, it's me. *My car won't start.* I think the battery's dead. I'm waiting for the AAA to come and give me a jump. I'm not going to make it home in time to—"

"Randall?"

She picked up.

"Oh. You're home."

"Where are you? We're supposed to be in Cambria Heights in fifteen minutes!"

"I know, baby. My car battery is dead."

"You nearby? I'll come get you."

"Naw. I'm . . . still downtown."

"Downtown?" she hollered in my ear. "You've been gone all afternoon! You promised you'd be home by six. Why didn't you call me earlier and tell me you were running late? I could've called the realtor and—"

"I'm sorry, I'm sorry. Time just sorta slipped away from me and—"

Click.

No, she didn't.

"Madison. MADISON!"

I slammed the phone back into the cradle, stepped out of the booth, and banged my fist against it in disgust—at myself. Moped back inside the theater and settled back into my seat.

"Everything all right?" Myesha asked, resting her head back on my shoulder.

"Fine. Everything's just fine," I lied.

63

MADISON

Totally pissed now, I threw on some sweats and put Noah in his stroller. I didn't feel comfortable going to this showing alone. I was too anxious about finding a new home. I needed a nonemotional, objective person with me to bounce things off of. The kind of thing I needed my *husband* to provide.

Wait. Maybe I could ask . . . naw. Ya think?

I grabbed the phone.

"Hi. It's me again."

"What's wrong?"

"Everything's fine. Sort of. You busy?"

"I was just about to call Fatima to see if she wanted to go to dinner. Why?"

"Remember that appointment with the realtor I mentioned?"

"At six, right? Shouldn't you be on your way?"

"Randall's not going to be able to make it."

"He didn't get home yet?"

"No—and I'm so upset with him right now. But that's another story. I really don't want to do this by myself."

"Mmm . . . want me to go with you?"

"Would you?"

"It's not going to take too long is it?"

"Fifteen, twenty minutes tops."

"Cool."

"Thank you, Dirk. You're a sweetheart. We need to be there like pronto, though. You dressed?"

"I'm decent."

"Great. Let me give you the address and you can meet me there."

64

RANDALL

It was a quarter past eight when I pulled up in front of our apartment building. Prepared for a confrontation, I was one part relieved, and one part perplexed not to see Madison's car on the block. I went inside and headed for the fridge to see if she had left a note for me. She hadn't. Maybe she was still mad at me and needed some extra time to cool off.

I quickly got out of my clothes and jumped in the shower to get rid of any scent of Myesha's perfume from my body. Unlike my last visit to her crib in Queensbridge, I didn't have to leave with my face in my back pocket this time. The same honey who once told me not to let my skin touch hers seemed *hell-bent* on letting me hit it.

But I didn't. Somewhere in between that short phone conversation with Madison outside the movie theater and anticipating the music I'd have to face when I got home, I lost my enthusiasm to get it on with Myesha. Today anyway.

I shut off the water, toweled dry, and got cocoa-buttered up. Heard Madison come in. I cautiously stepped out of the bathroom to gauge her disposition and to offer the mea culpa I had rehearsed over and over on the drive home.

"Hey, baby," I said, taking my son out of her arms and giving her a kiss that barely grazed her cheek because she moved her head. "I messed up. I know. I'm sorry. I did a poor job of keeping track of the time. I couldn't help what happened to the car, though."

"Did AAA come and give you a jump?"

"Turned out not to be the battery after all. The connection was just loose. I figured it out before they showed up."

"Mmm-hmm."

"What? You don't believe me?"

"What I don't believe is how you could have possibly forgotten our appointment," she said, snatching Noah out of my arms and rolling her eyes at me.

"That makes two of us. How did the house look?"

"I loved it. So did Dirk."

"Dirk?"

"I asked him to accompany me in your absence."

"You two barely tolerate one another."

"How 'bout that?"

"Can we afford it? Do you want to put a contract on it?"

"I'm tired. I'm putting Noah to sleep and relaxing," she said, ignoring my question.

"You hungry? Want me to fix you some—"

"Dirk took us to Red Lobster."

What the . . . ?

"Okay. What's up with all this sudden chumminess between you two?"

"Problem? You did say you wanted us to get along, am I right?"

"Yes—"

"Well, we're getting along. I hope whatever you did today was truly worth it, Randall."

"*Whatever* I did? You know exactly what I did today."

"Do I really? Show me the suit you bought. That is what you said you were going downtown to do this morning."

"I didn't buy one. Didn't really see anything that blew me away."

She laughed. Not the "hardy-har-har" variety. The "you're full of shit" variety.

"You've been gone all day today and couldn't find a single suit you liked?"

"If there's something you're trying to say, just say it."

"You're right. I think it's about time I did just—"

The phone interrupted us.

"Who is it?" Madison grunted, annoyed at the interruption. "Oh, hi." *It's your mother,* she mouthed to me. "WHAT!! Oh, my God, Eunice!" Madison's face lost what little color it had in it.

"What is it, baby?" I questioned her.

"When? How?"

"Madison. *What is it?*"

She took the phone from her ear and clutched it against her chest.

"It's your sister."

"Lori?"

She nodded.

"What about her?"

"She's . . . *dead,* honey."

My mother refused to say any more over the phone. I told Madison to stay put at home with Noah. Got in my car and sped down Francis Lewis Boulevard at least twenty miles over the speed limit, running lights along the way. When I got to Murdock Avenue, an ambulance passed me going in the opposite direction. Couldn't help but wonder if my deceased sister was inside it.

There were several police cars parked in front of my parents' house when I arrived, as well as a small crowd gathered on the street. Couldn't find a space, so I double parked and rushed toward the house. I was so numb, I couldn't even feel my feet touching the ground beneath me. I was met by an officer at the front gate.

"This is a crime scene, sir."

Crime scene?

"I'm Randall Crawford. This is my parents' home."

"Let's see some ID."

I yanked out my driver's license and showed it to the officer, who then let me pass.

The front door was open and through the screen, I could see several more police officers and a couple of people in plainclothes taking photographs in the living room. My parents were sitting next to each other on the front stoop. PC's head was in his hands and he was wailing like a baby.

"Jesus, Lord, Jesus . . ."

"Dad?"

". . . Help me, Jesus . . ."

"Dad!"

I turned to my mother. She shook her head, signaling me that she didn't want to speak in front of him. PC pulled himself together, got up, and disappeared back into the house without saying a word to me. I took his spot next to my mother on the stoop.

"What happened, Ma?"

She stared straight ahead into the faces of those milling about in front of her home, trying to determine the same thing.

65

DIRK

Madison was standing outside next to her Prelude with Noah in his stroller when I arrived. Her green eyes sparkled when they caught sight of me. Okay. Maybe I just imagined that part.

"Let's go, slowpoke," she chided me, hands on hips.

What I didn't imagine was this: At that precise moment, I felt the exact same rush I had a few years back when I spun around on that bar stool at the Red Parrot and got a glimpse of Madison for the first time.

I thought back to the seller's realtor who kept referring to us as *Mr. and Mrs.* Crawford, and how Madison didn't correct him until after he had called us that three or four times. Over the next twenty minutes, she and I walked up, down, through, and around that house. For every one of those minutes, I found myself wishing that I *was* her husband. The father of her child. That *we* were house-hunting. I stopped thinking about going to dinner—with Fatima.

It was awkward before, during, and after our meal, but only

because Madison and me were doing our best to conceal the fact that we were enjoying each other's company more than we wanted to admit.

French Fry knocked on my bedroom door, interrupting my recollections of earlier this evening.

"Come in."

He took a seat on the edge of my bed. He had on a linen shirt and gabardine slacks, and was bathed in Obsession cologne.

"Pee-yew! Where are you going?"

"To Sabrina Parker's crib in Rochdale."

"Who's she?"

"This honey I met in Roy Wilkins Park. She's a figure-eight, Dee," he laughed.

"Do your thing, playboy. Don't hurt nobody."

"Word up. Before I jet, though, I gotta tell you some bad news I just heard."

My heartbeat sped up.

"What happened, Fry?" I asked anxiously.

"I've just learned that Crystal's gotten engaged to another man. Can you beat that? Some other dude's gonna be playin' daddy to my little girl."

I thought he said he had some *bad* news.

My first inclination was to bust out laughing—but dude looked about ready to cry.

"See. You should've married her like she wanted you to."

"You're right, Dee. Just couldn't stop chasin' that ass."

"Been there, done that, and got this nasty scar to prove it," I told him, parting my hair and showing him the wound in my scalp that took twenty-four stitches to close. "But, hey, don't let it get you down," I said, patting him on the shoulder. "Everyone's a genius *after* the fact. Don't keep that honey dip waiting. And don't do nothing I wouldn't do."

I dozed off briefly after French Fry left. Awoke at 10:45. Surely Randall was home now. It was late, but this couldn't wait.

I had to put him on notice that we needed to have a serious heart-to-heart ASAP. Before I could dial, though, someone was calling me.

"Hello?"

"It's me."

Madison?

"Hi. I've been thinking about . . . thinking about whether you and Randall are going to buy that house."

Silence.

"Hello? You still there, Madison?"

"I'm here. I've got some really bad news, Dirk."

Geez. More bad news? Right. What is it now?

66

RANDALL

The turnout at First Savior wasn't large. All three of Lori's baby-daddies were there, though. Our family was quite pleased to see that. Even more pleased that all three came appropriately dressed and groomed. It had to be the first time that Lalisha, Shawanna, and Davonte saw their collective daddies in who knows when. Too bad it took *this* for *that* to happen.

Aside from family, most everyone else in attendance was there more out of respect to my father than anything else. I've never seen him so low. It's as if he's died, too. In a way, I guess he has. He had to step down as pastor of First Savior. That *was* my father's life.

It's ironic. Given their history, everyone in our family used to say that Dad and Lori were going to kill each other one day. But who could've imagined this?

I think my father now sees what everyone else in our family had been trying to get him to see for the longest time. That life—or death, as in this case—isn't always as black and white as the pages in the Bible he carries around with him everywhere. If it was, our family history headline would simply read something like:

REVERED PASTOR MILES CRAWFORD MURDERED HIS YOUNGEST DAUGHTER FOLLOWING YEARS OF CONFLICT WITH HER.

But that's not what happened.

This is what did.

My parents were awakened that fateful night by the sound of breaking glass and muffled voices. Already on edge from the previous break-in, my father grabbed his rifle—the one my mother had been begging him to get rid of for the longest time—crept downstairs in the dark, and came upon two intruders in his home. With only moonlight peeking through the open blinds as illumination, he said he couldn't ID either intruder. That, and because both were wearing hooded sweatshirts. All he could make out was that one guy was tall and fat, and the other short and thin. The tall guy was quick for his size. Too quick for my father's 70-year-old legs to give chase. He managed to escape out the front door. His smaller accomplice wasn't as lucky, however. He tripped and fell attempting to do likewise. My father cocked his rifle and ordered him to freeze. He wasn't going to chase this one. The short, thin guy refused to heed my father's command. Instead, he bounced to his feet and made another beeline to get out. I guess having his sanctuary burglarized for the second time in almost as many weeks, my father was simply mad as hell and not going to take it anymore. Guess he felt he needed to send a clear message to the next fool(s) who had an idea of entering his home unlawfully a third time.

I can't say I blame him.

There were no criminal charges filed against my father. The law saw the incident for what it was. A man rightfully protecting his loved ones and property. And a horrific, tragic case of mistaken identity. That short, thin guy was my sister.

As for the tall, fat one who got away that night, it turned out to be a recently released convict by the name of Theodore Barnes. Better known on the streets of Jamaica, Queens, as "Nero." Police apprehended him a few days later after he burglarized yet another home in East Elmhurst. Seems that when he got out of prison he promptly went right back to the MO that got him locked up in the first place. Nero confessed to burglarizing my parents' house on both occasions, and alleged that my sister had provided him with a set of keys the first time and the security code the second.

If that's true, it means Lori exited this world as bizarrely as she entered it. Saddest of all is that no one in our family will ever get to ask her the one thing she's left all of us grappling to understand. *Why?* Why would she participate in the burglaries of her parents' home? A home she was graciously allowed to use as a safe haven for herself and her three kids by three different men. Why would she do this to our parents, the only people on this earth who would unconditionally raise her children as their own if circumstances ever warranted?

I'm going to choose to believe that it was the mind-altering crack flowing through her veins at the time of her death. My parents had an autopsy done on Lori.

I mention that because Nero was also charged with cocaine distribution.

67

DIRK

Madison stood outside my apartment door looking totally hot in a pale yellow summer dress and red pumps. I welcomed her in. She took a seat on my couch and crossed her shapely legs, allowing those red pumps to dangle perilously on the tips of her painted toenails. French Fry was on a date with his new friend, Sabrina, and Randall—despite my serious heart-to-heart with him—was once again cavorting about New York with Myesha.

"Can I get you something to drink?"

"Sure."

I went into the kitchen and poured two tall glasses of lemonade.

"You're not uncomfortable being here, are you?" I asked, handing Madison her glass.

"Not anymore. We're friends now. I trust you, Dirk. I *am* safe with you, aren't I?"

"Friends. Who would've thunk it? Yes. You're safe with me. I'm harmless."

"Harmless, huh? I doubt your booty kills would say that."

"Now why you gotta go there?"

"I'm just kidding. See, Dirk, I can even joke about your 'out cold' behavior nowadays."

She reached out and began rubbing the back of my head with her free hand. I felt a hard-on coming.

"Those days are behind me, Madison. I'm dating Fatima now. Your best friend, remember?"

She stopped rubbing my head.

"Don't remind me."

"What's that supposed to mean?"

"Don't pay me any mind, either."

"That would be impossible for me to do."

She blushed. Her fair complexion turned red as the Devil's. She laid down her glass on the end table. I did likewise and inched closer to her on the couch.

"I was pretending. Trying to hide the obvious from you back then," she said.

"The obvious?"

"That I wasn't as attracted to you the night we met as I knew you were to me."

"So you decided to get with *Randall?*"

"Because I was attracted to him, too. Just in a different way. A 'here's a really nice guy who'll treat me right' kind of way. That's the kind of guy I needed. Not another—"

"Don't say it," I cut her off. "Well, seeing that we're being all honest with each other, I guess I can stop pretending, too. Pretending that I'm not jealous you chose Randall over me. More so than ever," I mumbled.

"What is *that* supposed to mean?"

"It means I'm falling in love with you, Madison." The room got so quiet I could hear my heart beating inside my chest. "Guess that's being a little *too* honest, huh? *Ooo-kay.* I'm totally embarrassed now."

"We're adults, Dirk."

"And you're my best friend's wife."

"And you're my best friend's boyfriend."

"Dirk?"

"Madison?"

"Nothing we say or do leaves this apartment, right?"

"Nothing *we do?*"

"Randall's probably someplace doing another woman as we speak."

"No, he's not."

"Stop it! You *know* he is. And if you love me like you say you do you'll stop covering for him."

She had a point. It was going to hurt me to my soul to have to give R up—but that was his fault. I warned him to do the right thing by his woman. His beautiful, sexy, supermodel . . .

"*Yes.* Randall's got a chick on the side. Two in as many months."

Oh, geez. What have I just done?

Madison's face turned red as the Devil's, but it wasn't from blushing this time.

"Two?" She placed her face in her hands and started to sob. I just sat there. Did nothing. Too scared to comfort her for fear of where it might lead. When she regained her composure, she grabbed my shirt in both her hands and ripped it open. Buttons went flying everywhere. Madison covered my mouth with hers. Our tongues wrestled in a fight to see whose could reach the other's tonsils first.

Hers won. Barely.

"I want you, Dirk. You fine, high yella, good-hair-having, pretty muthafucka. I've *always* wanted you!" she confessed through gritted teeth. "Make love to me like Randall won't anymore."

Whoa.

"W-wait, girl. *Wait!* We c-c-can't do this. It's wr—"

She slapped her hand over my mouth.

"*Shut up, Dirk!* You're ruining the moment. Just take me," she moaned.

I froze like a Popsicle.

"Boy, don't make me beg you. Do you understand what I'm saying? Do you, Dirk?"

"DIRK!!"

"Huh?"

"Wake up! We've got to get a move on."

Fatima was standing over me in nothing but her panties, with a toothbrush in her mouth.

Geez and holy sh—

"Okay, okay," I said, rubbing my eyes, trying to regain my coherency.

Yes. We made it "official" last night.

The two of us were taking Randall and Madison to brunch at Sylvia's in Harlem later this morning. A little something we thought of doing in an effort to brighten their spirits up a bit following Lori's death. Following brunch—and just as important if not more to me—was what the four of us had planned for the remainder of the day. Fatima and Madison were going to see a matinee performance of *The Piano Lesson* on Broadway, then have dinner at some restaurant they raved about in SoHo, leaving Randall and me free to spend the afternoon and evening engaged in a yet-to-be-determined activity of our own. The best opportunity I'd have yet to have that much-needed talk with Randall I'd been planning on having. And given the dream I just had, the sooner I could get Randall's mind back on his wife and mine off of her, the better.

68

MADISON

I was quite proud of myself. I was already dressed and making good time to pick up Fatima, and head back into Manhattan for the play.

"Which one of you is driving?"

"Dirk."

"Oh, good. Can I borrow your car, then? Mine's low on gas and I don't want to make any stops on my way to Fatima's. I started to say, "I think my battery's dead," but resisted the urge.

"Keys are on the coffee table. Please be careful with her. And don't be grinding my clutch!"

What-eva.

"What are y'all doing tonight?"

"I'm going to leave that up to Dirk."

"Well, have a nice time whatever it is and stay out of trouble."

I gave my husband a peck on the lips and grabbed my Gucci knockoff. He looked me over from head to toe. I was wearing a denim embroidered pantsuit over a low-cut blouse that exposed a lot more cleavage than I typically exposed.

"And don't you hurt anybody in that outfit."

"I'll try. Not to." I winked.

Fatima was ready and waiting for me outside when I pulled up in front of her place. Good. I didn't have to blow my horn. (I know it irritates the heck out of her neighbors whenever I do that.) She jumped in and immediately took out her eyeliner pencil to complete her makeup.

"Be careful with that. Randall is so anal about this car. Don't get nothing on these seats except your ass," I laughed. Of course no sooner did I say that than she dropped the pencil.

"Shit!" she sighed, unhooking the seat belt and feeling under the seat in an effort to find it.

"You got it?"

"Not yet . . . Got it."

When Fatima sat up, I noticed she had the eyeliner pencil and a business card in her hand.

"What's that?" I asked.

"Somebody's business card. It was under the seat."

"Whose is it?"

She held it to her face. "Myesha Coffey. Public Relations—"

"Give me that." I snatched it from her and tried to read it and keep my eyes on the road simultaneously. I couldn't recall taking her business card out of my Fendi bag since returning from my trip.

"Weird. I must've dropped that in here at some point." I stuck the card in that ashtray thingamajig and closed it.

"Who's she?" Fatima asked.

"That sista I met in Vegas. I told you about her, remember?"

"Oh, *her*. Ms . . . . ?"

"Know-It-All."

"Right."

"She was cool at first, but then she started getting on my nerves with all her philosophies on this, that, and the other."

"Such as?"

"For one thing, she claimed there was no such thing as a faithful man."

"Yikes! Let's hope she's not right about that—for your sake and mine."

"Yours?"

"I think I'm in love, Maddy."

"With *who?*"

"Duh! Dirk, silly. You didn't notice me cheesin' all up and through brunch this morning?"

"Is there something I should know, Fatima?"

"Mmm-hmm. I finally gave him some last night."

I nearly swerved off the road.

"Shit, heifer. Kill us, why don't you!" Fatima screamed at me.

"You *slept* with him?" I immediately regretted my tone. Quickly gathered myself in an effort to hide my disappointment. Disappointment I had no business even feeling.

"Uh, *yeah,* Maddy. I did. 'Bout time, don't ya think?"

"Congratulations." I could only imagine how disingenuous that must've sounded.

"So?"

"So?"

"So aren't you gonna ask me for details?"

Fatima knew me too well. Any other time, I would've been all up in her Kool-Aid.

No, Fatima. I don't want to hear you tell me how good Dirk was in bed. How he ravished you from head to toe. How he had your vagina singing a Teena Marie song—Ooh la, la, la.

"Fill me in later," I told her. "Oh, shucks!"

"What?"

"You just reminded me that I forgot to take my birth control pill again. That's the second time this week. Forgot a couple of times last week, too."

"Guuurl, if you think your marriage got rocky with Noah's arrival, you are *really* trying to become a single parent now."

"You know we're barely doing anything these days. And whenever we do he insists on wearing a condom anyway. Did Dirk use a condom with you?"

"Thought you didn't want to hear any details right now."

"Right."

"Dirk told me you asked him to go house-hunting with you. What? Things ain't working out with you and your man so you're trying to push up on mine now?"

"I-I'm sorry, Fatima. I-I didn't mean to . . . It's just that Randall wasn't around to look at the house with me, and I wanted to get a man's—"

"Madison!"

"Huh?"

"I'm *kidding*. Ha, ha, ha. Gol-lee. Loosen up, for crying out loud. Is there something you want to tell *me?*"

Other than your sense of humor sucks right now?

"Nothing at all."

We traveled the next few miles without talking until Fatima broke the silence.

"Yes, Maddy."

"Yes, what?"

"Dirk used a condom."

69

RANDALL

I had ironed a crisp crease in my jeans, slapped a fresh coat of Kiwi on my Florsheim flats, and gotten Grey Flanneled-up in anticipation of a big evening. So when Dirk showed up at my door with a six-pack of Heineken in one hand and a video cassette in the other, I was at a complete loss.

"You smell good," he said, waltzing into my apartment and handing me the beer. "Why don't you put these in the fridge and get that takeout menu for Hunan Delight."

"Why?"

"Because we're staying in tonight, that's why. No music, no hard liquor, no honeys. Too much of a distraction."

"Tell me you're kidding."

"No, Randall, I'm not. Think how impressed the girls are going to be with us when we tell them we stayed home, rented a video, and had some Chinese food delivered."

"Impressed with *you,* maybe. *I* wanna go somewhere and listen to some music, drink a little hard liquor, and peep some honeys."

"Peeping honeys is overrated, R. It ain't nearly as much fun if you can't touch 'em, too."

"All the more reason *you* should wanna be out doing the town tonight like I do. You and Fatima are only dating. *You* can look *and* touch."

"I ain't going out like that. I'ma do like Spike—do the right thing by my woman. Be the model boyfriend. Faithful. Honest."

I stared daggers at Dirk.

"Why are you looking at me like that?"

"Did somebody kick your ass again?"

"You got jokes. Negative, Grasshopper. Fatima and I made love last night."

"Oh. What you mean is, 'I waxed that ass last night,' don't you?"

"No, Randall, I didn't 'wax that ass.' Geez. Do you have to make it sound so crude?"

Uh-uh.

"Made *love,* Dirk? I'm sorry, but that's a mighty anomalous word to hear coming out of your mouth."

"What kind of word?"

"Strange, Dirk. Strange word."

"You're right. Love is a bit over the top for me. Fatima and I had sexual relations. Better?"

"My, my, my. I'd be expecting you to be bursting at the seams with excitement. You don't seem all that excited."

"Maybe 'cause I didn't feel the earth move. It was pretty . . . anticlimactic, to be honest with you. Hurry up, dude. Get that menu, I'm hungry."

"So what happened?" I asked, returning to the room with the menu. "The Nigerian princess couldn't do a full split while standing on her head?"

"You're just a regular Bill Cosby up in this roach motel tonight, huh? Fatima was great, R. The problem was me."

"You?"

"It was like I was there in the moment with her, but I wasn't."

"Don't tell me you wanted her to disappear afterward."

"No, nothing close to that. But what shouldn't be more memorable to me about last night is a dream I had earlier this morning."

"About?"

"You don't want to know."

"Know what I think?"

"What do you think?"

"That you've spent so much time being emotionally detached from those you've had underneath you that you don't know how to make love to anybody. There's a big difference between having *sex* and making *love*."

"You're trying to give *me* sexual advice?"

I ignored that.

"Take me and Bev, for example. That was just straight-up, unadulterated *sex* between two people."

"How could it have been unadulterated, Randall? Weren't you committing *adultery?*"

"Oh, yeah. Okay, okay. Bad example. Take me and Kat-the-Stripper. *That* was pure, unadulterated sex."

"Her name's *Sha-von-da,* dammit!"

"What-eva. *Be-yatch!*"

We hurt ourselves laughing.

"Speaking of your human birthday present, I gotta come clean with you. I really didn't knock that outta the park like I claimed to have. My first sexual experience was nothing short of slapstick."

"I know."

"You do?"

"Please. Shavonda told me *all* about it. How you almost knocked her out—literally. Put it in the wrong hole, came and went in less than a minute. Lawd, have mercy what I wouldn't have done to be a fly on the wall that night!" He laughed.

I could laugh at it, too. *Now.*

"Well, trust me. I've come a long way since. Betcha if I got a hold of Shavonda's half-black and half-Filipino ass today I'd knock it outta the park."

"Bet you would, *Short* Daddy Kane. *Wooo-hooo!*"

"Eff you!"

"What about you and Madison? Y'all make love or have sex?"

"We used to make love nearly every day. Until she had the baby. Now it's just sex—if you want to even call it *sex*—two times a month. I'm sure she'd agree with me on that. The only thing she'd disagree with is who's at fault for that."

Hmph. "That's too bad. I'm going to get the Shredded Beef with Garlic Sauce and fried rice."

A creature of habit, I already knew what I wanted. "Orange Beef with broccoli and white rice for me. Tell me something, Dirk. What were you going to tell me your pops said about marriage that day I came to see you in the hospital?"

"You didn't want to know, remember?"

"Humor me."

"He said he believed people are more likely to regret the decisions they make in their twenties than at any other time in their life. Said folks our age didn't have a clue what we wanted out of life on a week-to-week basis, let alone the rest of our lives. So he advised me not to get married in my twenties like he did . . . and you did. Told me to save those life-altering decisions for my thirties and beyond when I'll likely be able to live with them."

"I should've let you speak."

"What would it have mattered? Madison had your nose open wider than the Lincoln Tunnel."

"True, dat."

"You and this Bev chick. A minute ago you said it was unadulterated sex. *Was,* as in past tense?"

"I ain't messin' with her anymore."

"And Myesha?"

"You know honeys have put me in some 'situations' over the years, don't you?"

"I do."

"Well, Myesha Coffey took it to an entirely new level. She let me make a complete ass out of myself. She modeled linger-ee for me—"

"Linguine?"

"Lingerie, Dirk."

"Oh."

"Know what she tells me when her fashion show ends? She wanted to get my opinion on what she should wear to turn on some other dude she met."

"Geez. She really did let you make an ass out of yourself."

"Thanks, Dirk. But what goes around comes around and things must not have worked out between her and her West Coast friend. Now she's mine for real. I'm sure of it. I'm looking a lot better to her than I did before."

"You've given her the vapors, R?"

"I've got her *vaporized,* Dee."

"So, you just wanna pull a stick and move on her, is that it? There's no feelings involved?"

"I had feelings for her at one time. But it's just unfinished business for me now. A chance for me to get what she should've given me back when, and get her out of my system once and for all. Wanna label that a stick and move, so be it."

"And after?"

"After? After, I go back to being faithful to my wife—forever. I swear."

"You know what, Randall? A short time ago, I selfishly made my friends and family stand by and nearly watch me lose my life. Why? Because I just *had* to chase that ass. Just couldn't let it be. There's no way I'm going to let you make your friends and family stand by and watch you lose your wife and son for the same stupid reason. You just lost your sister, Randall. Isn't that enough? Get a wedding ring back on your finger and forget about Myesha. I gotta come clean with you about something." Dirk paused. Took a deep breath. "I've gotten to know Madison a little better now. Seen a different dynamic to her and I . . ."

"'I what,' Dirk?"

". . . I was wrong about her. You've got a good woman. I had my doubts in the beginning. Thought she was just some chick on a mission. The kind who've got to be married with kids by a certain age or they feel their life's a failure. I was wrong. She really loves you, Randall. She's told me as much. I believe her."

"You two seem to have buried the hatchet. I'm glad. I've always wanted my best friend and my woman to be able to get along. Madison would really be pleased to hear what you've just said about her. Mind if I tell her? Wait. Better yet. Tell her yourself. Y'all work a few blocks from one another. Take her out to lunch one day soon. By the way, I never did thank you for going with her to see that home. I messed up royally that day."

"Were you with Myesha?"

"Our date went into double overtime."

"Did you—"

"No. Noooo!"

"You're this close to getting busted, you do know that, don't you?"

"I do."

"This mackin' shit . . . it ain't your forte, R. Never was. That was *my* shit. You're venturing out of your realm—and getting sloppy at that. Which segues into the main reason I wanted us to stay in tonight. I needed to try and talk some sense into you. Reel you back in 'cause you've wandered out too far.

That would've been hard for me to do with us listening to music, drinking hard liquor, and peeping honeys."

"Reel *me* in? Ain't that something."

"Look, I know marriage has brought you some changes you weren't anticipating, but deep down inside, I know you love Madison, and you don't want to be with anyone else. So, no matter how hard you're trying to be a mack daddy, it's simply not in you. There's nothing wrong with being a 'nice guy.' They don't always finish last, either. You sure haven't."

Now I agreed with Dirk. Staying in tonight seemed like the perfect way for us to spend our few hours of freedom. I made that call to Hunan Delight.

Madison decided to spend the night at Fatima's following their "girls' day." That may have been a blessing in disguise because I awoke this morning with a renewed vigor about my wife, our marriage, and our future. I knew beyond any doubt now that things were going to work out just fine. That Madison and I are going to be together forever. So much so, that I thought about things like us attending Noah's high school graduation. Sending him off to college. Even tried imagining what she'd look like when that time came. She'd probably have a few wrinkles and a few gray hairs but still be able to weaken any man's resistance at a glance. My wife would undoubtedly be the sexiest 51-year-old sista on the planet.

I opened the bedroom blinds. Bright sunshine rushed into the room like it was in a hurry to get somewhere. That bright sun wasn't going to set today without me telling Madison how much she meant to me. Without me *showing* her how much she meant to me. Her fault, my fault . . . none of that mattered anymore. I was going to make passionate *love* to her like I hadn't since she gave birth to our child—no raincoat. If that resulted in us being part of that 1 percent again, so be it. Just hope it's a little girl this time. We'll name her Naomi.

Thank you, Lord. Thank you for helping me remember before it was too late that I'm no ladies' man. Just your average, conservative kinda guy. A one-woman kinda guy.

70

MADISON

Randall knows what you went through before. He promised you he'd never take you there. You've got a good man. You need to have a little more faith in him.

Right. I just needed to exercise a little more faith in my husband. And maybe while I was doing that, I could also figure out why I was inexplicably falling hard for his best friend. My best friend's boyfriend.

What else could've explained the jealous twinge I felt when Fatima told me she and Dirk had done the do? What else could've explained why I felt so compelled to know if Dirk had used a condom or not? For the record, I didn't ask out of concern that Fatima might catch cooties from Dirk or become his baby-mama—which *should* have been my main concerns, ya think? No. I was just hoping Fatima hadn't gotten to experience "bare-back" intimacy with Dirk.

The apartment was empty when I got home. Just a note attached to the fridge.

Hey, Baby,

Gone to pick up something from the store. I won't be long.
Don't cook anything. I've got a surprise for you. My folks are
keeping Noah an extra day, so just get comfortable and relax.

P.S. I know you haven't heard it enough from me lately, but I
love you. You're the best.

I melted on the spot. Began to tear up. Happy tears.
Searched for a tissue. Started to grin. Then chuckle. Broke
out in hysterical laughter. Ran into the bedroom, kicked off
the Bandolino Berrys on my feet, launched myself across the
bed, and let out a deep breath. I felt so much better now.

I raced into the living room when I heard Randall's key in
the door. He entered with a big shopping bag in his hand of
something that smelt heavenly.

"Hey, honey," I said, giving him a big smooch. He set
down that big bag of whatever smelt heavenly on the dining
room table, grabbed my face in both his hands, and kissed me
passionately.

"Don't move," he said.

He walked over to the stereo, turned it on, and hit the PLAY
button on the cassette deck. Our theme song began to play.

He came back over to me and wrapped his arms around my
waist.

"I missed you last night. I don't like sleeping without you.
Get my note?"

"Uh-huh," I giggled. "What's in the bag? It smells good."

"Dinner and dessert, courtesy of DEAN & DELUCA. And
this bottle of wine for celebration." He pulled the wine bottle
out of the same bag. "Hope you like Sutton Home."

"I do."

"Great. I'm going to put the food in the oven and warm
it up—"

"It's just four o'clock, honey. Sure you want to eat this early?"

"We've got a long evening ahead of us, baby."
That was even better music to my ears.

". . . I found lovin',
Since I found you . . ."

"What are we celebrating?"
"Technically, *we're* not celebrating anything. *I'm* celebrating something. *You,* Madison Mya Crawford. I'm celebrating how blessed I am to have you as my wife."
My husband's words made me want to make love to him right where he stood.
"Honey, let's make—"
"Ssshh," he said, putting his finger to my lips. "I don't think you heard me. I said we've got a *long* evening ahead of us."

Following a scrumptious meal of maple-cured ham, yams with banana rum, slivered almonds, and creamed spinach, Randall and I engaged in an act of lovemaking as intense as it has ever been between us. One minute we were being gentle and passionate with one another. The next, tearing at each other like carnivorous animals. I found it wonderful. Magnificent. *Long* overdue. In sexual exhaustion, we cuddled afterward just like we used to.
Don't know if it was a case of being caught up in the moment or what, but Randall didn't bother putting on a condom, nor did I bother to interrupt the spontaneity of our warm, tender moment to reveal to him how forgetful I had been in regard to taking my birth control pills.
When our heart rates returned to normal, Randall got out of bed, filled the bathtub with hot water, and added in my favorite bubble bath from Victoria's Secret. Lit a scented candle and placed it by the tub. I was expecting him to join

me, but he didn't. Instead, he bathed me like I was a three-month-old. After toweling my body dry, he told me to sit tight while he ran outside to get something from the car. He returned with yet another shopping bag. This one was smaller and read BLOOMINGDALE'S on it. He handed it to me.

"This is for you," he said.

Inside of it was a beautiful Louis Vuitton pocketbook. The *real* deal.

71

MADISON

My wonderful husband sure pulled out all the stops the other day. Treated me like the queen I am. Laid some incredible lovemaking on me. Had me in bliss like it was my birthday, Christmas, and New Year's Eve all rolled into one. So why, then, this morning, some forty-eight hours following all of that, do I feel like I'm on the verge of having another meltdown right here at my desk at *Trendy*? I'll explain. But first, I need to quote a phrase my father-in-law—formerly known as Pastor Crawford—loved to recite:

"*'The Lord works in mysterious ways.'*"

Check this out.

I get home from work yesterday, still floating on air. Immediately get dinner started, knowing my "wonderful" husband will be home shortly. Change out of my office attire into a comfortable pair of shorts and bedroom slippers. While doing so, I behold my beautiful new Louis Vuitton pocketbook resting on the top shelf of the closet. Then and there I decide to take it to work with me tomorrow—which is today—and be the envy of all these chicks at Trendy still sportin' Canal Street knockoffs.

I grabbed my old Fendi bag that I've been carrying around so I can transfer all my stuff from it to my new bag. I flipped it upside down and began shaking its contents out onto the bed. Out comes my wallet, loose change, subway tokens, makeup kit, checkbook, an unused Lotto ticket, the birth control pills I keep forgetting to take, Myesha Coffey's business card . . .

Myesha Coffey's business card?

Everything comes to a screeching halt. I pick up her card. Stare at it. This confirms what I had originally thought. I never took that chick's business card out of my pocketbook . . .

"'What's that?'"

"'Somebody's business card. It was under the seat.'"

"'Whose is it?'"

"'Myesha Coffey. Public Relations . . .'"

The air in my bedroom suddenly feels dry, hot, and humid. Like the air in Las Vegas.

"'What's your husband's name?'"

"'Randall.'"

"'Randall Crawford?'"

"'Mmm-hmm.'"

I get up, go over to the window. Crack it open to get some fresh air circulating. Think I'm going to need some—fresh air that is.

"'What a coincidence. I used to kick it with a guy by the same name . . . the guy I'm talking about had a . . . and a . . . oh, never mind . . .'"

"What, bitch? *An Afro and horn-rimmed eyeglasses?*" I shout at the four walls of my bedroom. They don't answer me.

I feel faint. Go back over to my bed, push aside all the stuff I've just emptied out on it, and splash down my face first. Close my eyes and count to one hundred—backward. My "wonderful" husband is going to be home shortly and I can't wait . . . to get my hands on his car keys!

Randall moseys through the door shortly thereafter and does what he normally does: lays his car keys on the coffee table, gives me a kiss, and sorts through the day's mail while asking me how my day at *Trendy* went before telling me how his was at United Trust. I keep on my "floating on air" face over meatloaf, string beans, and mashed potatoes. I don't let on in any way that I've officially gone into supersleuth mode on his short black ass. I'm married to a creature of habit, and so I can count on him to do what he usually does after a scrumptious meal I've made: grab something to read and head to the bathroom. Two things are certain when that happens. One, he's going to be in there a while, and, two, he's going to leave it lit up to high heaven when he's done.

On cue, Randall cleans his plate, grabs the latest issue of *Trendy,* and heads for the bathroom.

It's on.

I lay Noah in his playpen (feel horrible for leaving him unattended, but I'm hoping this isn't going to take long), snatch Randall's car keys off the coffee table, and bolt out of the apartment like a bat out of hell. Race down three flights of stairs, almost falling and busting my ass in the process 'cause I'm doing so in my bedroom slippers and they're those flip-flop kind.

His car's parked right in front of our building. Great. I dash to it. Meanwhile, from thirty feet away, some little snot-nosed neighborhood adolescent catches sight of me and comments on my shapely derriere.

"Dayum, miss. Can I get a steak with that onion?"

Okay. The shorts I'm in . . . they're booty cutters—but I hadn't planned on wearing them outside when I put them on. For that reason alone, I decide I'm gonna cut the little snot-nosed neighborhood adolescent some slack and refrain from cursing him the fuck out.

I sniff the cabin air inside my husband's car to detect the scent of a woman's fragrance that isn't one I own. (Am I getting into this supersleuth thing, or what?) I find what I'm looking for. It's right where I left it in the ashtray thingamajig.

Allow me to digress from my play-by-play account for a moment and say that at worst, I now knew Myesha and I were indeed speaking of the same Randall Crawford that night at the MGM Grand Hotel and Casino. At another time, I would have simply chalked up this finding to a simple case of my husband and this chick having had some type of a relationship in the past. One of those "small world" coincidences we all experience a number of times in our lifetimes. However, given Randall's un-Randall-like behavior of late, finding her business card under the passenger seat of his car *at this time?* She who was *so* sure of her claim that there was no such thing as a faithful man? RED FLAG. *Hello!*

Thing is, Randall was so anal when it came to his car. He washes, waxes, and vacuums it frequently. Frequently enough that I'd have to be one feather shy of a cuckoo bird to believe that Myesha's business card would have gone unnoticed by him under the front seat of it for any extended period of time. Unless, of course, it only found its way there fairly recently. My antenna was picking up its strongest signal yet. A signal pointing toward the confirmation of what I had been in fear of ever since Fatima put the thought in my head. My husband was having an affair. And I'll be damned if it wasn't with that young Ms. Know-It-All I met at the FMPA conference.

Aaarggh!!!

I couldn't confront him. Not yet. The evidence was too circumstantial. Short of catching him in the act—like I did my ex-fiancé—I was going to need better proof. Proof that would stick to Randall's cheating ribs like the meatloaf I'd just made for him.

Okay, so where was I? Oh. I remember. I stick Myesha's card in my pocket, race back inside our apartment building, and back up those three flights of stairs. Catch my breath for a few seconds before putting the key in the door and stepping back inside the apartment. Great. Noah's having a ball entertaining himself in his playpen.

And Randall's still on the toilet.

Now you know why I feel like I'm on the verge of having another meltdown right here at my desk at *Trendy*. Because all that lovey-dovey "I'm celebrating you" the other night was just smoke and mirrors. Same goes for the Louis Vuitton pocketbook I came struttin' into work with this morning. None of what had me floating on air thirty-six hours ago was really about me at all. Just the actions of a philandering husband whose conscience was probably beginning to whip him.

This was some bullshit!

The clock on my computer screen revealed that it was almost lunchtime. Time for me to get that hard evidence I was going to need. Knew just the person who was going to help me get it, too.

72

DIRK

"Ah . . . ooh, yes, oh, yeah, right there, Dirk, don't move . . ."

Fatima and I were doing it and doing it well. To put it in basketball terms (since she's such a hoop junkie), I started things off by letting the game come to me. Taking what the defense was giving me. The strategy worked because I was getting wide-open looks at the rim. Switched up and went zone on her. Followed that up with the box-in-one. I was about to apply the full court press when—

Riiiing . . . riiing.

"Let your answering machine get that," I told her. "Just keep doing what you're doing, girl. Take a brotha back to the motherland, yow mean?"

"You're so silly, Dirk. Aaah . . . mmm . . . oooh . . ."

Beeeeep.

"Fatima? You there? Pick up, it's Madison. I *really* need to talk to you."

"Maybe I should get that. She sounds stressed."

Is she kidding me?

Just like that, Fatima abruptly called time-out. A 20-second time-out, I hoped.

"Maddy? What's up? Aaaah. Mmm-hmmmmm."

There was a several-second delay between the "Aaaah" and the "Mmm-hmmmmm."

"Hold on, okay?" Fatima clutched the phone to her bare breasts. "This might take a minute. You mind going into the living room?"

"Are you serious? We're right in the middle of—"

"Dirk. Please!"

Geez!

So much for a 20-second time-out. This was going to be a full time-out. I pulled out—very reluctantly—and left her bedroom butt-naked, closing the door behind me.

The groove was gone. Destroyed. Given that I'd left my clothes on her living room floor, I went ahead and got dressed. I slumped on Fatima's sofa, picked up an issue of *Trendy,* and flipped through it while I waited for her to get off the phone. Wondered what Madison needed to talk to Fatima about that was so dang-on important it couldn't wait. Couldn't have been about our lunch date this afternoon. Although that would have really sucked, given that I hadn't bothered to mention it to Fatima. Not yet anyway.

Madison had called me out of the blue and asked if I'd like to grab a bite with her at a spot near Grand Central Station. Though I already had plans, I was too intrigued by her invite to decline. Besides, Randall did say she and I ought to go to lunch one day.

How extremely glad I was that I took Madison up on her invitation. She had no idea what a bombshell she dropped when she casually brought up the subject of her business trip to Las Vegas and the chick named Myesha Coffey she met while she was out there.

Talk about small-world coincidences.

What didn't make any sense to me, though, was why Randall had no idea that his wife and the current object of his lust had crossed paths in the desert. How could *that* choice nugget not have come up in his conversations with either woman? Whatever the reason, I'm just glad I was able to keep a straight face and remain cool as a cucumber throughout that part of the conversation.

I was anything but cool when I got back to work, though. Couldn't dial Randall's extension fast enough. Got his voice mail, unfortunately. Didn't want to leave a message. Naw. This was going to wait until I could tell him personally. I wanted to see *and* hear his reaction to this bit of news. It all but proved that my talk with R was not only the right thing to do but right on time!

I may have just saved your marriage, dude. Excuse me while I pat myself on the back.

Anyway, Madison's business trip wasn't all we talked about. I used the opportunity to tell her what Randall had suggested I tell her myself. That I thought she was a good woman and good for Randall. Why I didn't feel that way about her in the beginning and why I did now. I also apologized. Admitted to her that I knew she wasn't in the wrong that forgettable Thanksgiving night at Bentley's, no matter how shitty I tried to make her feel at the time. And last, that I considered her a friend now. A *close* friend.

While I expected her to be surprised at my candor, I didn't expect her to get all emotional and teary-eyed on me. But her reaction answered something for me that had been heavy on my mind since that day she spazzed out in the supermarket. I wasn't alone on an island in regard to how I had begun to feel about her. She had begun to feel the same way about me.

I was growing impatient with Fatima. Pissed off is more like it. I tossed the magazine and trekked to her bedroom to see if she had gotten off the phone yet. My intention was to knock on her door, but there wasn't a need to. Apparently, I hadn't fully closed her door behind me when I walked out. I could hear that she was still on the phone with Madison. I couldn't help myself.

I placed my ear in the gap between the edge of her door and the door frame. Didn't listen for more than five seconds. Five seconds was all the time it took for me to hear something that rocked me to my core.

73

MADISON

There was a knock at my door. Great. Randall finally decided to come home. Didn't understand why he wasn't using his key, though. I went to the door with Noah in tow. Looked out the peephole.

"Hi. What are you doing here? I thought you were Randall."

"He hasn't come home from work yet?"

"Nope. He called me before I left work to say that he'd be a bit late. That he was going to swing by his parents' house first. I just called Eunice and Miles and they say he left there over an hour ago. They're only ten minutes away."

"That's strange. What's up, little man?" Dirk asked Noah. "Mind if I come in?"

"Sure. But Randall might be home at any—"

"It's cool. I'll have a good explanation for my presence if I'm not gone by then."

"Is everything all right with you?" I asked, closing the door behind Dirk.

"Mind if I sit down?"

"Sure."

"Can I get a glass of water?"

"Yes—in a second. After you tell me what's up with you. Fatima said she got off the phone with me to find you gone. Said you didn't even bother to tell her you were leaving."

"I had to get out of there. Did you tell her we had lunch?"

"Evidently you didn't bother telling her."

"Damn."

"Are you upset with her?"

"Can you get that glass of water now?"

I did as he asked. He nearly drank it all in one long gulp. Something was obviously wrong, and I wasn't going to sit until he told me what.

"If something happened between you and Fatima, you know you can talk to me about it, don't you?"

"That's right, I can. We're friends now."

"We're more than friends, Dirk. We're *close* friends."

"I need you to be honest with me about something. Close friend."

I could hear it in his voice. He knew. Knew that I had somehow fallen in love with him.

Just tell him the truth. Don't try to hide it. Deal with the fallout later.

"What do you want to know?"

"Remember I asked if you thought Randall was capable of cheating on you?"

My heart became lodged in my throat.

Oh, my God. He's going to give me the proof I failed to get out of him over lunch.

"I said no."

"You said a little more than that. You said that you didn't think you'd be capable of . . . Why don't you go ahead and finish that statement? You never did."

Silence.

"I-I don't . . . recall that part."

"I think you do. YOU DIDN'T THINK YOU'D BE CAPABLE OF WHAT?" he hollered at me as he leaped off my sofa. His sudden outburst not only frightened me but my son. Noah started crying.

"You're scaring my child, Dirk. And me! What the hell is your problem? Look, I don't know what's gone down between you and Fatima, but don't be bringing your shit over here taking it out on me! *Ssshhh,* it's okay, Noah. Mommy's here," I said, trying to calm him.

"Sorry. That was wrong," Dirk apologized. "I don't mean to upset you or Noah. Please. Can I start over?"

"Actually, I think you ought to leave."

"You never thought you'd be capable of getting pregnant on purpose. Isn't that what you were about to say?"

My legs felt like they were going to give out from under me. Dirk took Noah out of my arms. He immediately stopped crying.

"Hey, Little Man. Big boys don't cry, don't you know that? Madison, can I go lay him down? Is that okay?"

I nodded my head yes.

I wanted to run. Anywhere, as fast as my legs would take me. But they felt like Jell-O.

Dirk returned from Noah's room. Stood directly in front of me and peered deep into my eyes.

"Why?"

I swallowed hard.

"I wanted a child. Two, maybe three. Randall knew that. I was turning thirty and I didn't want to wait another three or four years to become a mother. It's a female thing, Dirk. You wouldn't understand. I cannot believe Fatima told you."

"She didn't. I overheard . . . That's a lie. I eavesdropped on part of your conversation with her earlier."

"That was a *private* conversation, Dirk! Didn't you gather as much when she asked you to leave the room?"

"I was wrong to do that. There's a *whole* lot of wrong going around right now."

"How 'bout that?" I fired back sarcastically. "Exactly how much of my private conversation did you hear?"

"Just heard Fatima say that maybe it's bad karma coming back on you for getting pregnant without his knowledge. Do you know I vigorously defended your pregnancy to Randall? Told him that it was a fluke. That it wasn't like you were *trying* to get pregnant.

"Congratulations. Now you know the truth. Happy with yourself? Tell me. Do you still think I'm a good woman?"

"I don't know what to make of you right now. You betrayed my man—in a really sick way. You're out cold, Madison. I know that."

And that hurt. I began to cry. Dirk wrapped his arms around me and held me tightly. A gesture that let me know at the very least he didn't hate me. Our embrace seemed to go on for minutes, but in reality lasted only a few seconds. Our lips were only inches apart as we broke from our embrace. The chemistry was undeniable. I wanted him to kiss me.

He wanted to kiss me.

"Madison—"

"Dirk—"

"You first," I said, taking a step back from him and feeling as though I had just dodged a love bullet.

"Ladies first."

"Why couldn't you just mind your business, Dirk? You *can't* tell him. Please, don't."

"You realize the position you're putting me in?"

"Given where you and I started, yes, I do. But then we've come a long way, haven't we?"

Following a moment of reflection, a slight smile crossed his face. One that allowed me to breathe a sigh of relief.

"I better get out of here," he said.

"I agree."

I walked him to the door.

"So, Randall hasn't called or anything and you don't know where he is?"

"No. *Hmph.* Maybe he's with . . . oh, no."

"What is it?"

"When I got on the phone with Fatima, I was in the kitchen and I had the stereo playing."

"And?"

"During the conversation, I told her to hold on. I laid the phone on the counter because I had to go into the bedroom for something. I intended to come back to the kitchen and continue our conversation, but I got distracted and picked up the extension in the bedroom instead."

"You're rambling, Madison, and I gotta get out of here. Is there a point to this?"

"The point is, with me back in the bedroom talking to Fatima and the stereo playing out here, maybe Randall did come home after all."

"Well, wouldn't he have made his presence known and told you he was home?"

"Not if he came in and went straight into the kitchen first for some reason."

"I'm still not following you."

"I left the phone off the hook in the kitchen, Dirk."

74

RANDALL

Shit happens, huh?

"Hit me again," I told the bartender at Honeysuckles even though my nose and throat were still burning from the first shot of scotch. Though not nearly as much as my eyes from all the crying I had done on the drive over here.

Today had turned into the worst day of my life. Worse still, it wouldn't be officially over for another three hours.

"Here you go, champ."

Like the first, I creamed my second shot in one swallow.

No more, Randall. You're going to kill yourself.

I couldn't do that. Not before I went home and killed Madison first.

All I had wanted to do was put the peach cobbler my mother had made for us in the kitchen. It was a surprise. We were going to be in dessert heaven following dinner tonight. There it was, the phone. Lying on the kitchen counter unattended. I picked it up. Put it to my ear to check for a dial tone.

Fatima: *"Maybe it's bad karma coming back on you for getting pregnant on purpose."*

Madison: *"Pretending to be on the pill was wrong. But I've never been unfaithful to him with another man. He's the one who's been sleeping with another woman."*

Stunned beyond my comprehension, I laid the phone back down where I found it, stuck my mother's peach cobbler in the refrigerator, and left as quickly and quietly as I could.

So what if she had never been unfaithful to me with another man? I almost wished she had been. *That* would've been easier to fathom than *this*. I could've moved on from *that*. I couldn't move on from a *child*. A child that was now going to be a persistent reminder to me of his mother's duplicity.

I took care of the bartender, made my way to the men's room, and splashed some cold water on my face. I had to get out of this place, too.

I walked outside to a pay phone on the busy corner of 84th Street. Searched my pockets for loose change as the tears I was holding back at Honeysuckles began to flow freely again.

"Hello."

"She lied to me, man!"

"Randall?"

"Noah was no accident, Dirk."

"I know, Randall, I know—"

"You know?"

Honk, honk, beep, beep . . .

I could barely hear Dirk above the street noise.

"WHAT CHU SAY?"

"WHERE ARE YOU? RANDALL—"

"Aw-aight! Stop yelling. I can hear you better now. Outside of Honeysuckles."

"Stay there, dude, I'm coming—"

"Don't, Dirk. I'm leaving."

"You're going home, right?"

"Hell, no!"

"You been drinking?"

"Two shots of scotch. Straight, no chaser. How 'bout that?"

"Geez."

"I'm straight. I'm cool. Really."

"Listen to me, Randall. I know you're hurting right now and I don't blame you. But listen to me. Go back inside and get yourself a cup of hot tea or something. Clear your head. Then I want you to come straight to my crib, okay? French Fry's spending the night at Sabrina's. You can sleep in his bed if you want to. I'm gonna call Madison and let her know you're okay. She's worried about you."

"Puh-leeze! Her ass ain't worried about me. Her sole concern is *Madison*. What *she* wants and fuck how it may affect anybody else. Spoiled bitch!"

"Don't do nothing stupid, R. Just do what I said, okay? We've been down this road once before. And don't even think about . . ."

Beep, honk, honk, beep, honk . . .

". . . because Madison knows . . ."

Beeeeep . . . beeeeep . . .

This call was useless. I couldn't hear a damn thing on this corner. Fuck it. I was done talking anyway.

"YO, I'M OUTTA HERE!" I shouted into the phone, not caring whether Dirk heard me or not.

Click.

The ringing of an alarm clock woke me out of a semi-peaceful slumber.

Myesha's alarm clock.

She lay naked with her back to me. I thought that sleeping with her would ease the pain, but the pain nullified all the pleasure I thought I'd derive from sleeping with her.

"Does Madison know where you are?"

My heart skipped a beat. I thought I heard her ask me if . . .

"Did you hear what I said?" she asked, rolling over in bed and facing me. "Does Madison know you're here? Your wife. I know, Randall."

"*You know?* You know I'm married, Myesha?"

"Mmm-hmm."

I sat up in her bed. Shot up like the Apollo would be more descriptive.

"And yet you never said anything?" For the second time in several hours, a woman had left me stunned beyond my comprehension. A feeling that was getting old.

Maybe I'll kill Myesha first. Then Madison.

"Wait a minute. I think you've got it twisted here. Why didn't *you* tell *me?* I'm single. Free to fuck whomever I want. *Hmph.* You 'committed' guys crack me up," she scoffed. "Y'all are all the same."

"Am I supposed to know what that means?"

"It means you kept me in the dark for weeks so you could get what you wanted. So what's wrong with me keeping you in the dark so I could get what I wanted? Isn't that how the game's played? Don't ask, don't tell. You get yours, I get mine, everybody's happy? Worked for me."

"Is that what this was to you? A game?"

Myesha sat up. Grabbed her pillow and placed it between her chest and her knees. Ignored my question in favor of another one of her own.

"You cheat on wifey often?"

"How do you know her?"

"We met in Las Vegas at the FMPA conference."

"'I met him at the FMPA conference.'"

"'What's that?'"

"'A conference I attend annually for my job. Eric and I have been talking on the phone for several weeks now . . .'"

"The same conference you met that Eric dude at?"

She nodded.

Dammit!

I snatched Myesha's linens off my body and flung my legs over the side of the bed. Searched the room for the nearest window. Suicide seemed a viable option right about now.

"She showed me a honeymoon photo she had taken of you. I swear I didn't recognize the guy in the picture as you. The Randall I knew had an Afro and wore those horned-rimmed glasses. It wasn't until I ran into you that evening in the subway—after, what, four years?—that I put it all together. I looked at your hand while you were holding onto the same pole I was on the train. You weren't wearing a wedding band. After you asked me out on a couple of dates . . . Well, I'm not Jill Stupid. I knew what time it was. She never mentioned meeting me to you at all?"

"'Details, Randall. You never asked for any details . . . her name, what she looked like—'"

"She did. I just never got around to hearing the details."

I was too busy chasin' a different piece of ass at the time.

"Bummer. I suppose I could have leveled with you at some point over the past few weeks," Myesha said, sounding somewhat contrite, but way too late. "And I probably would have if wifey hadn't had it coming to her."

"What are you talking about?"

"She seemed real cool when I first met her. But then she started to get on my nerves. She seemed kinda self-absorbed. Pompous. Arrogant. A regular Ms. Know-It-All. She was so confident that . . . oh, never mind. Let's just say she needed a taste of humble pie. C-O-F-F-E-Y-flavored humble pie. I had to prove my point."

"That's what this was all about? Proving some point to my *wife?*"

"Wait. Let me guess. You thought this was all about you? Because you've morphed into a hot boy you thought I was all of a sudden feeling you like that? You thought I had caught the *vapors,* Randall?"

Don't know how, but I had done it again. I had allowed Myesha to let me make a complete ass out of myself.

I was livid. I hastily started putting my clothes back on. I didn't have to go home, but I had to get the hell out of Myesha's apartment—again.

"You're a real piece of work, you know that? Out cold! You're one fucked-up bitch, Myesha."

"Oh, that's great, Randall," she said, clapping her hands in mock applause. "If that's what I am, what are you? You came knocking on *my* door at almost 11 o'clock last night. Why? Because you had *feelings* for me? Or was it because you were pissed off at wifey about something and would've fucked *any* chick that would have opened her legs to you? Or was it because you just couldn't rest until you got from me what you thought I should have given you back when? Tell me your plan wasn't to get dressed this morning, leave my apartment, go back home to wifey, and erase any thought of me from your memory forever. How am I doing so far?"

Silence.

"You're doing just great, Myesha. Give yourself a big pat on the back."

She got out of the bed and came over to me.

"If you want to forget you even know me, that's cool. But don't leave here like you did once before thinking I played you—*again*. Especially not when you were trying to play me. I like you, Randall. I've always liked you. As a friend." She attempted to give me a hug. I wouldn't let her. "Oh. So it's like that now? Okay, Randall. I gotta get ready for work. See yourself out."

"One question before I do."

"What?"

"This point you had to prove to my wife. What was it?"

75

MADISON

"He knows, Madison. And I didn't tell him."

Dirk delivered the news I dreaded hearing but strongly suspected. Told me Randall was somewhere in Manhattan and was okay, but not to expect him home. He wouldn't let me get off the phone with him until I assured him that I was okay. Dirk was a huge comfort to me last night.

There was no way I was going in to work this morning. Not when I didn't get an ounce of sleep last night. I put a pot of water on the stove to make some instant coffee. Opened up the refrigerator to get the cream and noticed the peach cobbler pie sitting inside.

Damn.

Called my boss, Melanie, and faked a few coughs along with my message on her voice mail. Next, I called Eunice and Miles to let them know I wouldn't be bringing Noah over this morning. Didn't tell them their son hadn't come home last night. If they were aware, they didn't let on. Good. I wasn't anywhere near ready to deal with my husband *and* my in-laws.

Randall came through the door just as I sat down to drink my coffee. I bit my lip. Felt a knot form in my stomach. I expected to see disgust for me in his eyes. Instead, I saw a man who seemed relatively composed. Resigned to the inevitability of something.

"Hi," was the best opener I could muster.

He walked past me without speaking or even looking at me. Headed down the hallway of our apartment and into our bedroom. I followed behind him taking my hot cup of coffee with me in the event his composed demeanor was just an act and he had thoughts of going medieval on my ass.

He grabbed a suitcase out of the closet, opened it up on the bed, and began pulling various items of his clothing out of the dresser drawers and tossing them into it.

"Can we talk?" I asked.

"Is Noah at my parents'?"

"Your son's in his room."

"I was hoping you wouldn't be here." He still hadn't looked at me.

"I wouldn't have been able to accomplish a thing had I gone in today. I didn't sleep at all last night. How'd you sleep?" He paused momentarily like a VHS tape, then went back to pulling clothing out of the drawers. "You obviously aren't going in to work, either, I see. I'm glad you decided to come home, Randall. I've been worried sick about you. *Will you look at me, please!*" I closed the lid on the suitcase, interrupting his packing. He looked at me. Finally.

"You just couldn't wait, could you? Just a few years to let me enjoy being a husband. *Just* your husband. You looked me in the face and told me we had reached a compromise. I believed you."

"And you'll never know how sorry I am that I lost sight of all but my own agenda. That I allowed my selfishness to lead me into doing something unthinkable to you. To us. I didn't think any of it through. How it might affect you. I didn't even think through how it might affect *me*. Being both a wife and a mother this soon has turned out to be a far more difficult undertaking than I imagined it would be. You were right, Randall. We should have taken some time to enjoy being married without children. I should have taken some time to enjoy being a wife. *Just* your wife. Not that this is going to be of any comfort to you, but I came to this realization long before you overheard what you did. I was truly putting forth an effort to make amends. To make things better between us. I hoped you would have noticed the evidence of that. The changes I was making in regard to my character. How I was trying to be more balanced in my dealings with both the men in my life. This move back to Queens."

"I noticed."

"Good. Because I noticed some changes in you, too. Around the same time, actually. You didn't seem to care that I was making an effort. You didn't seem interested in much of anything related to me or your son. You looked me in the face and told me you'd never be unfaithful to me. I believed you, too."

"Seems this relationship is just *wallowing* in disillusionment, huh? Excuse me. I need to finish."

He went back to his speed packing.

"Were you with her last night?"

"No."

"Are you in love with her?"

He paused.

"Beverly and I were just kickin' it. There were never any feelings involved."

"Beverly?"

"Oh, I'm sorry. That's probably more information than you wanted to know."

"Not at all. You know I like to hear the details. So, how'd you meet this . . . Beverly?"

"I really don't think you want to hear this."

"No, I think I do. I think I *need* to hear this."

"Okay. If you insist. I met her a while back at Honeysuckles. At Dirk's insistence, I sent her a drink, she and I conversed for a bit, and that would've and should've been the end of it."

"But it wasn't."

"And I blame you for that."

"Me."

"I came home that night craving you, Madison. But once again, as had become the norm in our marriage since you got what you wanted—a child by your thirtieth birthday—you didn't even try to feed my craving. My frustration with that repetitive, tired scenario reached its breaking point. I reached out to another woman and things snowballed from there."

"So, that's your story? *I'm* the reason you had an affair with some woman named Beverly that you met in a bar?"

"An *affair* would denote that there were feelings involved. I just told you that wasn't the case. You're not listening. I'm outta here."

Randall zipped the suitcase shut and attempted to leave. I hurled my body in front of the doorway to prevent him from doing so.

"Move, Madison."

"No! Not until you tell me the truth."

"I just did."

"Don't try to play me for a fool. There's no Beverly. And I'm not to blame for you sleeping with 'her.' You've been fuckin' *Myesha Coffey* behind my back for who knows how long. That's the *truth,* isn't it, Randall?" I pulled her business card out of my pocket and flung it at him. "I found that under the front seat of your car the other day. How'd it get there, Randall? Was she riding shotgun around town with you often? Were you with her the day you were supposed to be with me looking for a potential new home for our family? The day your car battery supposedly died? Don't even form your lips to tell me you don't know who she is. She knows you. Know how I know? Because *I* met her in—"

"Las Vegas. I know." Randall set down the suitcase. Sat on the bed with his elbows in his lap and his face in his palms. "But you're still wrong. I've been sleeping with Beverly for weeks behind your back. I only slept with Myesha once. Last night."

I held my position in the doorway as my brain attempted to absorb this painful moment of déjà vu. My repeat perform-ance in the same bad movie I had starred in once before.

"I didn't think you knew about Myesha," he went on. "I wasn't going to bring *her* up. I wanted to spare you *that* amount of detail."

"My. How fuckin' generous of you."

"Not that this is going to be any comfort to you, but I didn't find out you two knew each other until after I slept with her."

I needed to sit down.

"Do you realize that bitch works just a few blocks away from me?" I asked from the opposite end of our bed that now stunk with the stench of adultery.

"Yes. And if your paths ever cross, I hope you don't assault her on the streets of Midtown. I was the pursuer, Madison. Myesha just allowed the pursuit. To prove a point. One she wouldn't share with me. She told me to give you a message if I ever confessed my involvement with her to you. Said you'd understand."

"Huh! What kind of message could that . . . bitch possibly have for me?"

"It's 'Told you so.' I have no earthly clue what that means. I don't want to know." Randall grabbed his suitcase and pre-pared to leave again now that I was no longer an obstruction in his path. "I'm gonna be staying at my parents' house until you and I can figure out how we're going to resolve the mess we've created. I'll be back at some point later to get more of my things. Give my son a kiss for me, please?"

"Wait. Don't you leave yet. I'm going to tell you what Myesha meant. You really *ought* to know." I stood directly in front of Randall. Looked squarely into those contact lenses I got him to wear. "She told me there was no such thing as a faithful man. A one-woman kinda guy. I told her she was young and green. That she was dead wrong. I was married to one. Make sure you write me a check for your half of the rent this month. *Now* you can leave."

LATER THAT EVENING . . .

76

DIRK

French Fry and I sat speechless, with the television providing background noise. Randall had just left. Told us he and Madison were separating. Told us about Myesha. Swore he didn't hear me above all the street noise on the corner of 84th Street.

Five minutes later, there was a knock at our door.

"I'll get it," Fry said. "It's probably Randall coming back for something." He opened the door. "Yo, Dee, it's Madison."

Madison?

French Fry let her in. She stood in the foyer absolutely wearin' out a pair of faded jeans that were slit open at her left kneecap. She looked worn. But still a sight to behold. I got up and came to her.

"Hey. You just missed Randall. He left here not ten minutes ago."

"I'm not looking for him. I'm here to see you."

French Fry's eyeballs swung back and forth between Madison and me like he was watching John McEnroe vs Jimmy Connors at the U.S. Open in Flushing Meadows.

"Is there something going on here I should know about?" he wanted to know.

"Aren't you on your way out to run an errand, Raymond?" Madison asked.

"Uh . . . no."

"What she means, *Raymond,* is she'd like you to give us some privacy."

"Hmmm. I suppose I could get lost. But I seem to be a little short at the moment," he said, searching his pockets for imaginary money.

Geez.

"Here, dude." I pulled a ten out of my pocket. "Don't spend it all in one place."

"Whoa. Big spender."

"Thank you, Raymond," Madison said.

"You sure there isn't something going on here I should know about?"

"Fry, go. Please!"

"Aw-aight." He grabbed his keys and jacket. "I'll be back."

"Don't rush."

As soon as French Fry locked the door behind him, Madison closed the distance between where she stood and I stood. I reached out to give her a hug.

"I'm sorry to hear about you and Randall."

Wham!

She slapped me in the face with all the strength I think she had in her.

"Don't worry, Madison. Randall's just got some stuff he needs to work out," she mocked me. "How many chances did you have to tell me what was going on with my husband? You knew all along Randall was sleeping with someone. *Two someones!"*

"I didn't know R slept with *Myesha* until twenty minutes ago."

"But you sure *knew of her* long before that, didn't you? You let me go on and on about her over lunch and you just sat there pretending to be clueless. You practically *encouraged* Randall to cheat on me!"

"On some level, I suppose I did. But I was in a totally different place then. That was before you and I got to know one another the way we have. When our relationship turned a corner, I tried everything in my power to talk some sense into Randall. I tried my best to get him to—"

Wham!

She slapped me a second time.

"I *trusted* you, Dirk! Against my better judgment, I trusted you. I had come to think of you as my rock. Do you have any idea how deeply I began to care for you? Can you even understand how incomprehensible that was for me?"

"Yes, Madison. I know how incomprehensible it was for you. I know because it was equally incomprehensible for me, too. I didn't lie to you as much as shield you from the truth. I didn't want to see you get hurt. I still don't—"

"Save it! I don't believe you. I thought you had changed, but you haven't a bit, since I met you. You're still an untrustworthy, conniving D-O-G—just in a brand-new way. I *hate* you, Dirk. I wished to God I never met you *or* Randall!"

"You hate me. Wow. And here all I was willing to do was let *your* sick secret remain a secret. Risk my lifelong relationship with my best friend for your sake. But I haven't changed? You hate yourself, Madison. Remember. All this shit . . . it started with *you*. Randall and I were living the good life before you entered the picture. So I'm even sorrier I ever met *your* ass!"

Madison lunged at me, arms flailing. I wasn't prepared to defend myself. Her manicured nails dug into the flesh on my face. I hollered in agony trying to get her away from me.

"FUCK YOU, DIRK. I HATE YOUR ASS!!" she screamed

while continuing her assault on me. I was suddenly in the middle of a cat fight that had only one cat in the fight.

I eventually managed to get a grip on Madison and bring her under control. She was a lot stronger than her frame would've suggested. I pinned her arms behind her back. Her body pressed against mine. She stopped struggling. I could feel all the pent-up anger and frustration she had with me, Randall, and herself evaporate from the pores of her skin. We stood motionless. Face-to-face.

I watched tears trickle down over her perfect cheekbones. Felt blood trickling down mine.

Then our violent confrontation erupted into passion.

77

DIRK

"C'mon, pick your chin up. You look like a third-grader who's been sent to the principal's office," Fatima said. Her arms were folded across her chest. She wasn't smiling, but she wasn't frowning, either. I sat in a chair a few feet away from her in her living room.

"Those are some awfully bad scratches on your face. Any idea of how you're going to explain them?"

"I'm gonna tell the truth. Just think. I wasn't even up to no good. I was actually trying to do the right thing this time."

"I know you were. For the record, I'm proud of you, Dirk. You've matured a great deal since we first met."

"Think everything's gonna work out okay?"

"If you can navigate your way through this latest minefield, and Randall doesn't murder you in the process, yeah. I think so."

"This isn't funny, Fatima."

"That's an understatement, Dirk."

"Please don't let this ruin your friendship with Madison."

"My friendship with Madison. Hmmm." Fatima rubbed her

chin. "Technically, my best friend did sleep with my boyfriend of less than sixty days. Which technically isn't on the same scale as you sleeping with your best friend's wife of two years—but it's still foul."

"Out cold."

"Yeah. That, too," she chuckled. "Sista girl and I are going to have to address this at some point. But don't worry about us. I'm really not even that pissed off, to tell you the truth."

"I notice."

"It's not like I've invested a lot of time in you or saw you as a prospective hubby or anything. I had a pretty good idea from the get-go that Maddy had feelings for you. You didn't believe me, remember? It was killing her that you and I were vibin'. In the beginning, because she *didn't* like you. Later, because she *did* like you. Didn't I tell you women are crazy?"

We laughed together. I sorely needed to laugh at something.

"I knew you were feeling her, too, Dirk. Got my confirmation of that the morning after we had sex for the first time. You were whispering *her* name in your sleep."

"Was I? Oh, geez." Fatima just looked at me and smiled. "I'm so sorry. And *why* are you taking this so well?"

"Because I'm not standing waist-deep in this colossal pile of shit the three of you have created." She rose from her chair and came over to me. "Well, you and me are a wrap, Dirk. You don't have to go home—"

"But I gotta get the hell outta here."

"Right on. Seriously, Dirk. I'm going to be pulling for the brothas to work it out." Fatima escorted me to her door like an employee who had just been fired. We shared a hug and a kiss.

"Get some peroxide on those scratches, pretty boy. *Eeeew!*"

I had never felt lower. Found myself wishing Columbus was wrong. That the Earth was indeed flat, so I could drive right off the end of it and never be seen or heard from again. *How do I even explain this to you, Randall?*

Halfway home from Fatima's, I detoured to 199th Street. Had an urge to see my mother and sister. It had been a minute since I was by for a visit. There are times when only family can bring a person comfort. This felt like one of those times. Figured all I needed was twenty, twenty-five minutes, maybe. But realistically knew I'd end up staying much longer than that. They both were going to be full of questions because I was telling them *everything*.

I parked and rang the doorbell. Rhonda came to the door with Rochelle in her arms. Her pale skin looked twice as pale.

"Where have you been?" she barked at me. "I left so many messages for you that I've lost count."

I stepped inside the house, taking my niece out of her arms. Feared Rhonda might drop her she was shaking so badly.

"What's all the urgency about?"

"It's Mommy!"

My heart sank.

"What happened, Rhonda?"

"She started drinking again this afternoon. But it wasn't her fault this time. It was all *his!*"

"Whose?"

"Daddy's! I tried to stop her, Dirk, but I couldn't put Rochelle in any danger. She got in her car, drove off drunk again, and now Mommy's . . . she's . . ."

"No, Rhonda, no. *NOOOO!*"

TWO YEARS LATER,
1992 . . .

FORGIVENESS

DIRK

I really like my new brother-in-law. Ain't the most hand-somest bruh in the world (and about as exciting to be around as watching paint dry), but I think he's going to be good for my sister. Think he's going to make a pretty good stepdad to Rochelle, too.

Edward's 32, nine years older than Rhonda and brainy just like her. She met Mr. Excitement when United Trust hired his consulting firm, which he owns and operates out of his home in Teaneck, New Jersey, to upgrade the company's computer net-work. Dude's one of those supergeeks. Really into that Internet thing. They say that Internet thing's going to change the world. Yeah, we'll see about that.

Ed's clockin' dollars. Not only that, he's making good money. Rhonda doesn't even have to work anymore. She's quit her job at United Trust and is now where she was sup-posed to be before getting pregnant on prom night—in col-lege. She's a freshman at Fairleigh Dickinson University. I'm so proud of Rhonda. I only wish our mother was around to see for herself how well her baby girl's fortune has changed for the better. But she's not.

She's in jail.

Something Randall said to me echoed over and over inside my head when Rhonda finally managed to get the words out that day. It hasn't stopped echoing since.

"'Let's keep our fingers crossed that your pops doesn't come back around and do anything to mess up your mother's progress.'"

True to form, my father showed up on the doorstep that morning with Amel. A seven-months-pregnant Amel. Claimed he was only there because he wanted his beloved baby girl to hear it from him first. That she was going to have a little brother or sister soon. While I'm sure there was some validity in his statement, I know that out cold state of mind of his simply couldn't pass up an opportunity to flaunt his pretty young thing in my mama's face one last time. One last time in *the* most insulting fashion. Sent my moms right back into the arms of Johnnie Walker.

Blasted out of her mind, she rear-ended a car on the North Conduit, killing a six-year-old boy sitting in the backseat. Her second DUI offense. Now she's serving a three-year bid for vehicular manslaughter.

Like he warned me, I warned him he might live to regret it if he didn't stop. Now he's got lots of regrets. I don't care. I will never have anything to do with my father again. There's just not that much forgiveness in me. Right or wrong, I will never recognize Hank Jr. as my little brother, either.

In between all the drama with me, Randall, Madison, and my folks, I lost my roommate, French Fry, too. It's all good, though. Raymond got hitched. No, not to his new flame, Sabrina Parker, but to Crystal, his old flame since tenth grade and the mother of his child. When word spread that she had ended her engagement, Fry told Sabrina to disappear, went running back to Crystal on bended knee, and finally asked her to marry him. She said yes (no big surprise there) and they got hitched ten days later without fanfare at City Hall.

I'd be remiss not to also mention that Fry actually walked in on me and Madison. I think we traumatized him. I told his ass not to rush back, didn't I? But I digress . . .

So, here I am, back on 199th Street in St. Albans. Alone now. I can handle it. The house is paid off, so taxes, utilities, and occasional maintenance are my only big-ticket items. I plan on taking real good care of this house so my moms will have a home to come back to when she's through serving her time.

I'm still at United Trust, too—with this caveat: I'm also in school. That's right. Dirk Francis is a college student now just like his little sister. I'm taking business and marketing classes at St. John's University. Don't know why I didn't think of this before, but as much as I liked to party—and knew *how* to party—I think I'd be a natural as a nightclub owner. Think I'm going to give that very thing a shot in the very near future. I've even got the perfect name for my new club: *The Booty Palace*. (Just kidding. Geez.)

Sometimes I really do regret blowing things with Fatima—twice. Especially since there's no special friend in my life at the moment. Mrs. Crawford was right. Fatima and me would have made a lovely couple. But then the first time I *really* fall in love, I've got to go and do it with my best friend's wife. *Duh!*

It kinda hurts that I'll never have a chance to be Madison's man. Though not nearly as much as me hurting Randall. Things got pretty ugly between us for a minute. Understandably so. The good news? We're working it out. Yep, that's right. The odd couple is going to make a comeback like bellbottoms. And our relationship's going to be better and stronger than ever. In fact, me, Randall, *and* Madison are slowly but surely digging ourselves out from under that "colossal pile of shit we created." For the first time in some time, I can say with confidence that that light I see at the end of the tunnel ain't another train coming, yow mean?

MADISON

I think about Dirk from time to time. Mostly trying to pinpoint the exact moment my feelings for him turned in a direction I never imagined they could. Think it was that day in the parking lot of Grand Union. When he used his hand to wipe away the tears that were streaming down my face. It was such a tender thing he did. So unexpected. So *un-Dirk*-like. But in retrospect, I don't think I was ever *really* in love with Dirk. More like in love with being cared about by someone when I didn't think the one I wanted to care did at all.

I had every intention of staying in Queens and buying a home. Just one ideal for Noah and me if that's how it had to be. Nothing much was supposed to change in my world.

Until I found out I was pregnant again.

Being pregnant with my second child should have been a blissful time in my life. Not something that had me so depressed I could barely get out of bed in the morning. Eat. Function on my job. But then I guess those sort of things go with the territory when you don't know if the child you're carrying belongs to your husband or his best friend.

I didn't tell a soul I was pregnant. Not Randall—damn sure not Dirk—or my family. Nope, nope, nope. As for Fatima, our friendship was on ice when I learned about the baby. Understandably so. Said she needed a break from me. That she'd let me know if and when she wanted to try and resume our friendship. I'm happy to say we're slowly but surely getting back in each other's Kool-Aid again. She and I have vowed never to let a man come between us again. We never will. Wait. I should know better than to ever say never again. Said I could *never* be unfaithful to my man. How'd that work out for me? Okay. I'm confidently optimistic we never will. Better?

I spent days and nights in an exercise of trying to determine the odds of whose baby I was carrying. I had bare-back sex with Randall and Dirk three days apart.

It was a pointless exercise.

The chances were 100 percent, however, that no matter who the father turned out to be, it wasn't going to be joyous news to either. My future outlook was looking bad (Randall's baby) and even *badder* (Dirk's baby). And, yes, I know there's no such word as "badder" in the English language. Although in this context, it's the most fitting nonword I can think of.

Following numerous unproductive days at work and sleepless nights at home, my soul simply gave out under the stress of my "whose baby is it?" dilemma. Mother Nature was only going to allow me to mask my condition for so long. I had to get out from under that ominous cloud of unrelenting angst. Get back to the life I had—or as close to it—before I met Dirk and Randall.

I had no other option as I saw it. Did the only thing I thought I could under the circumstances. Made that gut-wrenching decision an adult woman unfortunately has to make sometimes . . .

I moved back in with my parents. Damn, did I hate to have to quit my job at Trendy.

My old bedroom upstate in Newburgh used to seem humongous to me as a kid. Still seems pretty large to me as a 32-year-old woman.

I stayed a total wreck for weeks thereafter. Thank God I had my family around me for comfort. They assumed my crumbling marriage to be totally at the root of my stress. If they only knew.

My mother—as she did before I married Randall—offered her sage advice to me once again. Unlike the first time, however, this time, I followed it to the hilt. Now, I'm not a religious person, but I "threw my burden onto the Lord." Told Him I'd accept the outcome of my pregnancy whatever He saw fit to allow that outcome to be. If Randall was meant to be the father of my unborn child, I'd move back to Queens and do everything in my power to make our shaky marriage work for the sake of both our children. If my pregnancy was the result of a lone moment of unplanned passion with Dirk, well I'd learn to be the best *single* parent of two kids I could possibly be.

The Lord works in mysterious ways.

I miscarried nine weeks into my first trimester. The official diagnosis was a chromosomal abnormality.

Unofficially, I'd say it was His answer. I broke down and told my parents *everything*. Only them.

If you can believe that a woman could suffer a miscarriage and be *relieved* at the same time, that about sums up my mindset at the time. Sure, I had conflicting emotions about the outcome (c'mon, I lost my baby), but I also knew that *not* having this child was going to open the door to something that in all probability would have had little chance of happening had I carried my pregnancy to term.

Some forgiveness.

A chance for Dirk and Randall to heal their wounds and maybe a better chance for Randall and I to heal ours.

Randall and I are on the road to reconciliation. I truly believe that. Granted, we're taking baby steps, but even baby steps eventually help one get to their chosen destination. In the past two years that we've been living under separate roofs, I've yet to bring up the subject of divorce to him, nor has he to me. Guess sometimes the most significant communication between a married couple comes in the things they *refuse* to say to one another.

Bottom line? All he's got to do is let me *hear* it. *Tell me* he wants me back and I'm so there. I'm so going to quit my new job as an entertainment editor for the *Poughkeepsie Journal*—which is nowhere near the profile of working in Manhattan for *Trendy* anyway—pack up my things, and Noah's, leave this humongous bedroom, and head back to Queens.

Randall

I've got a great new gig at United Trust. But I'll come back to that.

First, let me say that First Savior has grown in leaps and bounds even without my father at the helm. So much so that they've even started a choir. You'll never believe who's singing in it. Yes. It's a miracle.

I've been attending church regularly for the past six months—and not just on Sundays. What I once viewed as an endless loopty-loop has now become something I actually look forward to. Of course, my parents are just tickled pink that I've "found the Lord." That might be taking it a bit far. Getting in touch with my spiritual side would be more apropos.

I can already see some good that's come of it, too. My relationship with my father is getting better with each passing day (he's a lot more humble himself now), and I'm learning a lot about a quality I never really gave much thought to before.

Forgiveness.

When I found out that Dirk had slept with Madison, I was

mortally wounded. Reacted just as one might expect a man in my position to react. I knocked Dirk's teeth out—literally. Well, a tooth. One clean shot to the kisser. No pun intended, but Dirk was out cold and *out cold.* (He's sporting a porcelain replacement in the space where his God-given enamel once was.) Has he taken his share of physical abuse over the years or what? A couple of Dominican guys beat him into a coma, Madison carves a tic-tac-toe board into his face, I knock out one of his teeth. I'll give it to Dirk, though. He's more than a pretty boy. He's a *tough* boy.

Following his admission—and my assault—we didn't speak for months. Things are better now. A lot better. We're communicating again. Making strides toward being the best friends we had been since elementary school. Time has allowed the emotional pain Dirk inflicted on me, and the physical I inflicted on him, to give way to a better understanding of not only what happened, but *why* it happened. It's like I said. I've known Dirk nearly my entire life. He's been a lot of things during that time, but a back-stabber has never been one of them. He wasn't scheming to sleep with my wife. He was trying to get *me* to sleep with my wife. He simply got caught up. Madison has that kind of an effect on a man. I know.

Dirk didn't blame anyone but himself for what happened between him and Madison even though there was ample blame to go around. A lot of which was my fault. I made Madison vulnerable to another man. *I* drove my wife into the arms of my best friend.

Life's ironic, isn't it? I was never keen on being a dad this early on in my life, but now that I am (never mind *how* I became a dad this early on), I've hated only being able to see my son on a handful of occasions on account of this separation between Madison and me. I've hated the prospect of Noah growing up without his father and mother living under the same roof with him. I wasn't raised that way and I didn't want to be the one to start *that* trend among the Crawford men. So, I decided to do something about it. Came home from Sunday service one afternoon, literally got down on my hands and knees, and prayed. Though I'm probably not deserving, I think the man upstairs is going to do me a solid anyway.

Which brings me back to my new gig I mentioned. Yours Truly is now payroll *supervisor* at United Trust. (Aunt Ethel's so proud of me.) Timing couldn't be better. Financially speaking, I'm doing a little better than just okay for a change. I've even got my own apartment now—roommate unnecessary. One more promotion or significant pay increase, and I'm looking to own something. Was thinking about a condo originally. Lately, I've been thinking about a house.

For me, my wife, and our son.

I've come to the conclusion that Madison and I still have the capacity to create a different type of good life together. Glancing backward at that life-altering decision of mine . . . well, married life wasn't really all that bad after all. Even for a dude still in his twenties.

Nobody said forgiveness was easy, but I'm going to forgive Madison for getting pregnant on purpose. Hope she'll forgive me for steppin' out on her before I even knew she had gotten pregnant on purpose. I'm feeling like the Little Engine That Could. I think I can . . . I think I *can* deal with being a young husband and father of one. *Just one* for now.

She doesn't know it yet, but real soon, I'm about to do like the Jackson Five and tell Madison, "I want you back." Because, like the words to my favorite song by the Fatback Band, I really did find lovin'. I've got a beautiful wife and son, good friends and a good job, and a close family.

Really. What more could a nice guy ask for?